Father's Day

Father's Day

———————

PHILIP GALANES

ALFRED A. KNOPF   NEW YORK   2004

THIS IS A BORZOI BOOK
PUBLISHED BY ALFRED A. KNOPF

Copyright © 2004 by Philip Galanes

All rights reserved under International and Pan-American Copyright
Conventions. Published in the United States by Alfred A. Knopf,
a division of Random House, Inc., New York, and simultaneously in
Canada by Random House of Canada Limited, Toronto.
Distributed by Random House, Inc., New York.
www.aaknopf.com

Library of Congress Cataloging-in-Publication Data
Galanes, Philip, [date]
Father's Day / Philip Galanes.—1st ed.
p.   cm.
ISBN 1-4000-4160-0
1. Suicide victims—Family relationships—Fiction. 2. Fathers—Death—Fiction.
3. New York (N.Y.)—Fiction. 4. Telephone sex—Fiction. 5. Suburban life—Fiction.
6. New England—Fiction. 7. Young men—Fiction. I. Title.

PS3607.A38M46 2004
813'.6—dc22   2003060570

Manufactured in the United States of America
First Edition

For my parents and for Michael

Father's Day

CHAPTER ONE

Loud Blouse

It wasn't so long after my father killed himself that Sheila Gray came to town and told me quite a story.

Wait.

Let me try that again.

And this time, I need you to pay attention to Sheila and the story she told me about my mother. That's what I wanted you to hear. The part about my father was just for chronology, but it felt like more than that, didn't it? It made more noise than that.

My father's death turns out to be like a very loud blouse, like a shrill leopard print or an acid Pucci pattern—nearly impossible to coordinate. It overtakes just about anything I put next to it.

It would have been simple enough, I suppose, to say that Sheila came to town after my father died. I could have left it at that, and his death might have floated by like a little silk blouse in that version— like an ecru blouse at that, just as unremarkable as can be.

Sheila's story about my mother would be front and center then.

But somehow I can't say that.

Time and again, I'm drawn away from the little silk blouse, toward the screaming colors of a Versace print: My father killed himself.

It feels almost like I have to tell you.

Once I've said this much though, I don't want to say another word. I want to retreat. Just this much, and not a word more.

I want to use his suicide like a stun gun—to shoot you into submission with it, have you defer to me because of it—but I know it doesn't work like that. This story doesn't make you docile.

As soon as I say my father killed himself, the question "how?" comes roaring back at me, as if the information I gave were disinformation, as if my confession just begged the real question: "So how did he do it?"

And that's just the beginning.

But after I've climbed so far out on a limb that I've actually spoken the word—suicide—all I want is to crawl back to safety, toward the solid trunk of a hundred-year-old maple.

I'd like to take a break then—tell you next that he was six feet tall, or that he had lovely gray eyes and smooth, smooth skin.

But I know how this works.

His faint smell of citrus is of no interest to you.

No, you want to know how he did it.

My father put a bullet through his head.

There, I've told you.

But now you might think he placed the gun at his temple, sideways, and fired.

That's not how it was.

You see, when you ask for the "how?" of it—the "where?"—you take me right back to the crack of the gunshot, when I'm nowhere to be found and everywhere at once. Like a man with an airtight alibi whose fingerprints cover every square inch of the murder weapon.

When the steel gray bullet with its shiny copper tip is loaded into the empty chamber. Click.

When the nicely manicured hand lifts the gun heavily upward.

When the jaw goes slack.

You can't ask for more than this: He shot himself through his open mouth and straight out the back of his head.

Happy now?

When Sheila Gray started talking, I most definitely didn't ask any questions. Not a one.

4

No, I receded. Let her tell me what she would.

I'd met her only once before, after all.

Think 1974.

She flew into town from New Mexico back then—some place she insisted on calling a colony—with long, center-parted hair and a gauzy red gypsy skirt that she wore three days running. She smelled of sandalwood and guessed all our astrological signs correctly. With one look, she saw straight to the heart of me, and still she gave me the highest grade: Libra, just like her.

So proud to be seen through, for a change.

Are you sure there's no mistake?

"No, no," she said. "It's clear as day."

Grateful not to hide any telltale sign of who I might really be—not from her anyway. No, she saw it all, and she liked me just the same. The pride and the gratefulness swirling together like tasty ribbons of Bundt cake batter—all my hidden worthiness baking into something delicious at last.

Then she left.

Good-bye, Sheila.

Only to return twenty years later—this past April—almost six months to the day after we buried my father like a tulip bulb in the fall, never to bloom again in any spring.

Within three hours and fifteen minutes of Sheila's arrival, my mother calls me at home in New York. "Darling," she whispers into the receiver, but loud, the way she whispers.

Shiny little needles prickle my cheeks and the nape of my neck. We're sharing secrets again!

"I would love to know what the hell she's doing here," she says, still whispering.

It's going to be all downhill from here, I know that. But it's so much fun at the start.

The idea of her: My mother!

She must be off alone in her dressing room, sitting on that spindly wooden chair without arms: A short, plump woman on a chair as delicate as she is sturdy, pinning it down. She'll have pulled the bedroom door closed behind her and the dressing room door too, but you can still hear her whispering anywhere in the house.

"It's turned nasty already?" I ask.

"What do you know about it," she says. It's supposed to be a question, I think, but it doesn't sound like one. Her voice stays flat at the end.

The picture of her eyes rolling on the other end of the phone is as clear to me as the little puff of frustration I hear through the receiver. She's worked up now and ready to accelerate. Given Sheila the slip, like the cleverest driver in the fastest car chase ever. I can either climb into the passenger seat or get the hell out of her way: Those are my choices.

"Life is a one-woman show for that woman," she says, not even trying to whisper anymore.

"She's come three thousand miles to visit you," I say.

Sheila and my mother have spoken on the phone nearly every Sunday afternoon since time began. She's my mother's oldest friend.

"But enough about me," she interrupts.

Really?

"What do *you* think of my Birkenstocks?" she asks.

Oh, I see. She was only joking, just mocking Sheila and her hippie sandals.

"I'd relax if I were you," I say, mastering the loss. "She's only been there for a couple of hours."

"Yeah," she says. "A couple of hours too long."

She's playing tough now. I've seen it a million times.

Once, we were parked at a service station, and she was arguing with a mechanic about brake shoes. He said she needed new ones. She said the problem was that he hadn't aligned the tires properly the last time she was in. Soon they were raising their voices and repeating themselves. They were escalation incarnate.

Then he called her a bitch.

I heard him. He said, "Lady, you're a first-class bitch."

She wasn't fazed though, didn't even blink.

"That's Mister Bitch to you," she said.

But I was with her when she drove away too, trembling from the danger so narrowly averted and the heavy price she paid standing up for herself. It wasn't as if there was anyone else to stand up for her—or for me either, for that matter. No, she was forced to become the man of the family. Taking care of everything as my father slipped quietly away. It wasn't her choice at all.

But I'm in New York now, safe in my own apartment. I try not to care whether she relaxes or not, whether she drives Sheila off or doesn't.

"I'll tell you one thing," she says. "She's drinking me out of house and home."

She's on a rant now. Doesn't mean a word of it.

"Just roaring through the liquor cabinet."

I've heard it all before: She offers people drinks, then holds it against them if they accept.

"Why her kidneys haven't packed it in by now is the sixty-four-thousand-dollar question around here."

"I know, I know," I say, mock solicitous, a singsong signal that I couldn't care less. I got it from her.

Defending Sheila is pointless now. Everything about her is horrible to my mother at this moment. Every defense would only constitute further proof of her horribleness.

You see, it's always black and white with her, and very black right now. But Sheila will be back in her good graces in fifteen minutes.

That's the trick: Never counting on her to stick with either one— neither black nor white—because sooner or later, every black reverses to white, every white to black, and never faster than when she has an opportunity to disagree with you.

There's just no predicting which end is up at any given moment.

Even if I took up her position right now, mimicked it as flawlessly as an expert drag queen, even if I carried on arguing for her in just the way she would argue herself, it would backfire on me.

"Listen," she says, "I'd better hang up before she gets into the cough syrup."

I adjust the white pillow behind my neck. Reach for the telephone and dial: 555-PUMP.

My phone bills have grown enormous, but I don't care.

"Welcome to the Pump Line!" a male voice announces, prerecorded and extremely upbeat. "New York's only phone line for men who are serious about their bodies! Hang up now if you're not serious about yours!"

Then he pauses, giving me a chance to assess my seriousness, I suppose. Don't worry. I'm dead serious.

"I'm Scott!" he says. "I'll be your guide!"

Like Virgil, I thought once, and now again too, like an echo.

"Calls cost fifteen cents a minute," he says. "Twenty-five for the first."

His whole rap is like a persistent echo.

"You must be at least eighteen years old to use the Pump Line," he says. "When you hang up, you will definitely be pumped!"

Somehow this call has wormed its way into my daily routine over the past several months, as inevitable now in any evening as brushing my teeth, or gazing at my face in the bathroom mirror when I do, checking out my sex appeal through toothpaste foam: The dark, wavy hair and slate gray eyes, the long sharp nose that's just like my father's.

"Let's do it!" Scott says. "Press 'one' to speak to other guys, one on one! Press 'two' to . . ."

I always press "one."

I'm not much interested in the alternatives to flesh-and-blood men. The other options mostly involve prerecorded messages from hustlers or invitations from hard-to-fit men with fetishistic specialties—tie me up, tie me down, take an orange, cut it into slices—that sort of thing, painfully elaborate rituals that just seem like too much work, especially at bedtime.

There are group calls too—press "three"—a free-for-all sort of party line, but I can never distinguish between the voices there.

I press "one."

"Hang on," Scott says. "I'm making your connection right now."

Then he gives away the golden key: "And remember, when you're finished talking to one guy, just press the pound key, and you'll be automatically connected to someone new."

The men appear and disappear too with the push of a button. With the push of a button we create and destroy. I try not to think too much about the ones left behind—the victims of the pressed pound key. It's

8

an individualized world here, a party of one really, with all manner of interior hot spots and land mines. The architecture designed for sexual efficiency—like pneumatic supermarket doors swinging open and shut with the pressure of an index finger on a dialing pad—hair triggers for the just-off detail, the not-quite-right tone of voice.

Everyone knows what it's all about here: Where were you when I created my sexy universe? It's hard to begrudge a man his pound key.

There's a short interlude of electronic music, then Scott again: "Here's the next guy."

The *next* guy?

I've got a connection.

But there was no *first* guy.

Never mind that now.

"Hello?" a voice says.

A real voice too, not prerecorded at all.

I'm on fire in a flash! Like Judy Garland at Carnegie Hall!

"Hello," I say.

My heart is pumping faster than a hummingbird's—a thousand beats a minute.

No response from my gentleman caller though.

My whole body is vibrating with excitement—thrumming on top of the snow white duvet.

Where is he?

My face feels as flushed as if I'd been in the sun all day.

I reach over and turn off the bedside light. I'm hot. Even that single bulb is generating too much heat for my racing metabolism.

"Hello?" I say again.

But I feel my heart in my mouth.

Feel my prospects dimming.

He should have said something by now.

"I'm here," he says.

That was a close one!

I feel a pain in my right hand.

Look down at it.

I'm clutching the receiver, squeezing it like a drowning man grabs onto the side of a lifeboat, bobbling along in the middle of the ocean.

"What's up?" he asks.

I loosen my grip.

"Not much," I say.

Careful to hide the thrill inside me.

"Just hanging around."

But my heart is racing still!

"You?"

I'm careful of my voice too, its pitch and tightness. Nervous that it sounds prissy, too controlled.

"I'm looking to get together," he says.

I like the sound of him—not like a friend, but not lurid either.

"Me, too," I say, trying for deeper, trying for looser.

"Where are you?" he asks.

His voice is exactly what you'd want in a boyfriend.

"In the Village," I say. "How about . . ."

Beep.

"You?" I ask, but it's too late.

He's already moved on to the next guy.

He pressed the pound key, which beeps loudly—painfully so, in fact—when you have the receiver at your ear, when you're still talking. I liked that one too, I think.

There are mysteries here, and you might as well get used to them. Maybe he's far away from the Village. Or maybe he didn't like the sound of my voice. Maybe his lover just walked into the room.

I'll never know.

Cut and switch, that's what I've learned here. You can't spend too much time worrying about the last guy.

I really wish they could improve that beep technology though—make it just a little softer for the recipient, hopeful still, receiver pressed against his ear.

"Here's the next guy," Scott says.

You see.

It's all about moving on.

"Hello," I say.

What's one false start?

"Hey, man."

"How are you?" I ask.

Revved up all over again.

"Great, man," he says. "How are you tonight, man?"

I'm not so sure about this new guy though—with his "man" this, and "man" that.

"I'm fine."

Hasn't he noticed that we're all men here? There's no reason to draw a thick red line beneath it.

"Yeah, man," he says. "I'm feeling real horny."

That's the nail in his coffin.

Beep.

I press the pound key. Just like that.

"Horny" has an expiration date, in my view, like milk: Sixteen, seventeen tops.

"Here's the next guy."

Bring him on.

"Hello," I say.

"Where are you?" he asks, very direct.

Geography is clearly the gating item for this one.

"Fine, thanks," I say, by mistake.

He doesn't seem to mind though.

Doesn't punch the pound key on me, at least.

"I'm in the Village," I say, self-correcting as quickly as possible. "On Twelfth Street," I add, making up for it with precision.

Sometimes I lose my place for a second or two.

"Chelsea here," he says.

Listen, even a professional's going to drop a line every once in a while. It's the recovery that counts. A pro keeps moving.

"I'm looking for a rough top," he says.

I pause for just a second.

Beep.

He presses the pound key in the gap.

The pause said it all: I'm not what you're after.

Several more connections follow quickly.

Beep.

Beep.

None are striking that easy, feel-good feeling that needs to be struck for this to work. It used to happen right off the bat, but lately it's taking longer—if it happens at all.

"Hang on for your next connection."

I'm becoming too demanding.

They all seemed charmed when I discovered this line a few months ago. But somehow they're dumber now, older, too far away.

I'm becoming the Leni Riefenstahl of the Pump Line.

"Remember," Scott says. "You can always push the star key and browse the messages in the personals locker room."

He must be running out of men.

"Here's the next guy."

Cue the orchestra.

"Whatareyoulookingfor?" he asks, so fast, running all his words together.

"Maybe get together," I say. "Maybe talk."

"Iwannagettogether," he says, even faster.

"Sounds good," I say.

I'm speaking at a normal pace, but it sounds ridiculously slow in comparison.

"Whereareya?"

I consider lying.

This fast talking is making me nervous. "On Twelfth Street," I say. "Near Fourth Avenue. How about you?"

Why don't I just hit the pound key?

"Whatareyouinto?" he asks, not one tiny bit slower, not answering my question either.

"More bottom," I say.

That should scare him off. Men rarely say "bottom" here without modifying it in some way, trying to lessen the shame of it. I only say it when I'm not interested at all.

"Me too, man," he says.

"Good luck."

Beep.

You see, birds of a feather don't flock together here.

Same with versatile guys, *maybe* more bottom—they tend not to mesh well either. Chalk and cheese. Two pretty versatile guys, *maybe* more bottom, are looking for something else entirely.

Out in the world—at work or over dinner with friends—I say that I'm looking for a nice guy, someone clever and funny. I might throw in handsome too, but without any sense of urgency. And I believe myself. I believe that I'm telling the truth about what I want. I've believed myself for over ten years now, since I first moved to New York—through more first dates than any ten normal people combined. Trust me: I've cornered the market on sweet and clever and funny in my day—with more than a little handsome thrown in too—but nothing's ever worked for me. No, my story may be carved in stone already: The calcifying spinster at thirty-five, ever watchful for his ten-thousandth suitor.

And my feverish excursions here belie that whole search anyway. I watch myself elevate the physical above everything else. Look at me, with a trowel and mortar, laying brick after brick. Building a soaring tower, pretending it's for me and the impossible specimen of my dreams. But that tower's so tall already—and I'm so far off the ground—that I'd never be able to make out clever or funny as I look down from above, telephone receiver in one hand, measuring tape in the other.

"Here's the next guy."

"What's your name?" he asks.

"Susan," I say by mistake.

Beep.

I was looking across the room at a book by Susan Minot. *Evening,* for what it's worth. I used to read.

Don't get me wrong: Even with these men on the Pump Line, I'll insist on clever and funny in due course. But the first cuts turn on the physical here: The embodiment of cleverness himself has nothing to look forward to from me but a beep if he's outside the range of acceptable height. Even now, my criteria are multiplying like a virus—voice, height, age, weight, sexual position, hair color. Spinning out of control like that blonde-haired Herbal Essence girl on old-time television, whose image multiplied arithmetically as she chanted, "And so on, and so on, and so on."

"Here's the next guy."

"You into muscle?" he asks.

This is getting depressing.

"Sure," I say.

This is the line for men who are serious about their bodies after all, but I can already smell incompatibility brewing here.

"I'm six feet four and two hundred and fifty pounds of pure muscle."

Two hundred and fifty pounds seems awfully heavy to me.

"Totally hairless," he says.

Like it's a virtue.

"Sounds great," I say, not meaning a word of it.

Liza Minnelli probably didn't even weigh two hundred and fifty pounds at her peak, and she was huge.

He probably wouldn't be attracted to me anyway.

"I'm into flexing and posing," he says.

I manage to feel uninterested in him and unworthy of him at the same time.

He doesn't even ask what I look like.

"You wanna worship my rock-hard muscles?"

I press the pound key. Even I have my limits. It's getting late. I should hang up now.

"Here's the next guy."

"Exhibitionist looking for a camera."

Beep.

Just a few more. I promise.

"Here's the next guy."

But Scott knows better: I'm on a bender. There's no stopping me now.

"Hi. I'm Peter."

Nice voice.

"Hi, Peter," I say. "How are you?"

"Fine, thanks."

A tad shy all of a sudden.

That's a good sign.

"You?"

"I'm fine too."

Maybe just a little slower this time.

"What's your name?"

With a little more feeling.

"Matthew," I say.

I never use my real name here, but I just did.

Kind of nice as a midtempo number.

As if my first name would help someone identify me better than my voice. But then again, this isn't my voice. This is a faux-butch simulation that slips into my real voice the second I stop monitoring it.

"Tell me what you look like," he says.

So I do. I speak my dimensions directly into the receiver, just like a military man singing out his name, rank, and serial number: Height, weight, hair color, age—all slightly augmented for telephonic consumption. It's the way we do it here.

"I'm six feet tall, and one hundred and eighty pounds," I say. "I have brown hair and blue eyes. Work out a lot."

It's all true enough.

"I'm thirty," I say.

Except that. I'm really thirty-five. But what's a few years between friends?

"How about you?" I ask, holding my breath.

I'm uneasy in the silence that follows my description.

Even before I've heard a word of what he looks like though, even before I have a single piece of datum on this Peter, I'm afraid he'll hit the pound key on me. I'm as afraid here as I am everywhere else in the world.

No beep though, not yet anyway.

"Sounds nice," he says.

And without a word of prompting from me, he begins to describe himself, restoring equilibrium, for the moment at least, to our transaction.

He's six-one and one hundred and eighty-five pounds.

Very lean, he says, in case you're interested.

He has a husky voice. Probably smokes.

Long brown hair, and he's thirty-two years old.

And then: "Eight-inch dick, cut."

That's unfortunate. I never include genitalia, myself. I might get further than I do here if I did, but I'll take the high road on this one. I don't like the image of myself with a ruler pressed into my groin, measuring out to the tippity-tip.

Plus, a dick is just not what I'm after here.

Trust me, that's not what's driving me onward like the original Christian soldier. I'm looking for a movie date really, with some hand-holding and some kissing in the balcony. Just a little romance with the handsome man in the velvet seat beside me.

But here I am, in the late, late hours of the night, looking for a boyfriend on a sex line. I don't think I could stop now even if I wanted to.

But at least his dick wasn't the centerpiece of his description, I think. Or painted in elaborate detail, like some I've heard. Plus, everyone has an eight-inch dick on this line. Saying that yours is eight inches is like saying that you have a liver, or that there are four food groups.

"Can I call you?" he asks.

"Sure," I say.

It sounds like comfort to me, leaving the Pump Line and its ever-present threat of the beep. A chance to speak with him directly, without Scott and his machinery of next guys.

"Got a pencil?" I ask.

I give him my number.

He repeats it back.

"What's your name again?" he asks.

"Matthew."

"I'll call you right back, Matthew."

The way he lays emphasis on my name, I can tell that he's making an effort to remember it.

He seems sweet, Peter.

Of course, that may not even be his real name.

I visit my mother most weekends since my father died. I take the train up from New York. Install the girl who watches the gallery for me at the stroke of noon on Saturday, then change out of my fancy art dealer clothes in the little bathroom at the back. Put on something more comfortable for the train—like a seven-year-old just back from school, out of his uniform in a jiffy and into play clothes, fast. I'm not heading out to play though. It's a tricky combination of guilt and hope that propels me onto that platform every week: A vague feeling that I'm somehow responsible for what's happened up there, that I might fix it too.

When the train pulls into the station, I take a cab from an old man who promises—every week—to give me a ride anywhere I want for three dollars. All winter, he wore a crisp white shirt and a snappy red tie, a cardigan like Mr. Rogers. I wish I could ride around with him all day, or take the long way home at least, but he drives straight to my mother's house and drops me at the end of the long gravel driveway.

How I wish I were someplace else.

I keep coming here though, keep trying.

Only each week, I realize all over again how absurd I was for thinking I might have been the help that was on its way. I never had the power to cause her even the slightest harm, much less rescue her. The minute I walk through the front door, I see how things are between us. It's very Gertrude and Alice: Very "Turn off the lights in the kitchen," very "Don't you have a nicer pair of trousers than those?" Very "That's the most ridiculous thing I've ever heard."

I close the cab door behind me.

"Thanks," I say.

The old man drives off.

Here I am.

It's a simple farmhouse, wooden and white. A rectangular box of rooms on top of rooms, with an old-fashioned porch that wraps around and a glass extension off the back—a dining addition that's rarely used. It's got nothing to do with the rest of the house, but it's beautiful just the same. Sunlight glints off the glassy walls in daytime; soft light from within keeps it glowing at night.

It's quiet here, altogether still but for the clacking of my shoes on the gravel as I walk up the drive. Like a movie sound track: *High Noon* with loafers.

The maple trees lining the long driveway are bare still, the needles left on the pine trees orange and brown. It's early April. When I'm almost there—just a dozen steps from the front door—I hear Maria Callas, like the first robin in springtime—like the first overwrought, squawking robin.

It's "Visi d'arte," turned up loud.

I live for art, she sings, *I live for love.*

When I was in high school, my mother asked me to make her a cassette tape with nothing on it but this, just this one aria in a continuous loop.

I live for art. I live for love. I harm no man.

I walk around to the back.

No, it's not about taking care of anyone here. It's about taking cover. There won't be any comfort either, only our dogged hope for it, and our ancient ways that keep bringing us back to each other, again and again.

Neither of them hears me when I walk into the kitchen, neither Sheila nor my mother. That's how loud the music is. But I can see them both, side by side at the kitchen counter, their backs to me. A valve opens in my chest—full throttle—when I see my mother. Excitement flowing unimpeded. This is what it's like for me to be near her, even now.

Somehow these women—together—aren't what I was expecting, even though they're exactly what you'd expect. They're older, practically the mothers of the women I was hoping for, as if their reunion might have conjured their younger selves, the 1974 versions, if not the ones from the photograph that's been on display in my mother's study since time began: The two of them sitting at a small table in a fancy restaurant.

Someone, not my mother, wrote "Morocco, 1955" on the back of it.

It's practically technicolor, that photograph, but saturated in more exotic colors than MGM ever dreamed up: Sepias and olives and browns. My mother wears a sleeveless blue dress in the photograph. The fabric shimmers. She's resting her hand lightly on her throat, not a ladylike pose though, not a pearl-clutching hand, more open and flat. Her shoulders are relaxed. Sheila sits beside her, grinning and looking at my mother out of the corners of her eyes, a flash of tight red twinset and sparkling earring (you can see only one) and sparkling eyes.

I've loved that photograph for years.

They're both about sixty-five now, more thickly set, shorter-looking. They've cut their hair short too into sensible gray bobs. Dressed alike in practical clothing, loose trousers and cardigan sweaters, no more tight bodices or tailored skirts, no shimmering fabrics. They're altogether wash and wear now.

My casual train clothes seem fancy by comparison.

Over the music I hear my mother laugh in a way I don't quite recognize. It's got to have been loud for me to have heard it over this music. It's not the laugh I think of as her real laugh, the one she uses with me.

That's a relief.

But it's not her social laugh either, higher-pitched and more measured by comparison. No, this one is somewhere in the middle, somewhere between authentic and counterfeit, and like the hand she rests on her throat in that old photograph, it's complicated too: Intimate and formal at the same time, inviting you to keep your distance and to come on in.

Eventually she notices me over her shoulder. She twirls around fast then, genuine happiness in her eyes.

I feel glad to be here.

But then she grows even more excited—like she's playing charades, acting out a natural disaster of some kind.

"Hello!" she screams, hurtling toward me.

"Matthew!" Sheila calls out. Then she rushes over to the stereo and lowers the volume.

"Why on earth didn't you call from the station?" my mother asks, breathless, heavy on the vowels.

The aria begins again, but softly now.

This isn't her real voice either. This is her company's here voice, slightly posh, more modulated.

She smiles at me and looks back at Sheila, watching her smile at me.

My mother's performing now, playacting for Sheila's benefit.

But everyone does this, right?

"The cab was just sitting there," I say, going along with her. "I didn't want to bother you." Playing considerate.

I take a cab every weekend.

I hug my mother, smile at Sheila.

"It's so nice to see you!" Sheila says.

But my mother doesn't let go of me, doesn't let me hug Sheila in turn. No, she kisses me hard on the lips, like she's always done, with a popping sound.

Most boys I know, older than seven or eight, kiss their mothers, when the pairs kiss at all. The mothers may initiate the kisses, turning their heads slightly, offering their cheeks, but it's the boys who do the kissing. It's the sons who brush their lips against their mothers' cheeks, like whispers.

That's never been my mother's way.

"Well, don't you ever do that again," she says.

Maneuvers her body so that she's addressing the room.

"I love picking you up."

She's doing distance work here, giving a performance that might look great from a hundred yards, from a seat in the mezzanine. But up close, the gestures are overbroad, and the stage makeup is unnerving.

Sheila doesn't seem perturbed by any of it though.

Maybe it's me.

"It's been such a long time since I've seen you," Sheila says. Even excited, her voice is soft compared with my mother's, everything about her is more diffused.

"I'm going to fix you some lunch," my mother says, with a strange upswell on the word "lunch."

She needs a dialogue coach.

"What would you like, honey?"

She runs her hands through her hair as if it were much longer than two inches. Stands in a sort of dancer's position, feet turned out slightly, as if she were modeling, as if her baggy gray trousers were sequined.

This act is beginning to bother me.

"How about an omelet?" she asks, upbeat, as if an omelet were something to aspire to.

At first, this felt like a trick we were playing on Sheila. We were in cahoots, she and I. I was willing to go along with her. But now I feel iced-out by this act that looks like attentiveness from a distance. It looks like warmth, but feels cold up close.

"I'm lactose intolerant," I say. "Remember?"

It's true, but I've said it to be mean.

She presses her lips together and squints her eyes, another stage expression: Of course I remember, it says. Do you honestly think I could forget? But annoyance radiates out from under the pancake makeup too, as if I'd arranged my digestive system to defeat her. There's a tinge of don't-fuck-with-me around the eyes.

Doesn't she remember the terrible stomachaches I used to get?

"Don't worry about me," I say, "I can make myself a sandwich."

Like I do every weekend.

"On a cold day like this?"

Why is she doing this?

She bounces back. "Soup?"

She'll outlast me. I know that. There's no way around her.

"Soup sounds great."

Sheila agrees.

There's half a bottle of red wine sitting on the counter. I pour two glasses, one for Sheila and one for me. I use the heavy Waterford goblets even. I know the woman playing the role of my mother would want that.

I don't even ask her if she wants a drink. She doesn't.

Plus, she has the salad spinner out, and since she's never used it before, she'll need to keep her wits about her.

When the salad is tossed and the bread is sliced thick and the soup is simmering on the stove just like it does on Walton's Mountain, my mother comes to join us at the table. She sits very close to me, like a girlfriend.

"It's so nice to have you back," she says.

"Where I belong?" I ask, naming that tune.

"Dolly?" Sheila says, finishing it off.

My mother ignores us both and takes hold of my hand.

I see the trace of a smile though.

She loves a show tune.

She interlaces our fingers.

I'm like a prop here.

And I don't know what I've done to deserve it.

"Sheila's just been to China," my mother says.

Then I see.

This is about Sheila. The real question here is: What has Sheila done to deserve this?

I feel even colder then. Gently untangle my fingers from my

mother's. I swear, that's all I do. But she looks all around, very quick, eyes darting here and there, terribly concerned about who might have seen. She looks straight at me with a singeing look then—an honest one at least—that transforms itself, in just a second, into one of hurt, then real sorrow.

I recognize her now, at least.

This is a woman I know.

She's so hard, my mother, and so soft.

Think of a chocolate-covered cherry, except instead of chocolate, think steel. A fortified steel-covered cherry, and just when you're convinced that its shell is impenetrable, that it could never break in a million years, it does. When she's whole, she steamrolls right over you, just flattens you out, but when she's broken, there's nothing but viscous red syrup spilling everywhere and seeping right into you.

And the transformation happens in a flash. Every weekend, I hear something like the crack of a gunshot—it's only an engine backfiring or the televised clap of a bat on a baseball, but it silences everything.

I turn to her.

She goes stiller than still then.

I don't know whether she heard the actual gunshot—my father's Virgo gunshot—or if she's just imagining that it must have sounded something like this. After the stillness, a look of panic comes. Her eyes go wide, wider, and she covers her mouth with both hands as if to muffle a sound that never comes.

She turns her face away from me, and her body begins to tremble slightly.

She's crying now.

I jump right in—embracing her, rubbing her wide back softly, like a baby's back is soothed and petted. It's these moments, I'm sure, that draw me to the train station on Saturday afternoons. I feel useful now, warm too.

But the moment doesn't last for long.

No, she knows the natural order of things as well as I do.

"Straighten up those papers on the table," she says, pulling away from the embrace. "I don't know what I'm running around here."

The crisis passes.

What doesn't pass is my fear—mixed with longing, I suppose—that she'll call on me like this, again and again, forever. Reminding me that we were the two who cleaved together in our little party of three, leaving my father out in the cold. We created this thing, and I'll never escape her now—or want to—as long as I live.

There's a large green pail.

It almost reaches my father's knee. It's plastic and filled with tennis balls. There must be thirty or forty of them.

All yellow.

Some are the color of egg yolks, creamy. Some are brighter, almost brand-new. Some fluorescent, some dingy with age—yellowish gray.

It's a rainbow of yellow balls, sitting in a green plastic pail.

Most of them are "live."

That's the term my father uses.

It means they bounce.

We weed out the dead ones as we go, picking them out by the hollow sound they make at their core when we hit them, or if they don't bounce high enough. I like the sound that the dead ones make, but I don't breathe a word of it to him. He wouldn't know what to say to that.

I must be eleven or twelve.

He hits the dead ones far off—in huge, sweeping arcs—into the field behind the tennis courts.

I stand at the baseline, facing forward. My right hand grips the racquet loosely, my left supports the weight of the racquet's wooden head. My father stands on the other side of the net, midway back, the pail of yellow balls at his side.

He hits them to me, one after the other. A forehand first, then a backhand, then another. He mixes them up. A lob next, then a drop shot. I've got to be prepared for anything, he says.

We're practicing my strokes.

He stands by the pail and hits the balls to me, one after another. Never returns the shots that I hit.

How dull this must be for him.

"Get your racquet back," he says, instructing quietly as we go.

Never any shouting, none at all.

"On the balls of your feet."

He speaks as if I were standing right next to him, and I hear him just fine.

"Turn sideways," he says.

"Make sure to follow through."

There always seems to be something I don't remember to do. Getting my racquet back or following through. Or most often: Finding my ready position—facing forward, knees slightly bent, racquet in front of me, ready for anything.

He hits me a forehand. Then another.

I wonder what it feels like for him when I pull it all together: The footwork and the preparation, the running and the stopping at just the right moment, the backswing and the follow-through.

Is it a victory for him then, when the ball sails low and even over the net? His face is so placid. It's impossible to tell. He's flat and steady like a well-hit ground stroke himself, bouncing even and nice, on the forehand side first, then the backhand.

I never know what he's thinking.

He's just as placid when I sail the ball into the net, upsetting its easy suspension, like a bird fluttering behind drapes.

When the pail is empty—after he's hit me thirty or forty balls—we gather them all up again, making fragile pyramids on the open faces of our racquets. Eight balls at the base, resting easy on the warp and weft of the racquet strings, five balls on the next level, three on the third.

We walk gingerly around the court, practically on tiptoe, gathering up the balls, careful not to upset the delicate pyramids. When we're afraid to add another, we tip our racquets into the pail and let the pyramids spill tumbling in.

We're cautious, he and I. Our pyramids are never very tall.

My mother would build a pyramid to the sky—throwing her head back and roaring with laughter when she'd gone too far, when all the balls came falling down, sliding off her racquet and bouncing away in every different direction.

We're more careful, he and I.

We tip them safely into the green pail. I love the hollow rumbling the balls make, tumbling against the walls of the plastic pail. It's like thunder. When all the balls are gathered up, we begin the drill again: He hits a forehand first, then a lob.

He must feel kindly disposed toward me to spend his Saturday afternoons like this.

A backhand now, then another.

But there's no sound track here, no dialogue at all. Just the sound of balls bouncing and the ping of racquet strings, the muffled sound of footwork. A forehand volley, then a lob. The instructional phrases.

Back to the baseline now: A forehand, then another.

"You've got to get that racquet back."

Now a backhand.

It would be so much easier to know for sure if he'd say something.

A backhand volley, then another.

I'm afraid of him.

Run for a lob.

Lob it back.

The gentlest man you can imagine, and still I'm afraid of him.

Find that ready position.

Does he know how I conspire against him?

Turn my body for a deep backhand.

He must.

Get my racquet back.

How I egg my mother on?

Hit the ball into the net.

He couldn't. No, he couldn't know, and still do this.

A deep lob, then an easy forehand.

What would he do if he found out?

When he hits a short ball, I run for the net.

"Dig, dig, dig," he says softly.

I think he wants me to make it in time, before the ball bounces twice. I'm almost positive he does, but I never let myself know for sure. I'm careful not to let myself grow too fond of him either.

"Nice job."

My mother doesn't brook disloyalty.

.   .   .

I have the portable receiver in one hand, and I'm waiting for the phone to ring with the other. Waiting for Peter. The slightest movement might break the spell I cast: The one that made him ask if he could call. I sit like this for almost a minute—which may not sound very long, but it is. It takes much less than a minute though to know he isn't calling.

Sometimes this happens.

Sometimes they don't call back, even after they've just asked you for your number, repeated it back to make sure they got it right.

I walk to the kitchen and shake a vitamin C pill from the container, swallow it down with a glass of water. At least I won't get a cold. I've got the telephone receiver with me, just in case.

I should be asleep by now. I like to wake with the birds in the morning, pretend I'm going off to the gym to exercise, but somehow start reading instead—the newspaper maybe, or better still, a fat Russian novel—then keep reading and reading until I've read so late that I have to rush over to the gallery to open up by ten.

The phone rings.

It's him.

"What happened to you?" I ask.

I wish I hadn't sounded so demanding.

"I had to feed my cat," he says.

I hate cats.

I'd like to believe him, but it's almost midnight—a bit late to be feeding a cat, no? He probably just stayed on the Pump Line, trolling for someone better, casting out his line and reeling it back in, over and over again.

At least he didn't find anyone.

"Tell me what you look like again," he says.

I repeat my statistics into the receiver, and even though I remember his precisely, I ask him to do the same, just to keep things on an equal footing between us. This request for repetition is common on the Pump Line, a stab at quality control: If a man can't repeat his alleged dimensions, keep them straight, if he can't stick to his story, you can be sure he isn't telling the truth.

Ages often increase by a few years in the gap between calls. Men who were nearly six feet tall become almost five-nine—shrinking Goliaths.

Once, just after I told some guy I was twenty-eight, he snapped back at me like a rubber band, "What year were you born?" I'm still surprised I was able to answer correctly, and I was only thirty-three at the time. I wasn't off by much.

But the cross-examination of Peter and me proceeds easily enough. Statistics are repeated in unwavering voices. Either we told each other the truth the first time, or we're lying again in the very same way, which may be all you can ask for under the circumstances.

"So how was your evening?" I ask, as if we knew each other, as if this weren't specifically an exercise in anonymity.

"Fine," he says.

Nothing more.

"What did you do?"

He doesn't answer immediately.

He probably thinks I want him to manufacture some specialized erotica for me. It won't even occur to him that all I really want is the trivia of his domestic routine.

"I just got back from a birthday dinner," I say, helping him out, just in case he's willing to have the conversation that I want.

More silence.

He can always hang up on me, disappear without a trace.

I don't have his number after all.

He's still silent.

Oh well.

"I went to the Film Festival," he says, tentatively.

Now he gets it.

"That's funny," I say. "I was supposed to go tonight too. I had a ticket to the John Maybury film." I did too, although coincidence concoction wouldn't be beneath me at this point.

"*Love Is the Devil*," he says, the title of the film. I hear the pleasure of a small coincidence in his voice.

You see, we have things in common.

"How was it?" I ask.

And when he answers my question, when he begins his critique of a film I don't particularly care about, I know I've won. I'm not even listening anymore.

Don't you see? I've turned the tide, parted the waters. We're having a real conversation now. This isn't the sex line anymore.

It's still precarious though: We're walking along a sun-dried ribbon of sand that was the bottom of the ocean two minutes ago, walls of water reaching up high on either side of us.

He's still talking about a film I'll never see.

He doesn't realize the miracle I've worked, doesn't feel the threat of all that water crashing down again either. And if I do my job right, he never will. I list some other films at the festival, just for momentum's sake.

He tells me which of them he has tickets to, which of them he's already seen. He most definitely doesn't invite me to any of them. It would be odd, I suppose, if he did.

"Back to the subject at hand," he says, apropos of nothing.

I don't know what he means. For a second, I'd forgotten about the liquid walls on either side of us, that the sandy path we're walking along is really just the ocean floor. We're still only one question away from the Pump Line.

The water won't stay like this forever. I need to put things right, and fast. There's not much time. I can swim, but I don't want to. I don't want him to hang up. Just let me think of what I need to say to keep him on the line.

He lets me know soon enough, calmly steering us clear of trouble: "So tell me again what you look like," he says, undoing all my handiwork, saving me at the same time.

I'm grateful for a second, then annoyed to be on the same old path.

"Again?" I say, mindless of my resolve to keep him.

Does he have Alzheimer's or something?

But now is not the time to challenge. Now is the time for me to say exactly what I need to say to keep him on the line.

"Humor me," he says.

I'd better watch it.

There are those who would have hung up on me a long time ago, as soon as I began that birthday dinner nonsense. So I describe myself again, ask him to describe himself again too, but I'm growing tired of this. I even ask a follow-up question about the length of his hair, just to be polite. But soon I venture off the prescribed route again. I can't help it. Ask him what he does for a living. I know I shouldn't have.

He doesn't answer.

Now I have a massive pause on my hands.

"Are you serious?" he says finally, his disgust palpable.

Now it's over. I've ruined it.

"I'm just trying to get the bigger picture," I say.

"Why?"

"Never mind. Question withdrawn."

"You don't care what I look like," he says. "Do you?"

As if that were a mortal sin.

"Of course I do."

"No, you don't."

His voice is harder now. He's grown impatient with me. He also happens to have got my number. I have stopped caring what he looks like.

I mean, six feet two, one hundred eighty-five pounds, dark hair and eyes, that can look so many different ways—gorgeous, ugly, in between. It hardly bears spending hours on the phone, making a mantra of it, trying to create a composite sketch. Especially when I need to cover other, crucial ground: Does he like Muriel Spark, for instance; does he play backgammon; does he have a boyfriend already?

"I care," I say. "It's just not the only thing I care about."

In truth, I don't care because now is not the time for me to care. Now is the time to get him to care. That's how I work it. Now is the time for me to disarm him with talk that doesn't feel like sex-line talk. To get him interested in me for something more than sex.

First, I need to reel him in. Then, once he's mine, flopping around in the dust at my feet, safely out of water, then I get to care. Then it's up to me to decide whether to keep him or throw him back.

"I wish you were here," I say, growling a bit like Eartha Kitt. "So I could show you how wrong you are."

I have no idea where it came from, but it probably wasn't a bad move under the circumstances.

"I'll tell you why you don't care," he says. My ludicrous, sexy line seems to have worked though. The hardness has left his voice. "I'll tell you, if you want me to." He sounds suggestive himself now, as if he were picking up where I left off.

"I wish you would," I say.

"You don't care because you're more interested in pleasing me. You care more about that than what I look like."

He waits for me to take this in. No one has ever seen through me this quickly before. "You want me to like you," he says.

That's exactly what I want, but he wasn't supposed to be aware of the manipulation.

"I like that," he says, almost whispering.

He seems turned on by this scenario.

But this was only supposed to be temporary, the holding pen on my way to liking him. I have a feeling that he wants a very bottomy bottom, a geisha almost.

"Will I like your body?" he asks.

Suddenly he seems very unavailable to me, more unavailable even than if he told me he had a boyfriend.

"I don't know," I say.

I feel tired now. I want to go to bed.

I picture my poor psychiatrist, Goldstein. See him in his office, sitting in his brown leather chair. The wale of his corduroy trousers so fine that the fabric looks like pale yellow velvet, like soft pants for a baby. I can already tell him everything he would need to know about Peter: I spoke with him on a sex line. (I could almost stop there, couldn't I?) The guy's fantasy is that my only pleasure is giving him pleasure.

I can see the disappointment mapped out on Goldstein's face even as he struggles to remain impassive, the slight wilting of his shoulders even as he wills himself to keep them still.

"So," Peter says, dragging it out a little. "Are you going to please me?"

But I just can't.

"There are so many—"

"Stop," he says, annoyed.

How do I know whether I'll please him?

"Let's just try this my way," he says.

He's very bossy.

"Take a deep breath," he says, but more gently now.

"Inhale," he says, with so much conviction that I do.

I inhale deeply, just like he tells me to.

"Now hold it," he says, and again, I do.

He pauses.

I'm holding my breath.

"Now exhale," he says, and I push all the air out of my chest until it's empty. He tells me to keep breathing like this, and I do. I feel myself slowing down, almost relaxing. Is it really this easy? Pulling the air in through my nose, letting it fill my chest, swelling it up. I hold my breath for a beat, and then for one beat more. Close my eyes and push it all out—all the air, all my breath, everything—pushing it all out through my mouth, hollowing my chest.

"You don't have to control this," he says.

I don't say a word.

I just keep breathing.

"Relax," he says.

I'm thrown for a loop.

We're at such cross-purposes, Peter and I. He's nothing like the sort of man I'd go on a date with, but I'm sticking with him all the same.

"Let's just try it my way," he says.

I'm still not sure. Why would his way be any better than mine? I don't say a thing though. I just keep breathing.

I'm not at all aroused anymore. Feel strangely calm, in fact. All hollowed out in the stomach as if I'd just had a good cry. It's a nice feeling, empty after having been full.

It's not so unappealing either, giving up control for a change.

Not being responsible for everything when it goes wrong.

After lunch, my mother announces that she's driving into town to do some errands. She asks Sheila and me if we'd like to come along.

I say no.

There's no pleasure in running errands with her. She goes too fast. She won't let you browse. It's like running with the bulls in Pamplona.

Sheila says yes first, then changes her mind.

Yes. No, she wants to stay here after all.

My mother looks indifferent, very suit yourself. She's back to normal now, and whether people stay or go is not a matter of grave concern to her.

So she leaves, simple as that, picks up her purse and walks out of the room. The screen door clicks shut behind her.

Quiet everywhere. So much quiet it's hard to know what to do with it all.

Then I hear an engine start in the garage.

She turns the motor over and revs the engine; booming explosions bounce off the wooden walls and concrete floor as she pumps the accelerator up and down. She's a big advocate of warming an engine. Then the racket diminishes. She's letting the engine idle now. Finally, I hear tires crunching on gravel, and the ping of small stones kicked up and echoing around the chassis.

She's driving away.

Now she's gone.

We wander around at first, Sheila and I, both a little awkward. We're moving in concentric circles through the first floor of the house, intersecting from time to time. Something large is missing here. Think of your kitchen: Now imagine it with the refrigerator gone.

Eventually, I join Sheila in the living room, take a seat at the opposite end of a long chintz sofa. She's thumbing through a pint-sized journal called *Healing Arts*—smaller than *Reader's Digest* even—its title written in lavish purple script across the front. Something tells me she brought it with her.

I wish now I'd sat in the club chair, facing her, but I've already sunk to the downy bottom of a big chintz cushion, without a thing to say for myself.

The silence feels permanent.

Sheila looks up at me from time to time, smiling warmly. She has the patient, expectant look of a psychiatrist at the beginning of a session, waiting for me to begin talking, but not rushing me: You just take as much time as you'd like.

Why can't they ever begin?

I suppose I could bring up my anxiety over the silence. Possibly cute, right? More probably neurotic. I don't want to be taken for a patient here.

San Francisco pops into my head. Sheila lives there now. Then Alice Adams, a writer who lives there too, at least according to her dust jackets she does. Nothing more to go on than this: San Francisco and the photograph of a toothy, blonde woman in profile.

I don't know if I can make this work.

"I've just started the new Alice Adams novel," I say, from out of the blue, having rehearsed the line a few times in my head first.

In fact, I haven't started it. I've bought it, but I haven't begun reading it yet.

"Alice Adams!" she says, more than a little surprised. "I haven't thought of her in a million years. You know, she was one of the first people I met when I moved to San Francisco."

Imagine the odds—a coincidence!

This was no simple swan dive either. I've got some degree-of-difficulty points coming to me on this one.

"What made you think of her?" she asks.

"Well, the novel's all about San Francisco really," I say, searching for an interesting connection. "And you live there, of course," still searching.

I've got to come up with something better than this.

"And I've been thinking lately that I'd like to live there too," I say, never having thought of it before this minute, and not at all sure that I would.

"But I thought you were happy in New York?"

It's a reasonable question. Deserves a reasonable answer.

"I am."

"Oh, you are a Libra," she says, smiling and shaking her head slightly, savoring the Libra-ness of the moment. "We're very similar."

I'm thrilled, of course. I smile too, but I'm not quite sure what we're smiling at.

"You'll spend half your life wanting to be where you're not."

Oh, I see. It wasn't a compliment. We're bonding over a mutual shortcoming. I don't know how I feel about this.

She removes a lovely golden ring from the long ring finger of her right hand. It's the softest-looking gold. Looks as if you could squeeze it into the shape of something else with just the push of your fingers. She slips it onto the twin finger of her left hand.

More Libra fickleness in action, I suppose.

"I'm going to give you some advice," she says, "that I wish someone had given me."

I wait.

"But of course, someone probably did give it to me," she says. "I just wasn't ready to hear it."

I wait some more.

"That's the thing about advice, isn't it?"

She fiddles with the cuff of her green blouse.

I'm still waiting.

She appears to be unaware that she hasn't told me yet.

"You haven't given me the advice yet," I say, finally.

"Really?" she says.

"Well?"

"I've completely forgotten," she admits, laughing now, but not too embarrassed.

I'm glad.

"I was talking about San Francisco," I say, rehearsing the moment for her. "Wanting to move there."

"Well, maybe you should," she says. "I don't think it much matters where we live."

I do.

"Take it from me," she says. "I've lived everywhere, and it's all the same kettle of fish."

I find this hard to believe.

"Who knows?" she says. "Maybe a poky little town like this is where I'll really settle down."

What?

I look around, as if she's said she wanted to live here, in this very room. My eyes come to rest on a red Fortuny pillow that's been here forever, deep, satiny red against the matte chintz of the sofa.

I used to love this room, all dark carved wood and rich upholstery fabric—so fancy, unlike all the other rooms in the house. I wished we could have made them all like this. I could have spent my days re-arranging the furniture, shopping for fabric swatches and new wall-paper, but my mother let me know clearly enough—with just the slightest reprimand in her voice, in her look—that she had no use for such activities, and that little boys shouldn't either.

So I tried not to, plumping the cushions in secret.

"This room makes me feel very young," I say, rather than the truth: This room makes me feel like a flop as a little boy, having been found out here once too often showing slightly too much interest in a Murano ashtray.

"Well, you are very young," Sheila says, smiling.

She must see that I look disappointed.

"I'll trade," she says. "If you'd like," moving the ring back to her left hand. "I'd make that trade in two seconds flat."

We fall into a quiet moment, which is natural enough, I suppose. I'm sure it wouldn't distress most people.

She's looking out through the big picture window that opens onto a glade of pine trees and white elms, a brook.

I've failed. I can't engage her.

Not looking at me at all.

This view opens onto the spot where my father shot himself.

Somehow though it's never my father I see when I imagine the scene, never him at all. It's my mother, in a soft pair of flannel pajamas—that's what I imagine. My mother running frantically across the meadow just before the sun comes up, her bare feet and ankles all dewy damp, the hems of her pajama bottoms nearly wet through.

She's running toward a sound, maybe a feeling, the aftermath of a sound that she's not quite sure she's heard.

She would have been awakened from sleep by it.

She runs to my father, lying already dead, instantly dead, in the middle of the lawn at the end of the night.

I'm sitting with Goldstein—the psychiatrist—on the far, far reaches of the Upper East Side—him in his corner, me in mine. Relaxed but ready, like boxers between rounds. He's ancient though, far too old for boxing.

And when I say the Upper East Side, I don't mean Park Avenue, where all the other shrinks are. I don't mean Fifth Avenue either. No, it takes an intricate patchwork of subways and buses and cabs to get me here—as far north as you can imagine, and then even farther east.

"Do you hate me?" I ask, calmly, from out of the blue.

He's looking at me, silent still, but now I feel him come to life over on his side of the room. Eyes open wider, head tilts to the left. Snowy white hair, as full and wavy as a child's, tilts that way too.

I know this look: Continue, it says.

"You must," I say. "Why else would you choose the least convenient location in the city for your office?"

He smiles benignly at me, but I see his shoulders droop slightly. He's listening to every word still, but he's a touch deflated in his brown leather club chair. He was hoping we were getting down to work.

"And with the rates you charge," I say, "you could probably have a suite at the Carlyle by now."

"I'm just happy you remember how to get here," he says.

I think of Hansel in the forest, trying to find his way.

Of the twenty-five or thirty weekly sessions I've had scheduled with Goldstein since my father died, I've managed to cancel about half of them, with trumped-up stories about client meetings and art fairs, exaggerated tales of sinus infections.

"How could I forget?" I ask.

Which is to say nothing of the sessions I have attended, tossing them off glibly, like so many bread crumbs in the forest. But I just can't seem to find the path to my father here, and even when I come close—when Goldstein grabs me roughly by the shoulders and pushes me onto it—all I want is to run in the opposite direction, leaving him and Gretel in the dust.

Canceling is so much easier.

Today I fill our session with talk of Peter: Our promising conversation on the Pump Line and his sweet request to call me at home; the maddening delay in his calling back, my profound relief when he did. And now my latest predicament: Wondering and worrying over whether he'll ever call again.

We've logged a lot of time chronicling the Pump Line here since my father died. "I should just call him myself," I say. "But of course, I can't. I gave him my number," I continue. "He was going to call me. Didn't even ask for his."

"Hmmm." Goldstein hums over on his side of the room, nodding his foolish head of hair slowly.

"Sitting here now," I say, "I can't think of anything in the world more natural than asking, 'What's your number?' But I didn't ask him when I had the chance, so now I just have to sit and wait. There's not much more that I can do about it."

"Hmmm," he hums again. His face neutral still.

I'm supposed to wonder what he means by all this humming, of course—that's my job here. But I refuse to be deterred right now. I need to get the rest of this story out on the table.

"He even asked me if I wanted to get together that night," I say. "So I know he was interested. I mean, at least that night he was.

"But I put him off," I say. "A date should be well under way by half-past midnight, don't you think? I asked for a rain check instead, and he agreed. He said he'd call me the next day, we'd get together that night. But that was almost a week ago now."

Goldstein hums for a third time over on his side of the room, as if I hadn't heard him the times before. Not to worry, Goldstein. I heard you.

I don't say anything though.

"So what do you make of it?" he asks, tired of waiting for me, I guess. Tired of humming to no avail over on his side of the room.

"What do I make of what?" I ask.

"All this madness over a complete stranger." His voice as calm as you can imagine.

He's right, of course. This fixation on Peter is demented. I've never even laid eyes on him. But unfortunately, Goldstein's question is simply not the one I'm interested in right now. All I want to know is whether Peter is going to call me again.

"Who is this man to you?" he asks.

I keep quiet.

"Who is this stranger that you care so much about?"

We eye each other warily from across the ring.

I know what I'm supposed to say, of course. Any fool would. I wish I could oblige him too. Simply cry out—"My father, my father! The stranger is my father!"—and burst into a flood of tears, entirely overwhelmed by feelings great and small.

But somehow I can't do it.

All I can manage is another listless rehearsal of the tale of Pump Line Peter. So I launch into the chronology one more time. Try to rekindle the hope that he might still call.

Sheila and I walk toward the meadow, past the swimming pool that looks put to bed for the winter, a blue vinyl cover wrapping it up tight like a shiny blanket. The snow and ice that sat on top all winter are melting now in small pools filled with pine needles and bird shit.

Soon the cover will sag under the weight of the water on top.

My father was always vigilant about removing the cover before the detritus above polluted the pool water below. I should call the swimming pool man when we get back to the house. My mother will be back from her errands by then. She can tell me his name.

We walk into the meadow. The farther we move from the house, the softer the ground feels underfoot, almost spongy. It must have been somewhere around here that he shot himself, but I don't know for sure.

Sheila begins talking about some kind of therapy group she runs in San Francisco, except she calls it a healing circle. I hope she hasn't called it that in front of my mother.

"I was thinking of one of the men in the group," she says. "Really the gentlest man."

I don't know what to say to this.

"He killed himself a few months ago."

Now I really don't know what to say.

My mother probably told her that my father shot himself out here.

"He lived with AIDS for such a long time," she says.

Doesn't she have an ethical obligation not to tell me these things?

"He tried every protocol that came along," she says. "Nothing ever worked for very long."

She's walking a little more briskly now.

"I don't think he could live with the fear of dying anymore."

I haven't worn the proper shoes. I forgot to change into sneakers at the gallery this morning. I'm beginning to feel dampness through the leather soles.

Sheila's looking off into the distance again. I wish she'd look at me. She combs her fingers through her hair. It looks soft.

"I went around to visit him on the afternoon he died," she says. "We played honeymoon bridge," smiling slightly.

Then, after a pause: "Pills."

I wasn't asking.

I can picture myself playing cards with Sheila.

I used to play cribbage with my father, but not very well. He was always admonishing me: "Count your points." "Use your head." But I was far too busy keeping track of the silence between us, trying to dream up a conversation starter that would draw him in, as if all that had been missing between us was an opening line.

My father always won, laying his cards facedown on the kitchen table after he did, lacing very clean fingers together and placing them on top of his cards. He counted his points.

Who knows what would have happened if I'd counted mine?

Maybe that's all he wanted: A boy who counted his points.

Sheila and I are nearly at the brook now, walking along its banks on a moist carpet of pine needles and smooth gray stones, through a maze of pine trees with slender trunks.

"Do you think he was sick?" she asks, not even naming my father.

"Meaning, that would be why he killed himself?" I ask, knowing perfectly well what she means.

I'm being difficult. I know that, but I've been lured outside under false pretenses. She could have asked me this in the living room. No need to drag me outdoors and ruin my good shoes.

Maybe she thought it would be easier for me out here.

Or maybe she wanted to get off my mother's turf. But if she thinks she can elude my mother this easily—just by walking out the back door—she's dead wrong. I'm sure my mother knows about this conversation even as we speak. She always puts two and two together.

When I was very young, I used to rummage around in my mother's bureau, inspecting all the artifacts there: Elastic garters with rubberized buttons and pearly white girdles with a thousand tiny stainless clasps. Things I can't imagine her ever having used. Pale chiffon scarves. No matter how careful I was about replacing these things exactly as I found them, no matter that my mother hadn't used them for decades, she always knew somehow. She didn't forbid me, or even seem to care.

"Enjoy your little foray?"

She just wanted me to know that she knew.

"I read a study not long ago," Sheila says, not giving up, "correlating suicide with physical illness."

I'm sorry this is the conversation she wants to have.

"I found it distressing at first," she says.

So do I.

"The authors seemed determined to deny the power of depression."

I've been having this conversation for half a year now. It's practically the only subject people want to discuss with me.

"But in the end," she says, "I thought they did a persuasive job."

Everyone wants to tell me the latest thing he's read. None of the articles are very illuminating though, none of the conversations very satisfying. People want to focus precisely on the information I don't have: Why he did it. They're mostly indifferent to the things I could tell them: How it's been for me. Sometimes I think they want me to tell them what no one can: Don't worry, you won't kill yourself.

"No," I say, slowly, as if pondering her suggestion for the first time, as if this weren't everyone's first stab. "I don't think he was sick."

My mother would have known about an illness.

The water moves fast in the brook. It's high too.

"And I don't think he was broke either," I say, preempting the second theory that people tend to raise.

There's plenty of money still. And besides, money didn't mean that much to my father. It would be a different kind of man who'd kill himself over money—which sends me back to "sick?" in a binary loop, as if sick and broke were the only options here, as if miserable didn't exist.

I look over at Sheila, who's smiling now, for some reason.

It surprises me, that smile, hurts my feelings a little.

Makes her look unexpectedly pretty too, coarse wool and burlap notwithstanding. Her eyes are clear and cerulean blue, the corners of her mouth softly wrinkled.

"It's funny," she says. "Your father always seemed so orderly to me, so smug," still smiling, but shaking her head now too. "I would never have expected him to do anything so messy."

This doesn't seem so funny to me.

We walk away from the brook. The carpet of pine needles is too marshy. Walk toward a cluster of hydrangea bushes, their buds small and hard as pellets. Maybe they're not even buds, they don't look much like promise to me.

It's my turn not to say anything now.

"I should just be honest with you," she says. "I was never really all that fond of your father."

"Really?" I say, nodding and trying for nonchalant, but feeling a scramble of excitement and protectiveness and guilt.

"No," she says, looking at me closely now.

She moistens her lower lip with her tongue. Squints her eyes slightly.

My stomach begins to roil with worry. Will my crimes never end here? I can't even remember what I did to make her hate him. My mind is spinning. I feel prickly heat beneath my father's cashmere sweater.

But I can't have caused this!

I've had no access to this woman. And once I know that—once I know I'm not to blame—I begin to grow interested in her dislike of him, fond of it even. Feel the heat that was brewing in my body begin to dissipate.

"I'm probably just jealous," she says.

Of my father? That's hard to imagine, given the ending.

Maybe my mother then? Jealous of her life in the boondocks, saddled with a child and a husband who shoots his head off?

No, I can't work it out.

Maybe she's jealous that my parents stayed together for so long, almost thirty years. Sheila's always been single. But even this doesn't make sense: Sheila's always had wonderful romances.

I remember one story my mother told me in particular, about an affair Sheila had with a handsome, married doctor who was visiting from London. How they met often, whenever they could. Secret dinners at Sheila's apartment, the lights low, casting long shadows of simple objects around the table, a salt shaker writ large, cut flowers looming in projection. Long walks in Presidio park, always deserted when the sun began to set. When the time finally came for him to leave, Sheila drove him to the airport—holding his hand as she did, fumbling as she shifted gears. She couldn't bear to drop him at the airport though, so she brought him inside to the gate, hungry for a few more minutes with him. But she couldn't bear to leave him there either, so she bought a ticket and flew all the way to London with him.

I can see them on the plane together, sitting close as possible. Imagine them perfectly quiet, silent as stones. Sheila thinking, I cannot get you close enough. When they landed, she turned straight around and flew back to San Francisco. Left him like a Spartan, without a tear, knowing he would ride just a few miles to meet his wife and children, knowing that she herself had a very long journey to make to be completely alone.

Not much of a nursery story, I guess, but I liked it all the same. Curled up with it on many a night, happily picturing myself in Sheila's narrow coach seat, my handsome married doctor nestling close. I liked the story better, frankly, before I saw *September Affair*, starring Joan Fontaine and Joseph Cotten, with its curious echoes of Sheila and her married doctor, but even afterward, it's still a pretty good story in my book.

"'Jealous' is probably too strong a word," she says, stepping back.

I still don't understand. Wait quietly for her to continue.

"I can't help thinking," she says, "how different things would be if she'd just stayed with me in New York."

She's talking about my mother. That much I know. The two of them worked together there when they were very young.

"In New York?" I say. I'm lost still, repeating a name on the map as if the sound of it might help me find my way again.

She nods at me, then looks down to the ground, pushes a small stone forward with the toe of her shoe.

I can't see how staying in New York would have made anything so different. "If she'd stayed in . . . ?"

But then I feel a tug in a different direction—something in the concentration of her look, the way she keeps pushing at that stone. It's just beneath the surface, and not about geography at all.

"You and my mother?" I ask quietly.

She nods again, looking straight at me. She looks vaguely worried now too, as if we were standing out on the middle of a frozen lake, at the end of winter or the very beginning of spring: Will this ice bear us up?

"Really?!" I say, a little loudly.

I feel almost giddy at first.

It's a thrilling piece of information!

I look at Sheila. See the color rising on her cheeks and brow. We're on that frozen lake still, but she's heard the ice crack, felt that strange buoyancy you feel just after a patch of ice breaks underfoot. We're floating on an icy raft now, wintry lake water beneath.

"You didn't know?" she asks. She sounds alarmed.

I shake my head.

Now I see: It's a cat-out-of-the-bag problem for Sheila.

"I just assumed," she says quickly, flustered still, looking for an escape route now. "The two of you are so close," she says. "And you're gay."

"Don't worry," I say in a soft voice, trying to soothe her. "It's fine."

It really is, I think.

She looks despondent though.

"It really is okay," I say, stepping forward, rubbing the sleeve of her scratchy sweater. "In fact, I think it's nice you told me."

We stay quiet for a while.

I look back at Sheila, who must stand in some different relation to me now, her hair all white and cut very short, wearing a smock and a scratchy sweater, pull-on trousers with an elastic waist.

Of course, I think.

"We weren't together long," she says, trying to erase it now, trying to wipe it all away.

But it's too late to take it back.

"Just a few months," she says.

I know already that my mother was the one who left, that Sheila was hurt by her leaving. My mother was supposed to be unlucky in love too. At least, that's the conclusion I drew from watching her and my father all those years. That version made me comfortable with myself too, as if I couldn't expect any more than she'd had. But now I see my calculations were all wrong.

"It's a million years ago now," she says. "Nineteen fifty-five, nineteen fifty-six."

Nearly a decade before I was born.

Before my mother and father were married, even.

I wonder if my father knew.

Sheila's lips are pursed when I look back at her again, and she's nodding her head in quick little strokes. She appears to have finished confiding now, which is probably just as well. I'm starting to feel as if I were rummaging around in my mother's bureau drawers again.

CHAPTER TWO

———

Big Red Lip

I'VE GOT fifteen minutes.

That's all.

Fifteen minutes to show time!

I dash into the living room like a crazed cleaning woman, straightening and plumping, neatening and hiding as I go, all very fast. Only fifteen minutes to make this place and everything in it look nice and inviting—and that's including me.

Peter called.

Can you believe it?

Pump Line Peter, who was surely never going to call again.

Snatch up several days' of newspapers, all the sections lying in a jumble at the foot of the big blue club chair in the corner. Only the first and arts sections rumpled from any actual reading, the others pristine still, with that sharp-creased trimness that makes a newspaper so appealing in the first place.

I scoop them up like an infant from a burning cradle, not a second to lose, elbows out wide as I rush them into the recycling bin, just out the back door.

Newspapers, gone.

Now he'll never know how parochial I am—how business and

sports go unread for days at a time—at least not from my newspapers he won't.

Kick the brown leather ottoman back into place.

Only thirteen minutes left.

Hurry!

In the back of my mind, in a small compartment there, I know there's actually a liberal grace period tacked onto the end of this fifteen minutes.

Fifteen minutes means as soon as I can.

Fifteen minutes is still no guarantee that he'll show up at all.

But *fifteen minutes* is what he said. I don't care a fig for custom and practice—he'll be late, you know, if he shows up at all. I push those flutterings of doubt to a safe remove from my frontal lobes. I'm preparing for his punctual arrival in twelve minutes.

NASA never took a countdown more seriously.

Okay, okay. Peter called only in a manner of speaking.

It didn't work quite the way you're thinking, the way I might have led you to believe when I said, "Peter called." It wasn't me, lounging in my blue chair, reading an article in *Vanity Fair,* when the phone began to ring. It wasn't: "I wonder who that could be?" walking across the room to the ringing telephone. "Hello?" It wasn't Peter, out of the blue, almost two weeks later than he promised: "Hello, Matthew?" In fact, you might even say he didn't call at all.

Rushing back into the living room now—eleven minutes to go—with a sensation of moistness at my temples, I glide the long, white sleeve of my T-shirt over all the wooden surfaces—the long, low coffee table in front of the sofa, the two short windowsills on either side.

Sleevedusting!

Rush two coffee mugs into the kitchen.

Nine minutes.

Stack the CDs into neat little piles—taking just a second to berate myself as I do: You could do this as you go, you know, when you take one CD out and put the next one in. But I'm far too exhilarated now to begrudge my housekeeping or any of the circumstances that brought me to this wonderful place.

Peter's on his way!

In a strict sense, Peter's calling was more like this:

I called the Pump Line, looking for him.

Hello, Scott?

Well, looking for someone, hoping for him.

"Hello."

Beep.

"Village."

Beep.

"Fat dick."

Beep.

"Leather."

Beep.

Beep.

Beep.

Why hadn't this occurred to me before?

Return to the scene of the crime.

"Here's the next guy."

"Hello," he said.

And I recognized his voice. Something—its rhythm maybe, its pitch, its slightly nicer than run-of-the-mill quality—caused a certain knowingness in me to blossom: This is Peter.

I skittle over to the books now, only ten or so, lying on the table in the corner.

Hurry.

I need to get them back onto the shelves, pronto.

Don't worry though.

I'm right on schedule.

Even after I recognized his voice, I kept up all the phone-line rig-marole—What do you look like? Where are you? What do you look like again?

I wanted to hear all his answers.

Make sure he was still as right as he was.

He didn't seem to remember me.

I was afraid to remind him who I was. I mean, he didn't call the first time. Maybe I was better off on a clean slate.

But I couldn't help myself: "You know," I said, very casually, almost with a small yawn thrown in, "I think we may have spoken before."

"Tonight?"

"No, a while ago."

"Did we get together?" he asked.

"No."

"Why not?"

Not: You tell me, I've been waiting.

Not: You promised to call and never did.

"I can't remember," I said. "Something about your going out of town, I think."

"Oh, sure," he said. "I remember."

But he wasn't very convincing. It seemed as if he didn't remember most just when he said he did.

"Something about going to Boston?" I said.

"Well, I don't have to go to Boston tonight," he said. "How about you?"

"No trips to Boston on the horizon."

"Why don't I come over then?"

"Right now?"

"Yeah, right now."

It happened so fast.

I gave him my address.

"Give me fifteen minutes."

That's what he said.

Hightail it into the kitchen with six minutes left, shoving all the dirty cups and plates into the white plastic dish drainer, where freshly washed dishes are meant to air dry. Lift the whole lot of it—careful of the sagging plastic bottom—and slide it into the oven.

I sponge down the countertop in a flash.

I could get a cleaning lady, I suppose. For forty-five dollars a week, the plates would be clean. No heatless baking of plastic pails then.

But that's a question for another day.

I rush into the bathroom. Simple here. Just get everything off the rim of the sink and into the medicine cabinet. Toothpaste, hair gel, dental floss. Fast. Pull the shower curtain closed, and no one's the wiser.

I'm as fast as the wind.

So you see, Peter still hasn't dialed my number. He never called in the traditional sense—the way he promised—but I feel good about

48

this development anyway, as if I'd taken matters into my own hands for a change.

Only the bedroom left, with four minutes to go.

Make the bed in a jiffy.

Straighten up the desk.

I throw all the strewn clothes into a laundry bag at the back of the closet.

Done.

Now I turn my gaze to me.

Undress in a flash.

No time to bathe in the two minutes remaining, but I don't need to. There's plenty of time for a clean T-shirt and a pair of jeans—not too tight, not too loose. Tucked and fastened, belted and zipped. All done.

With a minute to spare!

Not a thing left to do. Only sit and wait—and fight the knowledge at the back of my head that keeps creeping inexorably forward; I'll probably wait three times fifteen minutes for Peter to show up—if history is any guide—and that's if he shows up at all.

It's already been more like half an hour. More like that than fifteen minutes. I'm sitting in the blue chair in the living room, on my second glass of wine now. Legs stretched out on the brown leather ottoman. A little less excited. He might not show, you know. Some don't. But I whisk that thought away. There's plenty of good feeling still. And Astrid Gilberto on the stereo.

Fresh air breezes in through the window that's open just a crack.

I still have my hopes. They might be unreasonable, but I've still got them.

The buzzer rings, and my heart pounds.

Doubting to thrilled in half a second.

I could go to bars, I suppose, or discos or any of the other, myriad places that facilitate men's eyes meeting—gay launderettes even—but the thumping in my chest right now explains why I don't.

I wipe moist palms against my jeans, walking to the intercom by the door.

How could anyone go to a bar with this juiced-up version of Mystery Date in the offing?

He buzzes again.

I press the speak button: "Hello?"

Listen button: "It's Peter."

I recognize his voice over the intercom even.

Speak button again: "It's the fourth floor, on the left."

Press the door-open button. Let it ride.

So what if this has never worked before?

My Mystery Date is here!

Everything's coming up roses.

And talk about pride of authorship. I created this man. From the thinnest waves of sound and a plastic pound key, I produced flesh and blood.

I know this is scotched from the start.

But my heart is racing.

I give you my word: Nothing near this exciting ever happened at a gay launderette.

Dash to the CD player in the living room and start Astrid Gilberto all over again. A fresh start is always nice.

I open the door when he knocks—no preview through the keyhole for me.

How could I ever think this would work?

Adjust my gaze downward slightly.

Oh no.

I thought he said he was six-one?

He's not what I was expecting at all.

My heart feels like a penny to me now, rattling around in a rusty old Budweiser can.

I was expecting perfection—the Platonic boyfriend.

"Come in," I say.

Why do I keep doing this?

He steps inside.

Groomed to within an inch of his life.

Such a waste of time.

What's he done to make himself look so odd?

"I hope you didn't have any trouble finding the place?" I ask, fake friendly.

It's the eyebrows.

"No trouble at all," he says.

He's plucked his eyebrows. Not a stray one in sight.

It's freakish.

I think I'm smiling still, but I wouldn't want to see the corpse of a smile that's lying on my face now.

He's not the only freak around here.

I can't seem to look away from the eyebrows either.

I can't believe this is Peter, who occupied my dreams for nearly two weeks.

He's slightly overweight too.

And I wonder what's holding me back in the relationship department.

We're standing in the tiny foyer still. Just a spindly table for keys and one small picture on the wall. I can't bear to invite him inside though.

I bet he shaves his legs too.

Maybe he doesn't like me either. Maybe this is a mutual no-can-do. That would work.

"Okay?" I ask.

He knows what I mean. Takes a step closer.

"Fine," he says.

I smile.

Want to be perceived as a good person, even as I usher him out the door as quickly as possible.

Say it: "You know, this isn't going to work for me."

He keeps smiling, takes a step backward.

"No problem," he says, without much affect.

"Would you like to come in for a second?" I ask. Now that it's been said—not you—it's easy to be polite. "Something to drink maybe?"

Beverage service as a runner-up.

"No, thanks."

Who could accept a drink under these circumstances?

"Sorry that I dragged you out for nothing."

"It happens," he says.

It sure does. It happens every time.

. . .

At about four o'clock on Sunday afternoon—the day after Sheila told me about her affair with my mother—I'm sitting on one of the twin beds in my childhood bedroom, the one nearer the window. I've got the door closed.

I'm thumbing through my father's high school yearbook, calculating the number of Groton boys I'd go on a date with, right now, if they were transported across time—all the way from 1951—and asked me out.

More than you might think, by the way.

When I started this exercise, I thought I might end up with about ten—ten boys, ten dates—but I'm at fourteen already, and I haven't even reached the S's yet.

My mother opens the door without knocking and walks into the room, a green silk scarf tied around her neck and a nylon purse dangling from the crook of her arm. She's just applied a fresh coat of red lipstick.

"Too much lippie," I say, closing the yearbook.

I feel caught, even though she can't possibly imagine what I've been up to.

"Why don't you mind your own damn business," she says.

She takes a Kleenex from her purse and blots off half the lipstick.

See. I was right.

"Damn Georgette Klinger for a son."

"I suppose you'd rather go out into the world looking like the Whore of Babylon?"

This kind of talk comes easy to us. Not saying much, but filling in the empty spaces.

"Maybe I would," she says.

This kind of talk is just a disguise. There's a brief pause, but I don't worry about it, not with her around.

"I've lost some weight," she says. "Have you noticed?"

She stands straighter, thrusting her chin upward. Smoothes her sweater at the waist, tugs at its hem. I don't see it even now that she's pointed it out.

"Two and a half pounds."

She's living in a fantasy world of minor, imaginary weight loss.

"That's good," I say.

The scales in her bathroom don't even have half-pound measures.

She turns her right leg out slightly, not quite perpendicular to the left, like an old-fashioned model. "Rome wasn't built in a day," she says.

We must have made a pact a very long time ago, she and I. So long ago, in fact, that I can't remember making it. She is always to be the subject between us. She tells me stories about herself and things that are hers—her weight, her friends, her car. Even when she asks me questions, they relate back to her: Do you remember the time I took you to the Washington Monument?

And I conspire. Pay attention, always ready with a follow-up question: Then what did you say? It's got to be more than just good manners on my part, this willingness to let her speak, to stay so silent myself, just as it's got to be more than mere loquaciousness on hers.

"Are you ready?" she asks.

My things are scattered all around the room still.

"Almost," I say.

We'll be leaving for the station soon.

"You don't look it."

"I'm just packing up." And I begin to do just that.

She sits down on the other bed.

"Need anything?" she asks.

She means money, I think, or some other thing—toothpaste or socks—but I could probably segue from here to need of a different stripe. Maybe I'm just supposed to introduce myself as a subject for conversation, take the lead.

Is that what normal people do?

Maybe we never made a deal about this at all. Maybe the problem isn't her lack of interest, but my lack of initiative.

"The lipstick's much better," I say.

I shouldn't wait for an engraved invitation, I suppose, but when I do tell her stories about myself—about doomed love affairs or job disappointments—when I look to her for something other than money or socks, she grows uneasy. She's quick to change the subject then. And I let it change, ashamed of myself then and angry with her. I don't know if she won't take care of me, or if I won't let her. All I know is that she doesn't.

She walks to the mirror above the bureau, checking the lipstick for herself. Smirks: Doesn't look like near enough to her.

"It's all about pared down these days," I tell her.

She likes a big red lip.

She looks at the framed photograph on the bureau, just below the mirror. It's a picture of the three of us—only five or six years old—she and my father and I, standing together in front of the Acropolis.

"Will you look at this," she says softly. "Your father looks good there, doesn't he?"

He looks great. In fact, if he weren't my father, he would most definitely have made the Groton shortlist.

Then in a big blonde voice, she says: "And I look pretty damn good myself."

When I look at that picture, I go straight to my father too, a lock of brown hair fallen down onto his brow, a slightly wrinkled, pale blue shirt, and a sweet shy smile, like a little boy.

"And he looks happy," she says. "Doesn't he?"

He does. He looks entirely manageable in that picture.

My father was an architect and engineer, a good one too. Towns all around New England hired him to come and look at their quaint old covered bridges. He would tell the city fathers just how long the structures could be expected to bear up under the weight of modern life. He designed all manner of brace and crutch for them too, shoring them up for as long as possible, staving off the inevitable.

It was on that trip to Greece, I think, he first said he wanted to scale back at work. Too much pressure, he said. Should we have known, my mother and I, just from that?

From out in the living room, I hear Billie Holiday.

Sheila must have turned the stereo on.

I'd forgotten all about her.

I guess my mother isn't telling me the important stories any more than I'm telling her. The story of Sheila, for instance. I've probably got competitors I haven't even dreamt of yet.

"So how much do you need?" she asks, unclasping her handbag and fingering around for the soft leather billfold inside.

She sits back down on the bed.

"You know," she says, "just to be comfortable."

I hate this part. Never know how much to ask for. I'm never sure how "comfortable" she means. If she gave me a million dollars, for instance, I could invest it and live off the interest. But I'm pretty sure she intends a shorter-term comfort than that. She means: How much until the next time?

This payoff is actually a carryover from my father. He'd call for me at the end of the weekend, just before my mother and I left for the train station. Sometimes we'd even have our coats on already, but more often we'd be touring the rooms of the house, checking for things I'd forgotten to pack.

I'd go to him in his study when he called. He'd be sitting squarely behind his mahogany desk with drawers that locked, sitting in a chair with roller-ball wheels. He'd say it was nice to see me, keep up the good work at school, that sort of thing. Awkward smiles all around. Then he'd hand me some folded bills, without a word, without a peep. He didn't want to embarrass either of us. A tape recorder wouldn't have picked up any of these transactions.

I'd thank him quietly and slip off like a dog with a bone, waiting to unfold the money and count it out in private: Always two hundred dollars, always in descending denominations of fifties and twenties and tens, all facing the same direction, like at a bank machine. I'd just slip the money in my pocket, no worse for the wear.

It's not like that with my mother though.

Think of the pickup scene in *Midnight Cowboy,* the one with Sylvia Miles. That's what it's like with my mother. Think of old Sylvia out on the street, walking a nasty white poodle and bumping into Jon Voight, so handsome and half her age. Think of Sylvia going all girlish even though she won't spit on fifty again. You can see that even she only half believes her sexy ingenue act.

She invites him upstairs to her apartment, and they have sex.

Jon Voight's a prostitute. That's what prostitutes do.

When it's over, he asks for money, but awkwardly. In fact, he doesn't even ask, he hints. Sylvia detonates at the suggestion: "Maybe you haven't noticed," she screams, "that I'm one red-hot chick!" She's not convinced though. You can hear it through the volume. She knows the way the world works.

"Of course you are," he says.

And in the end, she doesn't pay.

He does. In the end, he gives her money.

It's just like that with my mother and me, except I get the money in the end. I'm not so sweet as Jon Voight. Sylvia pays up in my version.

"How much?" my mother asks, sitting at the edge of the bed.

I know the response she wants: Gratis for you, baby. I pretend to be engrossed in my folding and packing.

"Come on," she says, wheedling.

She's an expert negotiator. Forces me to start the bidding, never tips her hand.

Why can't she just do it like my father did?

She fishes the wallet out of her bag and opens it, fingers her way through the bills inside, counting as she goes. I can't tell how much she's got. She hands me some.

"How's that?" she asks.

The money comes out in a jumble with her dry-cleaning slips mixed in.

Four twenties.

"Thanks."

"You've become an expensive little houseguest," she says, smiling. Just a spoonful of medicine to make the sugar go down.

"I didn't ask for it."

I don't even need the money anymore.

"I'm only kidding," she says. Look who's sensitive now, the little prostitute from down the lane.

I only take it because it's what she's offering.

"I'd give you the world," she says.

So how come it feels like she gives me Rhode Island?

"Don't forget your laundry," she says.

Maybe she's saving it all up for a rainy day.

I walk to the dryer and collect a few things.

When I come back to the bedroom, she's thumbing through the Groton yearbook herself.

"Where's Sheila?" she asks.

"In the living room," I say, "reading the paper."

"Still?" she asks, with a raised brow. "She's no Evelyn Wood, is she?"

Sheila's probably mortified to be here now that she's told me about her affair with my mother.

"How long is she staying?" I ask.

"Just a few more days, I hope."

After I finish packing and find Sheila to say good-bye, I bring my bag out to my mother's car, a small silver Mercedes.

Sometimes when I slip into the passenger seat, I pretend I'm on a hot date with Alain Delon. Think Rome, 1960. But sooner or later, I look over to the driver's side and see my mother sitting there, seat pushed as far forward as it will go, both hands on the wheel.

"Do you have everything?" she asks.

"I think so."

"I'm in no mood to ship," she says.

She had to Federal Express my contact lenses to me once.

"That only happened once," I say.

"Once was enough."

I buckle my seat belt.

"Do you have the money?" she asks.

I nod, patting the front pocket of my trousers.

"I wish you'd put it in a wallet," she says.

She says this every time.

"You're going to lose it."

She turns the key in the ignition and starts the car.

I should just get a wallet.

"It must be awful to be you," I say, looking at her in profile. "All the pressure of knowing so much."

"You know," she says, eyes still dead ahead, backing the car out of the garage with an efficient three-point turn. "It is."

"Maaa-thew!"

It's my mother, screaming, upstairs.

I'm sixteen years old. Obliged to respond.

I can hear there's trouble afoot, but still I don't run. The harshness in her voice lets me know she isn't hurt. There's been no bout of tachy-cardia here, no accident flipping mattresses.

I say good-bye to Gene Rayburn and the crew from *Match Game*. Turn off the television. I doubt I'll be back soon. Her voice tells me everything I need to know: I've done something wrong, and she's discovered it.

I walk to the stairs and climb them slowly, one step at a time. Prepare myself to meet my fate. I find her in front of the cedar closet in the hall, where we store our winter things out of season.

It's June.

An ancient trunk from sleepaway camp lies open at her feet.

Oh no.

A *Playgirl* magazine flopping in her right hand.

She doesn't say anything right away. She's too agitated to speak. Looks down at the magazine, back at me.

Why on earth would she be going through the winter closet in the middle of June, through a trunk I haven't used since I was eight years old, no less? It's like she has radar.

"Where did you get this?" she asks, agitated still.

When she speaks, the magazine flutters slightly in her hand. I can see the edges of the pages inside—a pair of tanned legs with just the right amount of hair, an advertisement for a battery-operated sex toy. I know everything about this magazine by heart. I've had it for six months now, look at it only when she's safely away.

"From a friend," I say.

That was stupid.

"No, you didn't," she says. "You stole it, didn't you?"

She's right: I shoplifted it from the Price Chopper in Vernon. But that can't be the problem here, can it? The source of the soft-core pornography.

"How could you do this?" she asks, angry and hard. It doesn't sound like a question though, not the way she says it.

"I just wanted to see what it was like," I say.

Maybe I can still get away clean: No need to worry, Mom, just experimenting.

"How could you do this to me?"

Oh, now I see.

I don't say anything at all.

I watch her eyes calming though, watch her posture grow more relaxed too.

She must have known about me long before this.

"Are you okay?" she asks, in a quiet voice now.

I hear the warmth radiating from deep inside her, like the wood-stove in winter, sitting cold now in the kitchen downstairs.

"I'm fine," I say.

She steps toward me and hugs me tight. She's almost a foot shorter than I am, but I'm entirely protected here.

"I just wanted to see what it was like," I say. "Really."

Feel the shiny cover of the magazine slide down my back. Smell the faint scent of talcum powder mixing with her warm skin.

We stand like this for a long time.

"Are you sure you're okay?" she asks as she pulls away.

I nod.

"Listen," she says. "There's a man in town, Dr. Esty. I want you to go see him."

I nod again.

"I want you to talk this whole thing through, okay?"

She had this all planned out, I bet. Just waited for the opportunity to present itself.

Now a pang of worry, feel it stab at my chest.

"You're not going to tell Dad?" I ask. "Are you?"

I don't think I could take his blank expression staring back at me.

"Of course not," she says, looking at me as if I were crazy.

Must be two or three winters ago now. Creeping across Thirteenth Street like the French Lieutenant's woman, bundled against the cold with so many layers that I was scarcely visible. Shrouded like Meryl Streep in a long dark overcoat, gray woolen hat pulled low, thick scarf wrapped twice around my neck and as much of my face as I could manage.

Just a small patch of skin, that's all, only a narrow strip of brow and cheek and nose. Everything else hidden away.

And beneath all those layers, and the layers beneath them, an adhesive film of ForPlay Sensual Lubricant was crusting on my skin, encasing my genitals in secret, as I slipped quietly across town.

I was walking back to my apartment from a lunch date that morphed into an extremely unsatisfying sexual experience.

Apparently "lunch" can be a euphemism.

A very tall German I'd met at a Christmas party, smelling nicely of eucalyptus, had called me that morning and invited me to lunch at his apartment.

Maybe I should have known that lunch was never in the cards—just a wink between consenting adults—but I was far too busy trying to puzzle together what I could remember about him: There was the eucalyptus smell, of course, and his height, which bordered on the extreme. Silver-rimmed glasses. Lovely hands with long, slender fingers and a complicated network of veins, like the ridges and valleys of a purplish topographical map set against pale skin.

Lunch, he asked.

I'd love to.

When I arrived at his apartment, nicely spruced—for a date after all—a small host gift tucked into my coat pocket even, I didn't smell any cooking smells, no onions browning or chicken roasting.

Just the eucalyptus again.

You tell me: Should I have known then that lunch was never being served?

Maybe he was ordering in.

He led me into the living room and invited me to sit down on a chrome sofa with black leather cushions, designed to look like Corbusier, but definitely not.

There must have been something nice about that apartment, something I could mention now—there always is, but all I can remember is the rough leather of the sofa cushions.

He didn't offer me a drink right away, and when it became clear to me he never would, I asked for one myself—to put things right. As if a glass in my hand that he had put there, three tinkling cubes of ice inside, would somehow correct the atmosphere of this lunchless lunch.

He was the one who said lunch.

And even if I had known, what should I have done then—turned tail and walked out?

So I sat down on the couch, and he sat down too—close, but not too close. The black leather cushions, filled with foam, rose up slightly on either side of us when we sat.

I asked him how he'd been.

Fine, he said.

He slid in a little closer.

Oh no.

I don't remember now if he ever even gave me the drink I asked for.

He was on me in a flash—all over me and around me— a profusion of hands and tongue, all anxious and untrained, like fifteen Labrador puppies bounding on top of me.

Not much in the way of pleasure.

But I didn't stop him.

I could say now that he was so single-minded that Hercules himself couldn't have stopped him. But that wouldn't be true. It would probably have been as simple as a whisper, a murmur would have stopped him dead in his tracks.

One of the cushions slid off the sofa.

The beautiful hands were still as beautiful as I remembered them— even as they mauled.

I kissed him back.

Of course I did.

He wasn't forcing me. I'm sure I seemed perfectly game to him as he made his move, as we moved through his move.

I don't blame him. I couldn't really, even if I wanted to. I wind up in scenarios like this a little too often for me to lay the blame at anyone else's doorstep. Its blueprint must be written somewhere on my body.

When the second cushion tumbled off the sofa, he suggested we move into the bedroom. Now that we were in the realm of language, I really could have put an end to this business. It would have been as simple as: "Let's get some lunch" or "I should get going," maybe even simpler: A furrowed brow, a squinted eye.

But I calculated that just finishing up would be a lot easier. The energy required on the side of finishing would be as nothing compared with the wrangling and confusion of my saying no to him then, and the argument that would ensue, or the silence.

Maybe this is how they do it in Germany.

So I followed him into the bedroom and out of my clothes. I climbed into bed with him like Mary, Queen of Scots, climbing down from the Tower of London after all those years, so brave.

This is when the ForPlay Sensual Lubricant appeared.

He smeared it on me, cold at first and thick as paste, over my lower abdomen, like translucent toothpaste almost, the way it squeezed from the tube, and onto my dick. The gel softened as he worked it in circles, grew warmer. He spread it on my inner thighs too.

He began working his body against mine for friction, the gel becoming clear and even warmer, almost silky then.

It really was easier just to play along.

And some of it felt very nice.

In fact, I almost let myself believe in lunch all over again, just that it was coming afterward.

Then a surprisingly loud slap on my ass that stung.

No, no lunch here.

I felt the imprint of his hand on my ass for a long time, the reverberation and the sharpness, in waves.

Then a remarkably warm kiss.

More of the nice friction.

I know there's nothing wrong with this, lunch or no, it's just not what I had in mind that afternoon—the aromatic fantasy of garlic roasting like a lovely promise.

His lips curled into a sneer of pleasure.

I felt his dick very hard against my stomach.

I saw the closeness building on his face.

Then he grunted, warm sperm on me.

All done.

I raced to be done too—with him and my ambivalence and my dream of lunch, and soon I was.

A caressing hand again—my own—wiping myself up.

He offered me a shower, but I refused. I wanted to be gone.

He might have invited me out to eat, or whipped something up for me there—scrambled eggs maybe—if I'd been slightly jauntier about the whole business, afterward.

But somehow I couldn't be.

I drank a glass of cloudy tap water instead, and reassembled all my winter clothing. Layer by layer, I rebuilt my protective shell.

Didn't have enough Mary, Queen of Scots, in me after all.

The phone's ringing when I unlock the gallery on Monday morning. Probably just my boss, Harry, calling to check up on me from his house in the country. We're mounting a new show this week. Lots to do here.

I'm running late this morning too. It's not a big problem though. Ten o'clock on Monday morning isn't exactly prime time for an art gallery. But watch, it'll be a huge problem for Harry. He hates to think of my getting away with anything. Even now—after ten years here, my slow climb up through the ranks—he acts as if I might run off with the petty cash box any minute.

The phone rings a second time.

I pull my key out of the lock.

I pretty much run the place now. Harry dips in from time to time, of course, and we have a girl who helps out in the afternoons.

We show photography here.

It's a great job: Choosing the pictures and making a show, hanging the photographs strategically around the gallery. Like telling a story without any words. That's not why I've done so well here though, my curating abilities. No, it turns out I'm a born salesman. Who'd have guessed? Turns out I can sell ice to Eskimos—sweet-talking the up-town ladies and coaxing the Japanese collectors. Oh yes, they all leave with pictures by the time I'm done with them.

The phone rings a third time.

I run for it now.

Fuck you, Harry.

"Hello?"

"Good morning, sweet prince."

It's my mother.

I slump into the guest chair in front of the reception desk.

"You didn't call last night," she says.

I was supposed to call her when I got in, let her know I arrived safely, but I'm not in the mood to apologize now. I don't say anything. Just cross my legs and wait. It won't take long.

"What are you up to?" she asks.

"Oh, you know," I say, "working away."

"You are not," she says. "I called no more than five minutes ago, and nobody answered."

I feel even less like responding now.

"I must have been downstairs," I say.

There's no downstairs here.

"What are *you* doing?" I ask.

"I just went jogging," she says.

I know she didn't.

"That's nice," I say.

The very idea of it is ridiculous, but I have only my suspicions, no alibi-busting dirt from any previous call. I gaze up at the photograph on the wall in front of me: A black-and-white picture of an old woman in a nightgown, a paper mask covering most of her face. I sold it just last week, for almost double what Harry wanted for it too.

I really don't have time for her right now. I'm late as it is.

"I went into town this morning," she says.

Now we're getting somewhere. I can hear it.

"I'll never do that again."

"Why?" I ask.

"Six months later," she says, "and you should see the way people around here look at me. Big cow eyes."

I cradle the phone between my shoulder and my ear. Begin reorganizing a large stack of catalogues into two smaller stacks.

"They pity me."

They probably blame her, actually.

"I'm never going into that town again."

I wish I had a coffee. This is going to take a while.

"People feel bad for you," I say.

"But if I don't go in," she says, ignoring me, "how will I get my mail?"

"It takes time," I say.

But she's not even listening to me.

"I wish I never had to go into that town again," she says.

"You should move here if you don't want people to give a damn about you," I say. Then I panic when I realize what I've said. She must never, ever move to New York.

"I'll always be the woman whose husband killed himself."

At least she didn't hear my invitation.

"You're right," I say. "You will be, but after a while, a million more things are going to happen to a million other people, and everyone's going to forget about you. Even you're not going to think about it so much."

Could this be true?

"I hate it when people say stupid things like that," she says.

I feel stung, but I know she feels worse.

We're both silent for a minute.

"How do you know that's what will happen?" she asks, softer now.

"I don't," I say. "Not for a fact."

I feel myself opening to her.

"But I've got to imagine this is going to be vaguely like everything else in the world."

"They blame me," she says.

This is what it's all about.

"Honey, you're not to blame."

"No?"

Her voice is childlike now—wide open and vulnerable. I wouldn't even be able to identify it if I heard her on the Pump Line.

"Of course not."

How could she be to blame?

How could she feel she isn't?

She sighs.

"This is definitely not your fault."

Another long pause.

"Definitely," I say again, with real firmness now.

I can hear her on the other end of the line, breathing softly, not saying a word, only relishing not being to blame. I can practically see her shoulders relax and drop.

"Oh honey," she says, so grateful. "I love you like a mother."

"You can't say that," I tell her, soaking it up, deflecting it too. "You *are* my mother. You could only say that if you loved me like a mother,

65

but weren't actually my mother. That's the whole point of the expression."

"Quite the wordsmith," she says, back to normal now. "Aren't you?" Case closed.

But I see an opportunity now too. The door's open, just a crack. Just wide enough for me to squeeze my body through. "Listen," I say. "I talked to Uncle Andrew again last night." My father's brother. "About the memorial service for Dad."

She doesn't make a sound, but I know I've stolen her momentary relief from her. The hand that giveth.

"I think we should do it in early October," I say, as if the only question were the date. "It's so beautiful up there then. Just around the anniversary too."

More silence.

"So what do you think?" I ask.

"I think you're both crazy," she says, even harder than I was expecting.

No choice now but to wait.

"Your father is dead and buried," she says. "We gave him a lovely funeral, and now it's time to let the subject drop."

We gave him a private funeral three days after he killed himself—just her and me and the minister from the church in town. My uncle was away. We didn't know how to reach him. Couldn't even tell him until he got back. We didn't invite any of my father's friends either. Somehow we just didn't have it in us then.

"No," I say. "We have to have a memorial service."

"Why?" she says, snappish now.

"So people have a chance to say good-bye."

"You mean, so people can stand around blaming me," she says.

"People don't blame you," I say.

"Yeah," she huffs.

"They don't," I say.

But this exchange is entirely different from the one forty-five seconds ago. I can already tell that I won't make an inch of headway this time, not even a dent in her armor.

We both sit quiet on the line now, receivers pressed up against our ears. It's a telephonic standoff. There's nothing more to say.

. . .

Out on the street, some sort of meteorological miracle has taken place, turning the frigid day into a sunny trailer for springtime.

I was inside for only an hour! But all my layers are as dispensable now as the silver salt and pepper shakers I carried with me as a host gift for the German, nicely wrapped in craft paper still, in my coat pocket.

I feel foolish when my fingers find them there.

Don't be silly. We just had a misunderstanding, the German and I. Everything's fine now.

The sky blue sky is proof enough of that.

I buy a bagel to soothe my rumbling stomach and put the lunchless lunch behind me once and for all. Feel the warm sun on that exposed strip of brow and cheek and nose.

I stop beside a young blond woman on the sidewalk playing "Hey, Big Spender" on the flute, her velvet-lined case lying open on the street and a cardboard sign propped up against it: THANKS.

I'm glad to peel my gloves off and give her some change. My fingers were a bit sweaty inside the gloves anyway. I take my hat off to her too in the sunny afternoon.

I love a show tune.

> *Wouldn't you like to have fun, fun, fun?*
> *How's about a few laughs, laughs?*

It's here, standing alongside this Gwen Verdon with a shiny silver flute, that I first notice a change in the pedestrian traffic.

A chic woman with beige hair alights from a cab, a well-dressed little boy in tow.

They're the first ones.

Then a young woman, very plain, with two beautiful children walks by—a little girl by the hand and a baby in a stroller.

> *I could show you a good time.*

An old black woman with a little white boy walking toward us.

Children swarming, like bees.

Finally a father—there's one—with a little girl in a fancy pink coat. This must be a school zone, but I don't see the school.

They're all converging on a small brick building just ahead. There's a sign above the door: EDUCATIONAL ALLIANCE.

But it's after two o'clock. Too late for school, right?

They march in nevertheless, the adults all businesslike and efficient, the children willing enough.

Except for one little boy, who looks about five or six—but don't count on me here. He could be three; he could be eight. What do I know? He's small, somehow even smaller for the tiny yellow parka he's wearing. It's almost miniature, photoreduced from a normal piece of clothing. His mother is dragging him by the sleeve of his puffy yellow jacket, pulling him toward the building. He manages to stop her just short of the door.

The blonde flutist packs up her case and walks to the coffee shop on the corner. I can't say I'm sorry to see her go. A little a cappella flute goes a long way.

This looks like a better show anyway.

The little boy's face is astonishing, more the suggestion of features than features themselves, just the buds of a nose and mouth. He's everything you could want in a little boy, except he's miserably unhappy.

"I don't want to go," he says.

"Tu dois aller," the mother says brusquely.

She's not going to engage him. Just stating the facts, in French.

"I don't like it a bit," he says, sounding very adult to me—but again, I know very little of the conversational styles of children.

"En français," she says sharply.

Why is an American woman speaking French on Thirteenth Street?

Her voice is loud and strict, and she's wearing a long down coat with a horrible plaid pattern on it that makes her look gargantuan beside the tiny yellow cloud of boy.

"But I hate it," he says with a catch in his voice—just a small sob, like Linda Ronstadt on "Blue Bayou"—ignoring her command to speak French. He's on the verge of tears, but fighting them.

"*En français,*" she says, even tougher.

She seems so dictatorial with her crazy Frenchness, laying down the law just because she can.

He turns up the volume: "*Je déteste la classe,*" but slowly, pausing between each syllable.

I'm transfixed, watching a duel unfold.

"*Tu sais que tu l'aimes quand elle commence,*" she says.

"What?" He's impatient now, snappish.

"*Écoute,*" she says, and begins to repeat herself, more slowly this time. "*Tu sais que tu l'aimes . . .* "

"I don't understand you," he says, interrupting her loudly.

He begins to cry now, and not the false cries you hear from children in supermarkets when their mothers refuse them a box of cookies, or the attention-seeking cries of children who want to be carried, too lazy to walk. These cries are for real. I can hear his misery.

Suddenly the mother softens. She bends down to him and speaks quietly into his face. "Honey, I thought you liked to play upstairs." In English, at least.

He stops crying. "Sometimes I do," he says. "*Quelquefois,*" to please.

She kisses him.

I feel relieved.

She wipes his face gently.

I guess she's not so bad.

Softly still, "Why don't you give it a try, sweetie?"

We both see her trick at the same moment, catching flies with honey.

My stomach drops.

He begins to cry again.

"Please don't make me," he begs. "Please. I hate it."

He presses his back up against the redbrick building, arms out-stretched. He looks as if he were on a ledge, fifty stories above the city, terrified of falling. The downy yellow parka, pushed flat in back, puffs out farther in front. He looks even smaller now, frozen in place, sobbing.

Other mothers and other children walk into the building, the mothers trying to act as if nothing unusual is going on. But the children are transfixed; they have to be dragged, gaping, from the scene.

"*Calme-toi,*" she says, no longer bending to him, standing so much taller it's as if she's lording her size over him.

He's hysterical now. "I want to go with you," he screams. His face contorted, eyes panicked.

"Fine," she says, defeated now, but it's most definitely not fine. "Okay," she says. "Let's go."

She looks repulsed by him.

He doesn't rejoice at his victory either. He crumples onto the sidewalk, exhausted.

She just watches. Doesn't go to him, doesn't lift him up.

He lies there for quite some time, and then he stands, trying to compose himself. He's stopped crying now, but his breathing is jagged still. He straightens his jacket, dusts himself off.

He's old enough to do these things.

He calms himself, partly victorious and partly abashed by his victory.

He's old enough to go to school.

I can see that now.

He'll remember this scene, I bet, even if he forgets the details. It will be imprinted on him as surely as the mark her hand made on the downy sleeve of his jacket. He'll remember her desire to leave him behind. His weakness and his fear, her ultimate benevolence mixed with disgust.

I promise you he'll remember his shame.

She had the power to make him go, but didn't, like a pardoning executioner. But she was more than that. She was implicated in his crime too. It was she whom he wouldn't leave after all.

She's thrilling to him, and he'll remember that too.

Sometimes he'll love her for her kindness, and sometimes he'll despise her for her power and her ancient knowledge of him.

They walk off together, but not hand in hand.

His parka is dusty at the back from where he pressed himself up against the brick building.

They're moving separately still, decidedly so.

As they walk though, he'll inch back toward her.

I know he will.

Slowly, she'll take him in.

· · ·

I'm sitting in the living room, in the throes of a fierce war of wills with the cordless phone on the chair beside me. I will not call the Pump Line tonight. Not after last week's debacle with Peter. But the phone just sits there, mocking me, black molded plastic screaming out what it knows: You're desperate to dial.

The Pump Line never works. I know that.

But shouldn't there be one guy in that legion of men who lives up to the dream, one lovely guy who leaves his eyebrows alone, just sitting there on the line now, waiting for me to call?

Yes, I decide. There must be.

Lamplight shimmers off the shiny handset like moonlight off a slinky evening gown, a black dress for Jean Harlow.

It never works.

Back and forth, back and forth. But I already know I'm going to call. So I do, brimming with shame as I dial. Those who forget history are condemned to repeat it, you know.

I'm back in the saddle in a flash—weeding and sorting, beeping and flirting. And in the mood I'm in, it doesn't take long tonight either. I find my pearl among swine, although this one sounds more like Mr. Tonight than Peter ever did.

Not much later, my buzzer is buzzing.

"Fourth floor, on the left," I say.

Astrid Gilberto gets another fresh start, but she's sounding a bit tired to me now.

I wait by the door. Lean my forehead against the cool metal door frame. I could use a rest too. Hear the elevator cranking away as it hauls my gentleman caller up to me.

I look through the peephole this time, when he knocks. This one's taller than I expected, more handsome too. Now we're talking.

I open the door.

Dark hair and eyes, very good looking.

I warm to the Pump Line all over again.

He's dressed in simple dark clothing, a backpack slung over his shoulder.

"Come on in."

Eyebrows intact.

He walks in awkwardly though. Doesn't know quite where to look. He can still reject me, you know. I put his awkwardness down to indecision. "Everything okay?" I ask, closing the door behind him.

He keeps me waiting for a response. Maybe he's still not sure.

Indecisive, I think, turning back to him, but toward an altogether different version this time.

What's the matter with him?

His eyes are like slits, so narrow that I wonder whether he can see me through them. His mouth pressed shut so aggressively that I can see the muscles of his jaw flexing and fluttering beneath his skin. Everything closed up tight.

"Are you okay?"

He punches me in the stomach, very hard, without a backswing or any preparation, a straight jab to my gut.

I feel my breath hurl out of me, grunting.

What did I do wrong?

I lurch into a C-curve, wrapped around his fist.

It hurts.

This is my fault. I know it.

Will he hit me again? I'm doubled over still, too afraid to stand, even though I could. But I know already: I know this guy will hit me again, that he's here specifically to hit me.

He punches me again, again very hard, but just under my eye this time, just north of my cheek. I hear a cracking sound—like in the movies—when his fist connects with my face. I've never heard this sound in real life.

I fall backward, into the hall table, reeling back and falling down. The table falls with me. The little Persian rug slides out from under my feet. I'm lying on the floor now, curled into a ball.

He kicks me, first my leg, then my side.

I haven't done anything to him.

He kicks me again.

Astrid sings coolly in the distance.

As long as he's kicking me though, he's not killing me. They keep coming—kicks to my back and side, kicks to my stomach and my chest.

See his bag on the floor beside me. He could have a gun in his bag, you know, or a knife.

He stops kicking.

I hear him murmuring vague obscenities now. Maybe he's been murmuring them all along. Maybe I'm just now hearing them. His voice grows louder as he kneels, still cursing as he does. I don't believe he's cursing me though.

Then he punches me.

His eyes don't even seem to take me in as he punches. He's in a world of his own. I curl myself into a tighter ball, hands covering my face.

Finally I summon the courage to speak. "Stop," I say, just that, quietly at first, then louder, "stop."

And he does.

He stops.

Surely it can't have been this simple, just asking.

"Shut the fuck up," he says.

They're the first words that I've been able to make out since our sexy phone chat. I could hear every word he was saying back then.

He reaches into his bag, pulls out a black circle.

What is it?

It's not a gun.

Tape. It's a fat roll of black electrical tape.

I don't understand.

I am not afraid of tape. I'm afraid of kicking and punching and guns.

He rips a long piece of tape from the roll, and he bends down over me. Slaps it over my mouth.

I was wrong not to fear this tape. When this happens on television, the guy with the tape on his mouth usually ends up dead.

He pulls me to my feet and shoves me into the hall closet. Closes the door behind me. He doesn't slam it though. He closes it normally, the way you would after you'd hung up your coat.

"Keep your fucking mouth shut," he says through the door.

I haven't been saying anything.

"And don't you fucking move."

But he hasn't bound my arms or my legs. What's to keep me from removing the tape? Nothing, I suppose.

Nothing but my fear. There's plenty of that.

I stand stock-still in the darkness, brushing up against my winter coats, not removing the tape, not moving at all. Feel pain blooming under my eye and in the small of my back. My shoulder feels like it's floating. That can't be good.

I stand in the dark and wait. It smells musty in here. I wait for an unaccountably long time. I have no idea how long it is though.

I don't hear any noise in the apartment. But I haven't heard the front door open or close either.

I'm too afraid to move still.

After a very long time—after what I imagine is an hour—I open the closet door, gingerly, electrical tape still firmly attached to the right side of my mouth, flapping on the left, where the heat and moisture of my breath has undone it. I press at it repeatedly, trying to reattach it, but there's no more adhesiveness there.

It's not my fault.

I see the evidence of our struggle in the foyer. My having fallen down looks much nobler now than I remember it. The room is a wreck, the table fallen, the carpet doubled up on itself. The picture by the door has fallen too, glass cracked.

I stand very quietly, trying to locate the sound of him in the apartment, but I don't hear a thing.

I force myself to walk into the living room, quietly as I can, careful to keep the floorboards mute. It's just as tidy here as it was.

No trace of him.

No trace of him in the bathroom either or the bedroom.

I check the kitchen.

I check all the closets and under the bed and every place he could be hiding and even places too small for him to hide.

He's gone.

But I never heard the front door open or close.

So I check all those places again, just to be sure. No trace of him.

I lock the front door.

Nothing's missing either. My wallet's in my pants pocket still. The envelope of cash in the dresser.

I sit down in the living room.

Remove the tape from the right side of my mouth.

My eyes begin to tear, as if from onions or from allergies. I'm not crying. It doesn't feel like crying anyway. My eyes are just tearing. But then my back rocks forward slightly, forward and back, in time with quiet bursts of exhalation from my chest. Now I'm crying, and it builds. I'm racked with tears and sobbing, and I give myself over to them.

My nose is running, and my forehead is wet.

The front of my T-shirt soaked through.

All the water inside me wants to be loosed on the world, wants to leave me high and dry, just a heap of skin and organs and bones.

I cry through all of Astrid Gilberto—through all ten tracks of her, and even through the beginning of her again, thanks to automatic repeat. My heart will stop beating before she does, my crying too.

There's no end to this.

—

CHAPTER THREE

Tennis Whites

MY FATHER WOKE UP early in the mornings, long before six. Never an alarm, he just woke up. Creaked down the stairs and made himself a coffee. Stood waiting in the kitchen, watching it brew.

I can see him now in a watch-plaid robe, belt slung low.

He took a mug with him outside and sat on a yellow lounge chair by the pool, the dark greens and blues of his robe popping nicely against the shiny vinyl cushions, like an iridescent horsefly landing on a daffodil.

He looked lonely to me.

I'm not sure how I know any of this. I certainly never walked alongside him out to the pool. Never stood in the kitchen with him either, listening to the sputter and hiss of the coffeemaker. I don't even remember spying on him from an upstairs window, but I know he did these things.

He swam after the morning coffee—even well into the fall and much too early in the spring, when it was altogether too cold for swimming. Just untied his robe and slipped it off. Naked underneath. He dived into the pool without so much as dipping a toe into the water first.

There was always something not quite right about that, if you ask me, just diving into icy water that way.

These days—after the gunshot—people go on and on about how sensitive he was. A delicate flower, too fragile for this world. But I can't square that version with the one that dived into an icy pool on Columbus Day. Maybe he was just the opposite of sensitive, in fact. Maybe he was numb, trying to feel something. The chilly water just a prelude to the bullet.

After the swim, he came back indoors. I can hear the screen door clicking open and the long, slow arc of its close, the maddening delay of its final snap shut. I must have been vaguely awake, I suppose. He poured himself another coffee then and went back into his study, closed the door behind him.

I can see that watch-plaid robe more clearly than the newspaper on the seat beside me, the horizontal greens and the vertical blues. I can see the fabric clinging to his strong thighs and back, the water from the pool pasting it onto his skin.

He played records then: The Mills Brothers and Dinah Washington, Louis Armstrong, and Blossom Dearie. They were my alarm clock: The Gershwins and Harold Arlen, Cole Porter. Every morning.

Remember that balancing arm on phonographs—the one that steadied the records in place, floating up above the turntable? Just lift that arm up after the record had fallen down, and the music would repeat forever. That's how my father listened to records, always with the arm lifted up.

"A Tisket, a Tasket" until you could just about die.

Seven o'clock in the morning, no less.

The same eight songs over and over again, for hours at a stretch, several days running sometimes, until a new record appeared magically from the library of old ones, long after my mother and I knew those first eight tracks cold.

It didn't take a bullet to know that something wasn't right here. Of course it didn't. The solitary coffees and the chilly morning swims, the same eight songs repeating endlessly at the crack of dawn. Anyone could see something wasn't right—a child of six could see that. Did, in fact. The harder question is what, precisely, was wrong: Did he see our crimes against him: How I coaxed my mother into running him down, how I wished him gone when he came home to us at the end of the day? Or did he simply reject us for no reason at all?

Early one evening—back in sixth or seventh grade, it must have been—the midsummer sun just beginning to sink like a stone, I remember crunching through the parking lot in special baseball shoes. My uniform just a little too neat, the cap sitting precariously on my head.

My mother and father were walking on either side of me. We were heading to the playing field on the far side of the lot. Butterflies of nervousness fluttering inside my chest and stomach.

The baseball shoes clattered noisily against the gravel.

"Pick up your feet when you walk," my mother said.

But it wasn't so easy walking in those shoes—plastic bumps spaced evenly along their soles like hard, black tumors. The loose gravel in the parking lot made it even worse. Easier to walk in high heels, I thought.

We were running late that night, as we often did for baseball. I'd stalled at home for as long as I could—turning the house upside down, pretending to search for the baseball glove I'd hidden under the guest-room bed earlier that day, hoping for an easy way out. My mother found it for me. Pursed her lips when she handed it back.

Just as the three of us were about to part—them, climbing the bleachers to watch the game, and me, walking miserably to the dugout that smelled of mildew, spilled soda sticky underfoot—a dirty little boy approached us.

The butterflies turned more insistent then.

Jimmy Parker, his name was. He lived in the trailer park at the edge of town. His uniform looked as if it hadn't been washed in months. He smelled unclean too, a cocktail of sour milk and urine.

"We was hoping you wouldn't show up," he said to me, hard as slate, right in front of my parents.

I froze. Felt my mother's body tense beside me. Felt the blood behind my cheeks and the thickness of my tongue.

Could I pretend it was a joke?

"Bad news," Jimmy called out—to no one in particular. His voice was far too mean for joking. No one to hear it but us. All our team-mates were warming up already, playing catch in the soft green grass by the dugout. "Mathilda's here."

I looked at my father then, standing beside me on the gravel. What-ever my response would be, it would be for him. My mother and I would simply carry on, just as we always had. But I needed to do something then for him, somehow make this right. He just had to tell me what it was. His face looked almost serene though, the hint of a secret smile around his lips. Not much information there.

"Mathilda, Mathilda," Jimmy sang out then. "The strikeout queen."

I kept my gaze trained on my father. Something needed to be done here—and fast. Jimmy seemed ready to go on like this forever.

My father didn't move a muscle though.

"That'll be enough," my mother said, her voice nonnegotiable, stepping forward even in a vaguely menacing way.

Thank God for her.

Jimmy slinked off, of course. That's all it took. I watched him walk away, smelly and victorious. I watched my father too, standing silently beside me still, just gazing off into the distance, looking as blank as the scoreboard at the other end of the grassy field.

It's hard to know now what all that staring was about. Maybe he was mortified for me, just trying to pretend it wasn't happening. Or mortified for himself: Maybe it's not any less shameful being the father of a twelve-year-old sissy than it is being one yourself. Maybe he was thinking secret thoughts all his own.

I'll never know.

And it's hard to begrudge him much of anything now anyway, seven months after the bullet.

"Daaaaa-rien," the conductor calls out, holding on to the first syllable forever—three beats at least—tossing out the rest in a flash.

"The next stop on this train will be Daaaaa-rien." And he sings out the name in that same strange way again, like Harold Hill in *The Music Man,* singing the name Marion.

Maaaaa-rion.

Everything else as normal as you please.

I've been napping for a while. Half an hour or so, I think.

I'm on the train again, heading north like always, my body failing to conform in all the usual ways to the rigid vinyl seating here, entirely familiar with the stale air circulating through this car. But I'm not going to visit my mother this time. I'm on my way to Connecticut. I'll be there in just over an hour. I'm going to visit my uncle Andrew, my father's brother.

I should be hard at work by now—dreaming up a story, an alibi for my battered face. Something dramatic, but not too far-fetched, probably nothing involving any sort of fifteen-cent-per-minute chat line, or strangers you think are knocking on your door for sex, but come wielding electrical tape instead.

It feels awfully nice just sitting here though, letting my mind wander after a lovely little nap, gazing idly out the window at the pretty scenery passing by.

Feel rested too, lolling still.

I'm tired of not sleeping. What I've been doing lately has been less like sleep and more like an enforced hiatus from the bathroom mirror. Lying in bed for five or six hours, hoping for a miracle cure or at least a marked improvement for my battered face—the time so suffused with longing that there's no possibility of rest in it. I might as well be working on an assembly line for all the rest I get.

Then out of bed and hobbling straight to the full-length mirror inside the closet door. Hunched over and geriatric, favoring the side that took the worst kicks.

Stand up straight!

But I can manage it only for a second or two.

No one would ever notice my posture anyway, not with this riot of color and swelling on my face. I stood in front of that mirror for small eternities at a stretch, staring at the bruises that devoured my left eye and cheek. I'm steeped in a new familiarity with my face: The precise cast of olive skin, the beaky nose that—truth to tell—looks better slightly swollen.

I hid out all week. Called in for groceries, watching the bruises change—from red to orange, from purple to brown. Like the foliage at my mother's house in autumn, when the roads are so crowded with tourists that it takes half an hour to buy a quart of milk.

Perfectly normal, Dr. What's-his-name told me, without a trace of sympathy, when I hobbled over to St. Vincent's Hospital. But a broken rib can pierce the lung, you know. It can cause magnificent internal damage. Bruised ribs, he said, that's all. Probably not even broken, poking me hard on the side that hurt. No X ray, nothing. And nothing to be done for it even if they were broken, he said. As if that would put an end to my worrying, the fact that nothing could be done for me in any event.

What about internal bleeding?

He looked at me as if I were certifiable.

I wouldn't worry about that, he said.

I called in sick to the gallery all week: Terrible flu, I said.

I called the police the next day. Left everything exactly where it was though, so that when they did come, they could dust for prints, uncover clues of untold subtlety: Since you fell to the right, our man must be left-handed, that sort of thing—very *Murder, She Wrote.* But they didn't look for fingerprints when they came—two of them—or do much more than step over the debris in the foyer. Didn't invite me down to the precinct to look at mug shots either. Just told me that it wasn't a good idea to let strangers into the apartment.

Really?

I told my mother the flu story.

"Of course you're sick," she said. "You don't get any fresh air."

I left it at that.

The train screams to a halt.

Daaaaa-rien.

It's almost picture-postcard: A red dirt road and a tunnel of green foliage.

I'm nearly eighteen.

The light is turning dusky as it filters through the white oaks that line the road. I've got a wooden tennis racquet under my arm. Its cover is wooly and blue and decorated with a needlepoint design—my initials in sunny yellow against the navy background. Every now and then I grip the racquet's handle and twirl it, Billie Jean King at the service line.

I see the play of long thigh muscles beneath the surface of my skin, rippling like wings in flight as I walk. My legs feel heavy with fatigue. I've played already. I'm walking away from the tennis club.

Walking slowly, one foot in front of the other. White sneakers and white socks, tanned legs. When I place my foot down on the road, a fine cloud of brown dust explodes all around it, rains lightly onto my shoe and sock, the lower part of my shin.

I'm tired.

My mind is quiet, satisfied just to record the small explosions of dust around my feet, to watch my progress down the dirt road as dusk grows all around me. Like a neutral observer watching my passage from the side of the road—watching a figure in white pass through a tunnel of green and brown.

I've just played tennis with a Frenchwoman called Sylvia. It's getting to be a regular date. She's in her forties and wears stylish tennis outfits and brings a translucent plastic container filled with ice and lemon wedges—no water, just ice and lemon—and as we play, the sun melts the ice, making a cold lemony drink for us to share. This drink is more ingenious to me than nuclear fusion.

My mother hands me two quarters for the soda machine.

I used to play tennis with boys my own age or my father. Only with men—with their big serving motions and their lust for the net. They unnerved me. I could never get my racquet back in time. But Sylvia's long, smooth ground strokes just keep coming. She never rushes for the net. I hit the ball straight back to her. Why make her run? I follow through every stroke now. Prepare myself for the next shot as quickly as I can. It feels like I'm playing tennis at last.

I don't kid myself: I'd still choke if you dropped me back down onto a court with Billy Gillespie and his overhead smash, but that doesn't worry me right now. I'm just walking now, just watching one foot step ahead of the other, watching the small explosions of brown dust at my feet.

I hear a car approaching from behind. Move to the side of the road. A small sports car pulls up alongside me, its engine purring. A fancy, little red thing. I can't see inside though. The windows are closed, and the sinking light of early evening reflects off them.

Just me and the little car idling quietly beside me, like an exotic animal—like a lynx, nothing you'd ever expect to encounter on the side of a dirt road, so close up.

Then the window on the passenger's side opens in the even, automated way of a finger on a button, no rolling down of any window here. It opens all the way, an Eagles song tumbling out to greet me: *Don't let the sound of your own wheels drive you crazy.*

"Hi there." It's a man, a stranger to me, leaning across from the driver's seat, speaking to me through the open passenger's-side window. "Were you just at the tennis club?" he asks.

Two hundred yards from a tennis court, dressed in white, a tennis racquet under my arm, and *that's* his question?

I nod.

My mind begins its whirring and hopping again. That's probably just the buildup to his real question.

"I thought I saw you there," he says.

His face is good-looking, even-featured.

Strange, I think. I didn't notice him.

He's leaning his weight onto his left hand, almost trying to square himself to the open window. I wonder what he wants. He has a man's hand, a silver Rolex like my father. He looks younger than my father though, older than me. He's probably thirty-five or so.

"I think I'm lost," he says.

It's a girl, my Lord, in a flatbed Ford slowin' down to take a look at me.

He has lovely gray eyes.

"I'm looking for Orchard Street."

That's easy enough, I think.

"I know where that is," I say.

Proceed to give him directions that sound much more complicated than it is to get there. But directions are often like that, much easier to follow when you already know the way.

He looks perplexed.

"Let me try again," I say.

It's a trip of only two or three miles. Not complicated at all. I do slightly better on the second try.

But he still looks perplexed.

"I don't know," he says slowly, as if he were trying to locate the precise spot along the route where he lost his place.

I stand waiting.

"Would you ride with me?" he asks. "You can direct me."

But how will I get home?

"I can drive you wherever you're going after you show me the way," he says.

Seems overcomplicated to me. It's only a three-mile drive. But I open the passenger's-side door anyway.

"Thanks a lot," he says.

You really have to bend down low to open the door, even lower to get inside. I feel barely off the ground when my seat belt's buckled, and we're ready to go. A stone on the road could be a big problem for your ass in this car.

The dashboard looks like the *Apollo XIII,* buttons and knobs and gauges all lit up in cool green lights. He's probably terribly proud of this car. Men are like that, you know. Most boys would be jumping for joy to ride around in a fancy car like this. Most boys could probably tell you the make and model too. At least, the boys I know.

"I really appreciate your doing this," he says.

I'm embarrassed to think that he might have seen me playing tennis with Sylvia, lobbing the ball back and forth for an hour and a half.

He drives off.

There's not much navigating for me to do though until he gets to the intersection up ahead.

He's wearing rumpled tennis whites, red clay–stained, like mine.

"I didn't see you playing," I say.

"I was with the pro."

That explains it. The pro's court is tucked behind the clubhouse.

"What's his name again?" he asks. "Todd?"

"Tom," I say.

I've taken tennis lessons with Tom for a hundred summers. He has dyslexia, my mother told me. "Mot," we call him, she and I.

"Yeah, that's right," he says. "Tom."

We're getting close to the intersection now. I rehearse my first instruction to him, silently, inside my head: Take a left at the intersection.

"I just got into town," he says. "I was driving by the courts, and stopped to see if I could get a game. Luckily, Todd was free."

Tom, I already told him.

"Take a left up there at the intersection," I say.

Very smooth.

Hear the steady clicking of a directional light. It sounds different from the ones in my parents' cars, more like a bomb ticking. He waits for an oncoming car to pass so we can make the turn. Scratches the top of his leg lazily, leaves a long white trace. He keeps looking out into the intersection. He has fine, blond hairs—like down almost—at the crest of his cheekbone. You'd never see them though if you weren't so close.

"Where do you live?" I ask.

"Boston."

"That must be great," I say, but I have no idea why.

He nods, smiling.

Not the dumbest thing in the world for me to have said.

"I'm here to give a paper at the Commons."

I feel my stomach drop. The Commons is a mental institution. I'm driving around with a lunatic in a tiny, closed vehicle. "Oh."

"I'm a psychiatrist," he says.

I relax. I love a doctor. I wonder if he knows Dr. Norton Esty, the psychiatrist my mother sent me to when she found the *Playgirl* magazine at the bottom of my trunk in the cedar closet.

"Now bear left at the fork," I say with considerable authority.

It turns out I'm quite good at giving directions.

"Just here for a few days," he says. "It'll be a nice break from the city."

I turn my head to look at him in profile, just slightly though. I don't want him to know I'm looking. He has a little bit of stubble coming in on his chin. I can't imagine needing a break from the city. The skin at his temples looks soft. I get us to Orchard Street without a hitch. Here we are.

He's driving slowly now. Pulls into the driveway of a house that looks like a ski chalet. It's got large plate-glass windows unbroken by mullions.

"Mission accomplished," I say, like my mother does when she pulls into our driveway.

"I couldn't have done it without you," he says, smiling.

His teeth are very white.

"Let me give you a drink for your troubles?" he asks.

"Sure."

I'm glad to go inside, have a look around.

"Then I'll take you home."

"Whose house?" I ask.

He leads the way, through the front door. "It belongs to the Commons," he says. "But I don't think anyone lives here."

I don't either.

Everything looks too perfect: The furniture is all sleek and low, like a picture of a room in a magazine. The place is more like the idea of a house than an actual house itself.

"There's some beer in the refrigerator," he says, "Would you like one?"

Sure, I nod, but I wouldn't. I'd rather have lemon and ice from a plastic container. Or a Fresca. I'd love a Fresca.

"Go on in and sit down," he says, nodding toward the living room.

I hear him opening the refrigerator door, hear the sound of suction breaking.

Boys love beer.

I head for a chair that's covered in fur of some kind. It's curly lamb, I think, like at a petting zoo. Nothing in this room is like my house. I sit in a simple beige chair instead, shaped like a cube, with just a small opening to sit in.

He walks into the room—pausing in the doorway first, filling it up. The beer in his hands looks daunting. Two tall glasses, brimming full, each with mountains of foam on top. If it were wine, I could hold the glass the way my mother does, with just two fingers on the stem.

"I don't know your name," he says, matter-of-fact, when he reaches me in the corner.

"Sorry," I say, standing to shake hands. "Matthew," I say, extending my right hand, "Matthew Vaber."

"Jay Calhoun," he says, but both his hands are full.

He hands me a glass so we can shake hands, but I take it with the wrong one, my shaking hand. I notice just a second too late. We still can't shake.

He smiles.

This feels so much easier than I would have imagined, being in a strange room with a strange adult. Like playing tennis with Sylvia, so much easier than I ever let it be. Feels like swimming in a sparkling blue swimming pool. I'm floating on my back, flutter kicking as easy as you please.

I transfer the drink to my left hand, and now we shake. His palm is warm and dry, his grip firm. "Nice to meet you," I say.

We're about the same height, but he's broader than I am. He feels bigger than me.

"Nice to meet you, Matthew Vaber."

He makes it sound like a joke.

He might be making fun of me, with my Little Lord Fauntleroy handshake.

These are still new waters for me.

Was I too formal?

His smile looks genuine though, not at my expense.

We're standing in place.

I'm waiting for his lead now, now that I'm afraid of embarrassing myself, now that I see that the rules that governed little Matthew's old-time sweep through the living room no longer apply—all freshly bathed and pajama-clad, shaking the hands of my parents' friends one by one, Good night, Mr. Foster. Good night, Mrs. Foster.

His slightest movement will start the action again. But he doesn't move.

Neither do I.

"Nice to meet you," he says again, more serious this time, in a softer voice. No trace of a smile anymore. All the easiness has slipped away.

I've ruined everything.

He's staring now.

The sparkling blue swimming pool turns choppy and cold.

I haven't done anything that bad, have I?

He's nothing like my parents' friends, or Sylvia even—who could very easily have been a friend of my parents, I just got to her first.

He squeezes my upper arm.

Now I'm officially at sea—what I thought was a swimming pool turns out to be the middle of the ocean.

He leans forward and kisses my upper lip very softly.

I'm frozen in place.

Not my whole mouth, just my upper lip, and very softly.

Somehow, I find myself again.

Maybe it was the softness of it.

I know exactly where I am: Back on the dirt road by the tennis courts, strangely calm and outside of myself, merely observing my upper lip being kissed by a good-looking stranger, as if I were floating up above that tunnel of green foliage again, more a witness than a participant.

He stands back slightly to gauge my response.

But I don't know what my response should be.

I feel the breath moving smoothly into my chest and lungs.

Feel it leaving too.

This is simple.

Breathing in,

What made him think that he could do that?

Breathing out.

Could he tell just from looking at me, just watching me walk down a red dirt road?

Breathing in.

Is it that obvious?

He moves toward me again and kisses me on both lips this time, still very softly. They're gentle kisses, not tentative at all, but soft. Like he knows exactly what he's doing, and he's decided to do this very softly. So light, these kisses. Designed almost not to leave an impression.

I could walk away from them if I wanted to.

But I don't.

If I were Billy Gillespie, he couldn't do this. I'm sure of that.

I smell a faint aroma of citrus on him, mixed with dried sweat and the smell of his skin. I'm not much closer to him now than I was in his car, or when we shook hands, but this new closeness has unlocked these scents to me. Feel the heat radiating from his chest. Know the precise spot his hip bones would touch mine if he moved one step closer.

He wraps his arms around me now, still softly. One hand on my upper back, the other on my sacrum.

Very softly.

Not pinning me down—not at all.

He's supporting me, in fact, almost bearing me up.

He kisses me again, a little less softly now.

And this time, I respond.

I open up on the third kiss—like the third ring of the phone or the third knock on the door, like something out of a fairy tale: The third golden apple, the third prince.

Like magic.

I feel myself inside out.

That's how available I am to him and his kisses. Wonderful kisses, better than I could ever have imagined. Soft enough for me to feel them, and slow enough for me to know them while they're happening.

These are my first kisses.

My absolutely, first-ever kisses.

My very first steps down a new dirt road.

And now I panic.

I jerk backward against his arms, which tighten—only reflexively, I'm sure, not from any desire to hold me against my will. Careful to catch me if I'm falling. But the jolt of my back against his tightening arms, the little jab of breath inside my chest—they do me in.

I'm trapped now.

He loosens his grip.

My breathing is shallow, nearly ragged.

I move backward.

My palms feel moist against my thighs.

But I don't leave.

I only step backward.

I pick up the mammoth glass of beer again, all wet on the outside now, condensation running down the sides of the glass. This beer feels like salvation to me. How could I not have wanted it?

I sit down in the beige chair again, as if nothing had happened, as if I'd been sitting here all along. A blind man could see I haven't just been sitting here though—sitting people don't breathe like this. I don't know what to do. My eyes dart around the room, looking for an answer, but the instruction appears to have left off.

He looks calm still, standing right where I left him. Arms hang lightly at his sides. He looks prepared to wait me out, patient as you please.

I need to leave.

I know in a flash that I have to be gone from here.

Now.

I spring back to my feet. Feel my movements quick and choppy, as if all the lubrication had been drained from my joints.

"I should get going," I say.

He looks calm still.

"Thanks for the beer."

No stopping me now.

"Sure," he says quietly.

He looks concerned.

"Let me give you a ride home."

"No thanks, I can walk."

"Really," he says. "It's no bother."

This is probably the way he talks to mental patients—in a slow, quiet voice, but his eyes are intent, taking in everything.

"That was our deal, right?"

The deal's off. Can't he see that?

"Let me just get my keys," he says, "and we'll get out of here."

It's too late for keys.

I'm already lunging for the door. I'd never make it through the car ride home. I know that.

The keys, the unlocking, the buckling, the ignition—no, I'd never make it. I'm jumping out of my skin as it is. Normal modes of transportation are useless to me now. My hand reaches for the doorknob, smooth and cool.

"Bye."

I need to fly.

The air outside feels cool on my face, like the doorknob, like escape. I'm breathing easier too. I'll be okay now. I know that. It's dark outside. What a relief—the cool air and the darkness!

I'm halfway down the block before I know it. No one has ever walked this fast. I'm like a wild animal. I'm the lynx now. Miles from home. I didn't say good-bye to him properly. But I'm not going back. Going back is out of the question.

My tennis racquet!

I left my tennis racquet in his car. Oh no.

I'll tell my mother it broke.

What about the needlepoint cover?

I'm walking as fast as those middle-aged race walkers you see on running tracks behind brick high schools. I'm practically flying. Headlights over my shoulder.

Oh no.

Then I hear the animal purr again, see the same color red. He pulls to the side of the road just ahead of me. Like déjà vu. It wasn't so long ago that he pulled his car to the side of the road for the first time. But it's so different from the first time now.

What will I say to him?

I make a quick detour down Elm Street. I'm an idiot. Still walking so fast, just down the wrong street now, in the wrong direction. He's going to think I'm a fool. But I can't help myself. I keep walking very quickly in the wrong direction.

Did I have to kiss him, I wonder, as badly as I had to leave?

Just keep walking. He pulls up alongside me again. It's a car chase, only I'm on foot.

"Are you okay?" he asks.

"I'm fine."

"I'm sorry I upset you," he says.

"I said I was fine."

"I thought it would be all right."

Obviously, it wasn't.

"Let me give you a ride home," he says.

"I'm fine."

"I'll take you straight home."

"No thanks."

"I didn't mean to frighten you."

"Well, you did," I say.

The truth just pops out.

Surprises me, although it isn't much of a surprise.

He looks stunned.

"I'd feel much better if you'd let me give you a ride home."

"I'd feel much better if you'd leave me alone."

The truths are flying out of me now—like kernels of popcorn at the bottom of a pan. Hard little pebbles all closed up tight, sitting in a shallow bath of hot, hot oil, then exploded into fluffy white flowers, from nothing.

"I can't leave you like this," he says.

"Please."

Begging now.

"Just leave me alone."

He looks hurt. I don't care what he wants. The delicate skin at his temples looks bruised.

"I'm fine," I say. "Really."

He looks at me appraisingly. Wants to know if I'm fit to be left.

I look straight back at him, composed—conspiring.

It's my only chance.

"I'm fine," I say.

"I'm sorry," he says.

And then he's gone.

"What the hell happened to you?" my uncle squawks as I slip into his car.

Another luxury sports car, this one in black. Everyone's got them now, I guess. It's not just Alain Delon anymore. His voice is harder than I would have expected, almost aggressive, but I put that down to surprise.

I hadn't prepared him for my face.

Turns out we're even though. I hadn't prepared myself for his face either. He looks just like my father. Same gray eyes, same sharp nose.

"Are you okay?" he asks, still tough on the outside, but tender in the middle, like a perfectly cooked roast beef.

Sounds just like him too.

"I'm fine," I say.

How can I not have noticed this resemblance before?

I settle into the car, pushing and pulling at the various control knobs that regulate the position of my seat and the height of the head-rest. Stalling. He's staring at me, not even trying not to: Mouth hanging open, eyes searching. He wants to know what happened.

I fasten my seat belt.

"Well?" he asks.

"I was mugged," I say, looking right into his eyes.

I try not to look nervous at my lie.

His hands even look like my father's, wrapped loosely around the steering wheel, pinkish fingernails with little white half-moons at the base.

"Oh, Matty," he moans, brimming with sympathy.

All traces of hardness softened now.

Home free, I guess.

"I didn't think people even got mugged anymore," I say.

But it doesn't matter what I say.

"I thought the mayor had cleaned up the streets," I say.

He's already sold.

His heart's wide open to me. I can feel it, just sitting here.

"I'm so sorry," he says, voice heaped with kindness, ignoring all my chatter.

I feel so sad.

He looks just like my father, sounds like him too, but it's ten thousand times easier sitting here with him than it ever was with my father. No awkward silence that I'm desperate to fill, no kindly, vacant gaze from the look-alike sitting beside me.

He puts his hand on my knee, squeezes it lightly.

It's too much for me—like a banquet for a starving man, like filling a teacup with a fire hose.

He lets his hand linger on my knee.

"Is it painful?" he asks.

Turns out I worried for nothing. It's not—Where were you going? Or, What street were you on? It's not—What time was it? There's no challenge in his voice, no squinting to see beyond the picture I've drawn. He's only concerned. No need for further fact-finding.

"I'm so sorry," he says.

Then a flash of anger: What a fool he is!

He shakes his head slowly. Puts the car into reverse and backs out of his parking space. Reverses direction and drives off, out of the parking lot. Suffering my lies gladly.

I turn away from him now. Want nothing more to do with him. This must be what Billy Gillespie feels like, standing triumphant at the service line after an overhead smash: Slightly repulsed by his victim.

I gaze out the passenger's-side window. Not at all sure what I'm so angry about. He turns left at the traffic light and drives out of the small commercial zone, just the train station and a few shops really.

"Poor thing," he mutters, turning toward me again at the next stop sign, squeezing my hand now too, as if there weren't words enough to convey the depth of his feelings.

Such a moron, I think. Feel my eyes welling with tears just the same.

The liquid roundness of them resting precariously on the shallow ledge of my lower lids. I have no control over these tears, whether they overflow or not has nothing to do with me. Crying at my own lies. I turn away and wipe the tears from my eyes. Cheekbones still painful to the touch.

He's navigating the pretty residential streets now, all green lawns and manicured paths to tidy front doors. Everything under control here, all the little pathways lined with flower beds. Everything under control but me, sitting in the passenger seat crying.

My eyes replenish every tear I wipe away.

They just won't stop.

I hadn't banked on this.

Upstairs at my uncle's house, it's very *Me and My Shadow.*

He settled me into the nicer guest room, the one that looks out onto the Long Island Sound, and then left to exercise at his gym.

We agreed I should recuperate a bit longer before exercising again. Believe me, I'll take any excuse I can get. It feels a bit lonely here though, all by myself. I take a bath with lavender-smelling syrup poured in.

Now what?

I decide to begin the Muriel Spark novel I bought on the way to the train station. Set the stage before I even sit down to try, make everything nice: I open the window to a lovely breeze from the water, traces of bracing cold inside the fledgling warmth, wrap myself in a thick flannel robe from the closet, and sink into the downy armchair in the corner, even an ottoman for my feet. The velvet upholstery feels soft against my neck. A glass of water, in case I run dry. Everything's ready now, but me. I know it from the moment I open the book, even before I hear the surrender of its cracking-new spine.

But I press on. I concentrate on each word of the long first sentence, making each one out in turn—pausing over it, willing myself to—but none of them coalesces. I soldier on: The second one feels as if someone is shouting the words to me from a great distance. I can barely hear them. I don't even attempt the third. Close the book.

I spot a telephone by the bedside, and my heart quickens. Try to temper my excitement though: It's an old model, I tell myself. It might not work. It has to have push buttons, you know.

The phone is beige and squarish, with an old-fashioned whirligig cord. I'm sure it's much too old for my purposes. I keep trying to douse the rush of excitement I feel.

It really needs to have push buttons, you know, and a pound key. Don't forget about that.

I stand up and see that it does—push buttons and pound key both. A whole new world of Pump Line companions! Callers from posh Connecticut suburbs, dockworkers from the shore. This could be the start of something big.

The charges are going to be a problem though. I can't very well rack up charges on my uncle's phone, even if it is only fifteen cents a minute. It wouldn't add up to very much. Twenty-five cents for the first. No, it would be very rude of me. Out of the question, in fact.

Maybe I can bill the charges elsewhere.

I try my calling card. But it doesn't work. I try again, but it's still not working. The line simply lies there, dead. None of the numbers I'm pressing signifies anything to this phone.

An operator comes on the line after the third try, a man.

"May I help you?" he asks.

"Yes, please," I say. "I'm trying to charge a call to my calling card. A premium call," I mention discreetly, hoping to avoid any ugliness by using the phone company's own euphemistic parlance.

"You mean a five-five-five number?" he says, cutting to the chase.

"Yes," I say, hope we won't have to get into whether I'm a top or a bottom.

"Can't do it," he says.

He doesn't leave much room for hope.

"No way at all?"

"Sorry."

My mind whirrs, hunting for another solution, but I'm a bit out of my depth here.

"That's too bad."

"You can bill it to a credit card though," he says.

Telephone operators in Connecticut really are a cut above.

I can assure you I wouldn't have gotten any helpful hints like this in New York.

He walks me through the machinations of credit-card billing, which are breathtakingly complicated. Desperate times, desperate measures.

He assures me that no record of the call will appear on my uncle's phone bill. I don't believe I've ever been so impressed with a phone company employee. I've stumbled onto a bed of roses with this one. He even waits on the line with me to make sure that I get through. Excuses himself politely as soon as the automated voice begins.

Scott!

I press one.

"Hold on while I make your connection."

"Hello?" I say.

Silence.

"Hello?"

I'm losing faith.

"Hello?"

Press the pound key in mounting desperation, the traveler's aid: Press pound for succor. Of course, I know from experience that you have to be speaking with someone before pressing the pound key does much of anything for you.

But it works.

"Hello," a man's voice says.

And we're off.

I see a holding pen full of Chips and Parkers, blonds with even features and dark-haired men with sky blue eyes. I see them in full sailing regalia, with ropes and thick canvas trousers. Chalk-stripe suits fresh from the commuter trains.

"Hello," I say, trying for John Cheever.

"Where are you calling from?"

"Darien," I say.

Beep.

Some things never change.

"Hello?" another one.

"Hi," I say. "Where are you calling from?"

"Greenwich," he says.

His voice is nice—deep, but not too deep.

"Me too," I lie.

"Which side of the Post Road?" he asks.

No end of subtleties here.

I don't even know what the question means.

What should I say: Your side? The right side?

"The south side," I say, hoping for the best.

Beep.

I thought they all had cars here.

But still, this is fun.

And I'm really settling into this armchair now.

I haven't felt this alive since the night of a thousand blows.

"Hello," I say.

"Hey, baby," he says. "You sound sexy."

"Thanks," I say.

It sounds like he's drunk though, slurring his words together. And it's not even five o'clock yet.

"I'm looking for big cock, baby."

Beep.

Very down-market.

"Hello?"

"Top."

Beep.

"Hello?"

Beep.

"Bottom."

Beep.

Beep.

Same as it ever was.

Would it be like this in Minnesota too?

"Hello."

"Hi," I say.

"Where are you calling from?" he asks.

"Darien," I say, settling for the truth.

"Me, too."

"Really?"

"Uh-huh."

Thrill to my suburban victory.

I just hope he doesn't want to get into Post Road orientation.

"What's your name?" I ask.

"Henry," he says. "What's yours?"

"Matthew."

"What do you like to do, Matthew?"

"I'm pretty versatile," I say.

"Me, too."

I can't help the mounting feeling of success.

I force myself to picture a fat roll of electrical tape.

"What are you doing?" he asks.

"Just hanging around really, waiting for my uncle to come home," I say. "I'm here visiting for a couple of days."

"Me, too," he says. "I'm visiting my parents."

"Where do you live?" he asks. "In real life."

"New York."

"Me, too," he says.

I wonder if he's like me, inventing himself for the pleasure of a stranger on the other end of the line.

"What are you doing tonight?"

"Probably going to dinner with my uncle," I say. "You?"

"Same, I think."

Maybe he's a bit too same-y, in fact.

I want him to be a little different from me.

That's part of the pleasure.

"Maybe we could get together tomorrow," he says.

"Maybe," I say hesitantly.

I'm not so sure though.

"Nothing big," he says. "We could get a coffee on the Post Road."

Where else would we go?

"Okay," I say.

Trying to signal that I'll think it over, not that I agree.

"Good."

He sounds glad.

He gives me his phone number—probably made up in any event—and we agree that I'll call him in the morning.

I don't have to, you know.

And he suggested a public place.

"Bye."

I don't press the pound key this time. I hang up the receiver instead, finished with the Pump Line for now. I disconnect the corkscrew cord, wanting to unravel what looks like fifteen years of tangle. It takes almost no time to accomplish though, the cord practically unspools itself.

Now I'll be able to read.

I know it even before I pick up the book.

It happened pretty regularly for a stretch, nearly every night.

I'd be fast asleep, at first.

Sometimes a dream, even one of standing right in front of the toilet, a dreamy hand raising the seat like a good boy.

Sometimes no dream at all, just a sensation of warmth spreading.

So nice then, burrowing into it like a chinchilla jacket. Even cozier in the little twin bed. Not for long though.

Soon it turns chilly and damp.

Half awake then, rearranging my body, trying to find that lost coziness. But it's no use now. Doesn't matter where I turn, how I arrange myself. There are wet pajama bottoms and wet sheets, layers of wet like saturated paper towels laid one on top of another and applied directly to my bare legs and tummy.

I'm wide awake now.

Throw back the covers and stand.

The shame fires my upper chest like a too-quick sip of hot tea. I can feel the redness, even in the dark.

Entirely too old for this, that's what she always says.

I survey the damage. Is there no place left for me to lie? But my eyes can't make anything out. They haven't adjusted to seeing in the dark. So I feel around instead. Feel the bottom sheet and the contours of wet, like a map of Europe.

Peel off my pajama bottoms, sticking to my legs. I wad them tight into a small ball. It's a relief to be done with the insistent wetness. Throw them in the hamper in the bathroom—right next door.

Where all this could have been avoided in the first place. That's what she always says.

It happens nearly every night. He doesn't say a word about it, but somehow his silence is more embarrassing to me than her squawking judgment. Like when he caught me sitting in the cedar closet, sucking my thumb. Just nodded in acknowledgment and closed the door. Left me to my thumb and the aromatic wood.

There's a bitter smell, rising up from the damp geography.

There's really no alternative.

I leave my room and creep softly down the hall. All the way down the hall in the dark, past all the rooms in between. I pause before the closed door.

Why never one of those empty guest rooms in between, I wonder? Big beds there, all to myself.

Press my ear against the door. I need to hear the sound of sleeping breath before I take another step. Listen close. Yes, there it is. I gather up my courage. Place my hand on the chilly doorknob and turn it all the way, until I hear a soft click.

Not a peep from inside the room.

I pause again. Make doubly sure about the breathing. Yes, there it is. I push the door open now, just wide enough to squeeze through and not an inch wider. The hinges make a high-pitched squeak. Sounds awfully loud to me. I freeze in place. No harm though.

And not nearly as loud as the lower-pitched creaking the floorboards make as I tiptoe across them. I just need to get to the foot of the bed.

There they are, two blanket-covered lumps, like wooly mountain ranges.

Listen to the sleeping sounds they make. Snortling and exhaling, little sighs mixed in. I climb softly onto the foot of the bed, just the very foot. Careful. The mattress makes a small groan, but the easy breathing continues undisturbed.

I'll do well to remember these sounds too, for when I'm pretending. For when they walk into my room, and I go stock-still, feigning sleep.

Two sets of sleeping legs on either side of me at the foot of the bed, like the low-lying foothills at the base of a mountain range. I start to shimmy up toward the headboard. Slowly though, very slowly. Just inch my way forward. Softly too. Very good.

I slip under the blanket when I reach the top, between the dry sheets. They feel silky against my bare legs. No pajama bottoms now. Into bed with them—how nice! I curl up on my side, facing him. He's on his side too, facing back at me. Like bookends.

Sometimes I only look—thrilled by the size of him, the bulk and strength of a sleeping giant. The handsome prince who might carry me away. I slide in as close as I dare. Careful not to wake him though. Like Batman in his black tights.

Every millimeter creates a rippling wave in the bed, threatening to wake them both, like the vibrations of a tuning fork just daring you to hear them. But still they don't stir.

I've gotten very good at knowing how far I can go.

Just about here.

I can hear his breathing, see the blanket rise and fall.

Did I ever touch his chest, or did I just dream I did?

A stroke of genius on Saturday morning. I'm looking out the window at the sky blue sky and the matching blue water.

I can cancel Goldstein right now with impunity!

He'd never be in his office at ten-thirty on a Saturday morning. No tension for me either—hoping he's busy, praying for the answering machine. I'll just call now, and get away clean.

So I dial. Push down heavily on the numbers, hear a pretty little melody through the earpiece. This old phone has been like a lucky charm for me all weekend—first the suburban Pump Line, now this. Like a rabbit's foot with a superlong cord, just sitting here on the bedside table in my uncle's better guest room.

First ring. No salt for my shoulder, but I don't need any today. This is a foolproof plan. Now the second ring, and the third. But no machine yet either, and it always picks up after three rings.

"Hello," he says.

Shit.

"Dr. Goldstein?" I say.

"Yes?"

What the hell is he doing there on a Saturday morning?

"It's Matthew Vaber calling."

"Good morning, Matthew," he says heartily, as if nothing were out of the ordinary here, neither his being in the office on a Saturday morning, nor my calling him there.

Now what do I do?

Look down at the old phone—a fat old block of beige plastic. Nothing like a lucky charm. And I hate my uncle too for not updating it—with a cordless maybe, or a trimline model.

"I'm calling about Wednesday," I say.

"Yes?"

"I have some collectors in town that day." As good a lie as any. "I have to cancel our appointment."

Goldstein stays silent on his end of the line.

I wait.

"Matthew," he says finally, but in his grave voice now, "I'm concerned about you. This will be the third session in a row you've canceled."

"I know," I say. "I'm sorry, but—"

"Not to mention," he interrupts, "all the others you've canceled since your father died." He doesn't sound angry though, not at all. In fact, he sounds perfectly composed.

I stay quiet.

"I know this is a difficult time for you," he says. "And I understand your impulse to avoid our sessions."

It's not the sessions I'm avoiding, Goldstein.

"But if you're going to stick with this therapy," he says, "and I think you should, you're going to have to make the effort to get here."

It's not the sessions I'm avoiding at all. It's you, Goldstein—sitting there so smug in your leather chair and your worn-out corduroy pants. Wanting me to blame my father for everything.

"Why don't you see if you can break away from your collectors for an hour or so," he says. "You can let me know at the beginning of the week."

My father's not to blame.

"Good-bye," he says.

Dinner's at eight

My uncle and I drive to a restaurant that appears to be inside a mini-mall. "We're going to a restaurant in a mall?" I ask.

"No, no, no," he says. "It's way over there," pointing to the other side of the parking lot.

It doesn't seem like a significant distinction to me.

My uncle parks his car by the entrance, softly lit with imitation old-fashioned street lamps. Different from the lamps that light the rest of the lot. I think I get the picture. It's not so hard to make out, what with the raging fluorescence of the 7-Eleven right next door: Mall-adjacent fancy.

We walk to the restaurant's huge mahogany door. I pull it open.

Look onto candlelight flickering off crystal and ornate silver, starched white cloths on all the tables. This is fancy. There are oil paintings of house pets and scenes of animal husbandry in heavy gilt frames. And all strangely hushed. No one is making an extraneous peep here. Captains and waiters and all manner of assistant captains and demi-waiters are bustling all around the room in black evening suits and shiny shoes, and all as quietly as they can manage.

We're only a hundred yards from a 7-Eleven.

My uncle leads the way to the captain's table, beneath a huge spray of white gladioli. Do we look like father and son, I wonder, my uncle and I? The difference in our ages would make it the natural choice, the family resemblance too. But here, in this aspirational room, a father and son alone together doesn't seem likely. No, this is a room for overdressed women and their reluctant husbands, or suburban homo-sexuals who want everything nice. No father in his right mind would bring his son here. Standing at the captain's table, as the captain looks me up and down, I feel more like the lovely young paramour, the third wife.

The captain checks my uncle's name off in his huge leather book, with a brisk little stroke, and leads us across the room. He's so intent on making no sound—lifting his feet slightly too high with every step, placing them down so gingerly again—it's hard to imagine he has the energy to think about anything other than the threat of leather soles clattering against terrazzo flooring.

"The food's very good here," my uncle says as soon as we're seated, napkins in our laps and menus open in front of us. "Annie loved it here."

Annie is my uncle's ex wife. She ran off with the tennis pro. My ex-aunt. Got a big settlement too. He looks all around the room, expectantly, as if he might find her here still.

It's never a surprise to me when the husband runs off with his young secretary or the baby-sitter, and has to pay out. That makes all the sense in the world. He's the man of the family, after all, the bread-winner, buying his freedom from the bread-eaters. That's a straight-forward transaction. That's the way the world works.

But I've never understood my uncle's case: Annie left him for a handsome younger man. Shouldn't that change the equation?

Don't get my mother going on the subject of Annie: She's like a lawn mower running over a canvas sneaker that's been left out in the yard. Nothing left but grommets and tattered laces.

At least now my uncle's affection for this restaurant makes sense. An homage to his departed wife. Otherwise, this is the sort of place any right-thinking person would despise.

"My mother would love it here," I say, just to say something.

"Oh, God, no," he says, shaking his head and screwing up his face. I'm impressed he could work that out so fast.

"She hated it."

"You brought her here?"

I'm surprised again.

She's never mentioned coming to a hideous French restaurant in Darien. Surely in one of her diatribes against Annie—when her every fault is catalogued to a fare-thee-well—surely her inclination toward a restaurant like this would have been included, somewhere between her insufficient education and love of gaudy jewelry.

"Oh yes," he says. "Years ago."

I can't remember my mother ever visiting my uncle without me.

"When?" I ask.

Maybe I was away at school. But he isn't interested in the question. No, he's distracted now.

"I'd love a drink," he says.

He searches the room, looking for the waiter—eyes dancing randomly from place to place. When they come to rest, I know he's found him.

A handsome waiter scurries over.

"Gentlemen," he says, bowing. "May I get you something to drink?"

"A Tanqueray martini, please," my uncle says, all business. "Very dry, with olives."

"Straight up?"

"Please."

Alcohol is a mystery to me. Booze and olives don't sound very tasty.

"Sir?" the waiter says, looking to me now.

But I have no idea.

His head is angled slightly to the side, eyes importuning. He looks as if he'd hold this geisha pose forever, even if it took me a hundred years to tell him what I'd like to drink.

"I'll have the same, please."

"Thank you, gentlemen," he says, bowing again and backing away from the table, like a servant in *The King and I*.

My uncle turns back to me, relaxed and smiling now that the necessary business has been transacted. "So how are you, Matty?" he asks, sighing softly. His eyes look directly into mine. He's asking about my father. I can hear it in the quiet of his question, in the soft exhalation of breath.

"Okay, I guess."

I pause for a second, not sure what to say next. I decide to sigh too. Feel the pressure of air against my lips. "I still can't believe we missed it," I say. The words just seem to come tumbling out, all on their own. I don't script them or rehearse them either. "Right in front of us the whole time."

My uncle leans into the table, like he wants to shield me from something. He's nodding his head slowly.

He knows what I'm talking about. I can tell.

My eyes begin to well again, for the second time today.

"Getting ready to do what he did for God knows how long," I say. "And we missed it."

He runs his hand through his hair. It looks just like my father's. Parted on the same side even, a razor's edge of white scalp separating two fields of wavy gray hair. "Oh, Matty," he says, full of sympathy. "Your father was so shut down it was ridiculous."

It stings me—that "ridiculous." He's loaded with sympathy for me alone, I guess. Doesn't have a drop to spare for my father. It's not like anyone would choose to shut down, would they?

"You could never tell what was going on with him," he says. "Even when we were in grade school."

He sits back in his chair again.

He should know, I suppose. Still I don't like his tone. It's not for him to criticize my father. "You were saying you brought my mother here?" I ask, changing the subject.

"Yes," he says, but looks confused.

I suppose the shift was a bit abrupt.

"Annie and I brought her here when she and that friend of hers came to visit," he says.

I'm confused now too.

"What friend?" I ask.

"You know, the tall woman," he says. "The swimmer."

Bertie?

"My mother brought Bertie to visit you?"

"Bertie," he says happily, recognizing the name—yes, that's it. "Um-hmm." He nods.

"When was this?" I ask.

"Let's see," he says, eyes squinting slightly and looking off into the middle distance, searching for a landmark. "We still lived on Fithian Road then, so it must have been about twenty years ago."

I was a boy then, still at home. I should remember this.

"Are you sure?"

But I've lost him again. I see his eyes wandering off. He's following the waiter around the room again, not like a bee this time though, dipping in and out, more as the crow flies—in a very straight line.

The handsome waiter is carrying our drinks to us now, walking carefully. Glasses filled to the tippity-top, brimming with alcohol. He's guarding every last drop for us. My uncle watches him closely. He wants every drop. He and the handsome waiter are absolutely on the same page. The waiter places the glasses carefully on the table. Lovely glasses too, wide open at the top and tapering down to delicate little stems.

"Here's to you," my uncle says, lifting his glass gingerly and bringing it to his lips. "And your mother."

Why not my father? I wonder, another little surge of resentment coursing through me.

He doesn't sip his drink though. The glass is too full for that. He merely places his top lip in the clear pool of alcohol, like a bird at a birdbath.

"I think of you two every day," he says.

He's a good man. I know that.

"To you," I say, touching the skin at my cheekbone, just beneath my left eye. Tender still.

I'd almost forgotten about my face. Isn't that amazing? Before this getaway, I couldn't go two minutes without thinking about it, running off to the bathroom mirror.

"You've really got to be more careful," he says, looking thoughtful now. "New York can be very dangerous," as if he were sharing a secret.

It's not hard to imagine Annie pulling the wool over his eyes, playing tennis two or three times a day even. In the rain and the snow. Without a racquet occasionally.

I sit quietly.

Touch the bruise on my cheek again, feel my kinship with Annie.

"Any news on the memorial service?" he asks.

I sit up in my chair. He's caught me by surprise. This is what I should have been rehearsing this morning, my answer to this. But I didn't. I was too busy concocting an alibi for my face.

I don't know what to say to him.

My mother's not even close to agreeing to a memorial service. And the more insistent he gets about it, the less likely she is to agree. It's becoming a war of wills, a real *Battle of the Network Stars*.

"It's coming along," I say. I just hope he doesn't ask how.

I place my top lip in the alcohol too, copying him. I don't taste anything though. Just feel the icy liquid against my lip.

This memorial service has got me stumped. I don't know what to do. The funny thing, of course, is that I'm right where I usually love to be, smack in the middle of a conflict: Eliciting confidences, and then betraying them, stirring the pot. I don't love this one though.

"Looks like early October," I say, as if it were resolved.

We have to commemorate my father somehow. I know that. Send him off properly into the ether. I don't know how to do it though, or how to convince my mother either. It's no mean feat, getting her to do something she doesn't want to do.

"Okay with you?" I ask.

But I don't feel like any fireworks tonight.

He nods back at me.

"That'll be good," he says.

I smile at him.

We'll save the fireworks for another day.

Now that his drink's not filled to the brim anymore, my uncle picks it up and sips properly from the glass. I follow his lead. It's shocking this time though: Purely alcoholic. Nothing to mask the taste of it either, just a few olives sunk down to the bottom of the glass.

My mother would scoff at all this drinking: A waste of perfectly good calories, she'd say. "It's funny," I say, letting my mind wander back to her. "I don't remember my mother ever visiting you with Bertie."

Bertie was a neighbor of ours in the country, long since moved away. Just a summer neighbor really. She taught high school in Toronto during the school year, calculus or some other math that was light-years ahead of me at the time. She spent the summers in Vermont, in a little cottage not far from us. She ran the beach club during the summer at Putney Lake. She was very lovely, tall with shiny raven hair that hung down straight to her shoulders. An excellent swimmer too. That was how we met her: She taught me how to swim.

"Sure," he said. "They came for a quick visit once, to see the land we'd bought for the new house."

I take another sip.

The drink is growing less bad now, burning less against my throat, and glowing nicely in my stomach.

"Don't you remember?" he asks, sounding proud of his reconstituted memory. "They had car trouble and had to stay over."

"Yes," I say. "I remember that." And really I do. I'm not just remembering to be polite. I remember a maroon car that broke down. A lemon, my mother called it. I just don't remember Bertie being with her on that trip. Bertie is the sticking point here.

I take another sip. The drink is actually bordering on nice now, not tasty by any means, but a nice experience in my mouth and throat.

"Bertie stayed too?" I ask.

"Well, of course," he says. "Both of them."

That makes sense, I guess. If the car broke down, Bertie would have to stay too. I lay my hands flat, palms down, on the starched cloth in front of me. See the gold ring on my right hand.

"Funny," he says, remembering more. "We called our mechanic the next morning. Asked him to come over and take a look, but it started right up," he says. "No trouble at all."

Of course it did. That car was as dependable as the North Star. There was never a problem with the car. Lemon, my ass.

"Just a temporary glitch, I guess."

He really is a fool.

My face is on fire now. It must be flaming red again, like after the visit from bachelor number two. Like the foliage at my mother's house in October. Maybe he'll put it down to the alcohol.

My mother cocked up a breakdown to spend the night with Bertie.

I open the large menu and hide my face. The golden tassel falls into my lap. The overlovely script inside, loopy and black on the thick ecru stock, is enough to make me sick. I already know I don't want a single thing they have to offer here.

Sheila. Bertie too.

I'm as big a fool as my uncle.

She's had lots of lovely women. My mother.

I close the menu and place it carefully on the table.

"I'm going to have the rack of lamb," he says.

I have no idea what I'll order.

Maybe another drink?

I fold my hands in my lap. My fingers start to work the ring I'm wearing—twirling it and twirling it.

It's my father's wedding band. I'm sure of it, but I pretend I'm not. I found it in the top drawer of his bureau a couple of months ago. My mother must have claimed it from the undertaker and put it there. I took it, wear it sometimes, when the mood strikes.

She hasn't said a word about it yet, but I'm sure she's noticed it missing. I give her credit too, for keeping quiet. It's not her strong suit. She must be waiting, trying to work out what it means. It's awfully complicated, Oedipal almost beyond belief. Who does it marry me to? My father, who wore it for so many years, or her, wearing its twin even as we speak?

It looks lovely against my skin though, very rich.

Turns out I'm a gold person.

CHAPTER FOUR

——

Lemony Sweater

I'M SITTING IN a little bookstore café in Westport—walls and walls of books surrounding a small café in the center, only ten tables or so. I'd always thought this particular combination—coffee and books under the same roof—was a New York City phenomenon, scarce real estate and all, but I guess they have them everywhere now.

The bookshop itself is practically empty, just a couple of browsers poking wearily through the shelves, but the café is bustling, nearly all the tables occupied, lines of people at the "to go" counter.

Muffins are flying out of this bookstore.

We café patrons all have books with us at our tables. I've got a picture book of midcentury chairs with me. We'll muck them up with coffee and jam, and then just leave them behind without a thought, ruined. Books and food, together like this, have never seemed a very clever combination to me, but I'm clearly out of step on this one.

I'm sitting at a small round table, strangely tall for the chairs surrounding it. My chest barely clears the tabletop. You could dislocate your shoulder reaching for the sugar here.

I'm waiting for Henry.

Can you believe?

From the suburban sex line.

I called him this morning, after my uncle left to play tennis.

Live and not learn, that's my motto.

I should have it embroidered on a cushion—a very small one with intricate needlework, small enough so I can take it with me wherever I go. If I had a pillow like that now, I could sit on it. It would give me some height in this tiny chair. I'd hate for Henry to think I'm a midget at first glance.

It didn't seem like the dumbest thing in the world, when I called him this morning to arrange a meeting—it's a public place after all. He was so glad to hear from me too. But it doesn't seem like the cleverest move now, now that I'm actually sitting here, waiting for him to throw open the doors and disappoint me.

I can see it all already: There'll be me and some perfectly nice man who's definitely not for me. There'll be coffee and some baked goods too, no doubt dry and crumbly, but we'll soldier on and choke them down with copious amounts of butter as a last-chance lubricant, struggling to clear our passageways. We'll be struggling for air and struggling for words.

This whole thing really can't help but be a bust.

I should probably leave right now.

But my face is finally approaching normalcy this morning. It would be a shame to let that go to waste. You'd almost have to be looking for a black eye to see the remnants of mine this morning.

Wait— This could be him now.

No, no. False alarm. That one's meeting the lady in the corner. She's waving wildly for him too, as if she were trying to flag him down from the opposite end of Madison Square Garden.

I feel the hope draining from me, drop by drop. But I keep sitting here all the same, ass glued to this Romper Room chair.

How close do you have to be to tell someone's eyes are hazel? And isn't that just brown anyway?

My attention keeps drifting back to the mother and son a couple of tables to my left. I can't help it. My eyes just keep drifting back. She's wearing an eight-dollar wig, the mother—reddish brown synthetic curls springing out from every square inch of it. A real Zsa Zsa Gabor number. It might be the cheapness of it—the unreasonable optimism in the face of certain failure—that's created this tenderness in me. I feel it inside me like a solid mass, like a brick pressing itself against my chest, just beneath my heart.

At least it's not lopsided. I'll give her credit for that. She's got that wig on straight. She's got a shiny aluminum crutch too, and I don't think it's about a sprain or a stress fracture either. No, she's palsied in some way. You can see it in the way her hand topples over her wrist, like a waning sunflower, spilling over its flimsy stem. There's something plainly wrong with her motor skills.

Her little boy—seven, maybe eight—runs back and forth to the counter for her, fetching their drinks, then their muffins. Running back for the cream, then for a knife. So many trips for such a little boy. He's barely tall enough to reach the top of the glass counter.

Could my mother have some ice, please?

I'm afraid for him every time he races back to retrieve some new thing she wants. He picks up just a little too much speed for the short distance he has to cover. He looks as if he's going to smash into the display case every time. Someone should warn him. Put a small decal on the face of the glass. Maybe that would do the trick—a butterfly sticker, anything, just some small warning to let him know it's not the open road; if he's not careful, he's going to crash through to the other side, all cut up on a shelf of brioches.

He's going back again.

She's an awfully demanding woman. He doesn't appear to be the least unhappy with his lot though, springing up again and again, delighted to do her bidding. He doesn't appear to notice that there's anything wrong with her either. No trace of embarrassment in his smiles and giggles.

That'll come later, I guess.

He's focused on her too, to the exclusion of everything else in this shop that might claim his eight-year-old attention, thrilled to run for a pot of raspberry jam if that's what she wants.

Just a little boy in love with his damaged mother, like the rest of us.

My mother and I are standing in the playroom together. She's just asked me to do some little thing for her.

"What?" I ask.

I'm very small, six or seven.

I've fallen into the habit of asking her to repeat herself, even when I've heard her perfectly the first time. Just a little strategy for dragging out our conversations, prolonging her attention for as long as I can manage.

She even asked the pediatrician to test my hearing once. Afraid I might be slightly deaf—hard of hearing, she called it. But I always heard her perfectly. That was never the problem.

She obliges me though, repeats her request in a calm voice still.

"Will I get a surprise?" I ask.

She looks perplexed, pauses for a moment.

I may have jinxed myself

I'm afraid her voice will be brittle when I hear it next, her eyes hard at the sight of me. I wish I could retract the question, but there aren't any second chances here. I know that too. You either get away clean, or you don't.

A smile breaks out across her face, small and sly. "Absolutely," she says, smiling at me instead of everything I feared. Her eyes are velvety brown still and warm, no hardness there at all.

Relief blooms inside me, creates a jumpy dancing in my little body, a slight bouncing up and down.

The little thing she asked for—whatever it was—didn't merit a reward. I don't even remember it now, just some little thing a mother might naturally enough ask her young son to do: Put away his toys, find her cigarettes, listen to an involved story about her husband's inadequacies.

I do the little thing, whatever it is.

It couldn't have been very complicated.

I'm only six or seven, after all.

And I feel my legs rushing back to her again, breathless at her side now.

"All done," I sing out, happy to have done what she wanted. "I've done it," I say. Happy to please her and happy for the reward to come. "Yea!"

I see some hesitation on her face, some tension around the eyes.

She must be reconsidering her promise. Must see that the task was too small to merit a reward. I'll never concede the point though. "A promise is a promise," I remind her.

"Quite right," she says, nodding. "Yes, you are."

That's all it takes. I'm thrilled again, dancing my body from side to side, from foot to foot. It doesn't take so much with a little boy, you see?

"I think I might faint," I say.

And it's true, I feel as though I really might.

"Now, you lie down on the floor," she says.

What?

Her voice is neutral. I don't know how to read this request. There are no clues for me to make out here.

"And close your eyes, mister."

She must be warming up to this though. She's stretching out the process, letting the excitement build. This isn't like her. She isn't the sort of person to appreciate the pleasure of a surprise waiting to reveal itself, sitting in plain view but unknown. She's too impatient. Sometimes our birthday gifts aren't even wrapped.

Still, I go along with her. I jump onto the ground, onto my back.

"Now you have to give me a minute," she says. "I'll be right back."

I'm bursting at the prospect.

"Do you promise to keep your eyes closed?" she asks.

I squint my eyes shut. Purse my lips closed too, although she hasn't even asked for that. I nod with abandon. I promise. I really, truly promise.

She leaves the room. I hear the leather heels of her sandals tapping gently against the wooden floor, then the more muffled sound as she crosses the threshold onto the kitchen linoleum. She closes the French doors behind her.

She's getting my surprise now!

When the doors open again, my heart begins to pound. I feel a small breeze from the opening doors wash over the front of my body, clenched and tingling with excitement.

The beating of my heart is the only thing that keeps me from floating away, each pulse nailing me back down to the floor, my little-boy ribs against the planks of wood, grounding me as I wait.

"I'm back," she says.

"I know," I say. "I can hear you."

"Are you ready for your surprise?" she asks. I can hear the excitement mounting in her voice too.

I have no idea what this present might be. It could be anything. She must have spare gifts hidden away for moments like these, for when I've been such a magnificently good boy that an immediate reward is in order.

"Are you ready?"

"Yes," I cry out. "I'm ready."

I won't be able to contain this excitement much longer.

"Now keep your eyes closed."

I reach my arms straight up into the air like two radio antennae waving, fingers wiggling for optimal reception.

I just can't wait anymore.

"Please, can I have my surprise now?"

"Yes, you can," she says, almost giddy herself.

Something cold on my face and neck.

It's horrible! Hard and cold.

Wetness seeping through the front of my shirt.

My hand grabs at my chest.

Can it be?

I open my eyes.

It's an ice cube.

No, it's a bunch of ice cubes.

And cold water. She's poured a glass of ice water on my head.

I open my mouth to scream.

It's so cold. My heart is frozen.

"My surprise?" I cry out to her.

I don't understand yet that the ice is my surprise. No more surprises will be forthcoming.

She looks at me, smiling still.

"Not all surprises are nice, you know."

Henry hasn't shown up yet, but it's early still. There's a clock above the door. Five minutes to the hour now. I don't let myself look at that clock too often though. Just steal a glance every now and then. Fixating on that clock will only make me a nervous wreck, and there's no need to worry yet.

I'll let you know when it's time.

I order a coffee when the waitress comes around, a sweet-looking girl with the jitters in her legs and a tangle of frizzy blonde hair. She throws one hip out to the side when she stands in front of me, tapping her heel insistently against the carpet, like a bobbin on a sewing machine, a thousand little jabs in the space of just a few seconds. It's all the coffee racing through her. She must be a wreck by the time her shift ends.

"Would you like a muffin with that?" she asks, tapping away.

Must be instructed to push the pastries. Muffins may be more popular than books here, but they don't have half the shelf life.

"No thanks," I say. "Just the coffee for now."

She smiles back at me, drumming a pen against the side of her order book.

I won't drink more than a cup.

Look back at the clock again.

There's a large cardboard display by the cash register, featuring a book by Rosamunde Pilcher. A hundred copies, I bet. All neatly stacked inside little cubbies built into the display—a huge, sky blue sky, rendered in cardboard, and a cardboard couple too, locked in a feverish embrace. They've really pinned their hopes on this one.

I peek at the clock again. Still not eleven.

Look back at the little boy at the table down the way. He's playing a dangerous game now, tilting backward in his chair—balancing on just the back legs, giggling for a second, until he loses his equilibrium and the chair threatens to fall out from under him, tossing him backward, head over heels.

I don't let myself look back at the clock again.

The other patrons don't do much for me. Hardly take up any time at all: A pair of middle-aged women in colorful wrap skirts and identical beige haircuts. *Ladies of the Canyon,* Connecticut-style. A college student at the table next to them, a huge textbook open in front of him. It takes up nearly the entire table.

No room for a muffin there.

He's devouring that book too, face pressed up close, not six inches from the page. You'd think it was a Rosamunde Pilcher novel the way he's eating it up. An elderly couple behind him, buttering their muffins slowly and taking small sips from their coffee mugs. Peaceful as you please. Not saying a word to each other, just relaxing with a mid-morning snack.

I let myself look back at the clock now.

Now it's eleven.

He's still not here.

So far, the little boy's managed to right himself each time he loses his balance, landing all of the chair's legs firmly on the floor again despite the gravitational pull backward. But I know it's just a matter of time.

I should never have come so early. I was worried about navigating the Post Road though. I thought there'd be more to it. Who knew it was just an overgrown Main Street?

The little boy's mother doesn't intercede either. She's just gazing off into space, her face a wide-open stare. My mother would have put a quick stop to a game like that.

When the clock reads four past eleven, I let myself begin to worry in earnest. I'm afraid I can't make any more excuses for him now. He's probably not going to show up. He may never have intended to come at all. Or maybe he intended to come initially—when we were on the phone together, and maybe just after he hung up the receiver too—but then decided against it, at the last minute maybe, brushing his teeth in the upstairs bathroom, gazing vacantly at himself in the mirror as he did.

It feels ordained to me now: He'll stand me up. Making the question of how much longer to wait for him even trickier. Of course, I've got to wait long enough for him to arrive if he's en route, but not too long. Every minute too long I wait will make me even more foolish when he doesn't come, until I'm such a big fool that I won't be able to fit through the door to leave.

Five more minutes then.

Is that long enough?

I'm sure the Post Road gets awfully congested. All right, ten minutes, and not one second longer.

But he's not coming. I know that.

I'm not sure I blame him either. The genre almost begs for it. Think about it: The perfect anonymity, the overfrankness. Sexual truth-telling to complete strangers. Phone chat almost depends on not showing up. Turns out I've had this all wrong from the start. How could he ever recover the innocence to shake my hand and speak his name, when he's already put much more telling knowledge at my disposal?

It would be like enrolling in Engineering 101 after you'd built the Aswan Dam.

He'll stand me up. He has to.

I've convinced myself now. And just as I'm about to motion for the check—looking all around for the waitress with the jitters in her legs—Henry walks in the door.

I know it's him without the slightest hesitation.

I just know it.

He surveys the tables quickly, and walks immediately toward mine. Walking purposefully too, practically striding. He knows it's me. He extends his hand for me to shake when he reaches the table, without even asking my name. I feel an immediate pull toward him, a full exhalation of breath.

He showed up.

A strong pull, and an even stronger feeling of relief. It's not that he's so attractive, it's not the pull of sexual attraction. Almost the opposite: The pull to safety, toward the white Styrofoam circle with fluorescent nylon trim, the lifesaver that's bobbling along, up and down, in the middle of the ocean. You just need to get to it, that's all.

He's walking around this place like there's nothing he can't handle here.

Just slip your arms around it, or place your head through the opening at the center, if you prefer. He'll take care of the rest.

"Matthew," he says, smiling.

Not asking though. He's announcing it.

He's good looking. Light brown hair and dark eyes, just like he said. Even features and a strong chin, which he left out. Freshly shaven. Maybe that's why he's late.

I note a full set of eyebrows. A navy shirt that could do with a bit of improving, but nothing I can't handle in that department. Clear skin and a straightforward gaze. He's not going to stop any trains with his magnificent beauty, but neither am I. And frankly, gradations of attractiveness seem entirely beside the point now, as he stands in front of me at the tall café table with the too-short chairs. To me, it looks as if he's made of marble, that's how solid he looks.

I hope he likes me.

He sits down and catches the waitress's attention right away. He asks for a lemonade, which sounds appealing to me: A grown man with a little-boy drink. I abandon my coffee and order one too. Ask the waitress for a toasted scone—walnut, please—with lots of butter. Nursery food, all around.

"Sorry I'm late," he says.

"Not at all."

"I had trouble finding a parking space."

I just have to get through this part, the banal part. It's tricky for me. I get tongue-tied.

"Did you have any trouble finding this place?" he asks.

I get bored.

"Not at all," I say.

Just keep going, I think. Just get through this part.

"It was really quite—"

A tremendous crash: Furniture falling, a woman cries out. The little boy's toppled over, I know it even before I look. I knew it would happen. I saw it coming. Why isn't he crying? Tipping back on the legs of his chair like that. Of course he'd lose his balance. He had to fall over eventually.

That mother should have her head examined, letting him play like that. I see the little boy lying on the floor in a heap. The mother's struggling to get to her feet, but she can't negotiate it. Can't seem to fit her forearm into the holster of that crutch. It's all tangled up in her coat on the chair beside her. She's trying to do everything too quickly. That's her problem.

Henry's already sprung to his feet.

I'm astonished.

He's going to get involved.

Runs to the little boy and picks him up.

He never mentioned citizenship on the phone. Then again, I probably wouldn't have put much of a premium on it.

The little boy must have been too shocked to cry, too frightened. When he throws his arms around Henry's neck though, buries his face in Henry's chest, he lets himself go. He's howling now. There's no blood though. None that I can see from where I'm sitting anyway. I hope it's not serious. He's probably crying from the terrible surprise of it all, the shame of having fallen over, humiliating himself in a bookshop café in the middle of the Post Road.

Wait, little boy, just wait. It gets much worse than this.

Henry bounces him lightly, walks in a small circle around the mother, the boy in his arms. Keeps the mother always in the little boy's field of vision. Rubs his back.

Then he settles the boy in the chair next to his mother. She strokes her son's hand, kisses the top of his head. He stops crying now, only sniffling. He's regaining his composure.

Henry rights the fallen chair.

The mother thanks him profusely. I can't hear the words, but I see the gratitude on her face. There's no more trace of anything gone wrong.

The little boy's in love with Henry.

And what's more, the drama confers an exemption on us from any further exchange of banal information. It's like magic. We just skip over the dull parts: Parking on the Post Road, gone. Where we're from and what we do, vanished. Brothers and sisters, all skipped. For now, I don't even know where he went to college.

"I wasn't late because of parking," he says, almost as soon as he sits down again. His eyes look a little wide to me as they meet mine, as if he were surprising himself.

Must be the adrenaline still, coursing through his veins—all that rushing around, all those heroics.

"No?" I say.

But I don't know where he's headed with this.

"No," he says. "I almost didn't come."

I nod slowly—at a loss. Feel my stomach drop.

Maybe adrenaline's like truth serum. I don't know why else he'd tell me this.

"These things never work out," he says.

I keep nodding. Couldn't agree more really, but still I feel a little hurt. I've never been dumped by a superhero before.

"Well . . . ," I start, but I'm not really sure what to say. Does he want to stand up and leave now? What about the lemonade?

"I'm glad I came now though," he says quickly, smiling at me.

Nice teeth, for the record: Even and white.

But I'm even more confused. "Why did you tell me all that?" I ask.

"Just being honest," he says.

Oh, one of those.

I'm not so sure about this. But I can't help a slightly soaring feeling either. I made the grade, after all. He's glad he showed up.

The jittery girl brings us our lemonade and the toasted scone. I butter it for us while it's warm. Take a bite of the sweet cake, warm walnuts and butter melted in.

Henry picks up the picture book I was looking at before he arrived—the book of midcentury chairs. He flips through it, mentions an exhibit that he wants to see at the Cooper-Hewitt. My ears prick up at reference to future events.

"I haven't seen it yet," I say, careful not to force an invitation, but diligent to create an opportunity.

"I've heard it's excellent," he says. "Maybe we can go together?"

Well, that was about seventeen times easier than it usually is.

No, I take that back.

It's never this easy. Calling it seventeen times easier seriously understates things.

"How do I know you'll show up?" I ask him.

"You'll just have to take my word for it," he says, smiling back at me. "I guess."

My father sits in the passenger seat of a baby blue Volkswagen. Head nearly touching the creamy vinyl of the car's inner roof. He tilts his head slightly off to one side, slouches down in his seat too. Even so, it looks as if he might sprout through to the other side if we drive over any kind of bump.

He's much too big for this car.

He has his hands folded neatly in his lap, but I can see the pressure of his fingers bearing down, see the skin beneath his fingertips pressed white. I can tell he'd like to wedge them up against the dashboard, create some small protection from being thrown through the windshield as I buck the car forward.

I'm sitting in the driver's seat.

Fifteen years old. Learning how to drive.

We're in a large field on the far side of town. It's very early on a bright Sunday morning in the fall.

Seat belts hitched up tight.

I have a learner's permit already, so we could be practicing in a parking lot in town, but I know I'm not good enough for that yet. He would never say such a thing to me though, and I'm smart enough not to ask what we're doing out in the middle of a pasture at eight-thirty on a Sunday morning.

It's lovely here just the same. The entire field is surrounded by a ring of maples and sycamores and oaks, all at the red and yellow height of fall color, silvery aspens fluttering in the distance. I'm driving in large circles, trying to learn the syncopation of clutch and accelerator, releasing the one while pressing down the other.

It's a matter of timing, he says.

It's not coming easily to me.

"Smoother on the clutch," he says. "Let it up easier."

I try.

When I look over at my father, I see his cheeks are flushed. He doesn't raise his voice, but I can tell he's nervous from those ruddy cheeks.

I try again.

We lurch forward this time, bucking to an abrupt halt. The back of the car feels like a whipped-up bronco, furious and determined to kick its back legs up over its front. There's a bad grating sound too, the sound of innocent gears being stripped.

"Easier," he says. "Easy on the clutch."

I must have let it out too fast again.

When I let the clutch up slower though, pressing down on the accelerator too, we don't seem to move forward, not an inch. Just hear the revving of the engine, sitting stock-still in the middle of this field.

I sneak another glance in my father's direction. Oh dear. See the red from his cheeks, like the fiery maples at the perimeter of this field, spreading to his ears now. I continue driving in a large loop. Something in me wants to move for the brake when I shift.

"No brake," he says. "You don't need the brake."

So I try some more.

As bad as I am though, the odd thing here is that I'm not at all worried about the accelerator or the clutch. Sooner or later, I'll get the knack for driving. I know that. I'll learn to leave the brake alone. What worries me is the silence in this car when he leaves off from his calm instructional phrases. When he's not telling me about the gas or the clutch, the brake, there's not a word to be heard inside this powder blue interior.

This is the problem I want to fix.

So I sit in the driver's seat, mangling the transmission of this poor little car, scripting questions that might start some kind of dialogue between us.

When did you learn to drive? I think. Or maybe: Who taught you?

My eyes peeled on the grassy path our car has made in the field, trying to trace it again this third time around. My foot steady on the accelerator, hoping against hope that I might find the right question—the perfect one, the one that lets the clutch up easy, sends just the right amount of gas to the engine, purring beneath the powder blue hood.

"Was it easy for you to learn?" I ask.

He answers all my questions, of course, every single one.

"My father taught me," he says. Or, "I was about your age."

He's never rude.

But none of them open onto anything larger than their specific one- or two-word answers. They're all like little dead-end roads. I can't seem to locate anything like an open field here.

The questions aren't very original, I suppose. I hardly care what his answers are. I just want to bridge the gulf between the two bucket seats.

My father wants me to pay closer attention to the clutch.

. . .

Rii-IIIING.

Rii-IIIING.

I'll let it go a few more times. She's not as fast as she used to be, and I really need to sort out this business about the memorial service. I've let three weeks go by since I got back from Darien—it's June already—and I still haven't nailed it down. Already promised my uncle too.

Rii-IIIING.

"Hello," she says.

Good, she's there.

Now finish this business once and for all. And under no circumstances are you to mention Bertie, or any faux engine trouble in Darien, circa 1982.

"Hi, Mom," I say.

"Matthew!" she says. "I was just thinking about you. The Weather Channel said it's raining in New York."

"Why are you watching the Weather Channel?" I ask, legitimately curious. I've never seen her watch the Weather Channel before.

"Oh, I like to keep up," she says.

"With what?" I ask. "Low-pressure systems?"

"Sheila's leaving today," she says. "We were just checking the weather at Logan Airport."

"I thought Sheila left two weeks ago," I say. My mother told me she was leaving just a couple of days after my last trip to Vermont.

"She did," my mother said. "She went visiting some friends at the Cape, then popped back up again."

"Oh," I say.

Popped back up again?

"So what are you up to today?" she asks.

"Not much," I say. "Just looking at some old photographs actually."

There are no old photographs.

And it looks like I'm going to mention Bertie after all.

"That sounds pretty dreary," she says. "I wouldn't go knocking the Weather Channel if I were you."

"There's a great one of you and me," I say. "At the beach, it looks like. You know, that incredible seaside light. You and me and Bertie."

All made up.

"Mmmhh," she hums, feigning boredom.

"What ever happened to her?" I ask.

"Who?" she asks.

Maybe she wasn't feigning.

"Bertie!" I say.

"I have no earthly idea."

Oh well. At least I come by all this lying honestly.

Happily, at least, my newfound annoyance helps propel me onto the subject of the memorial service a little easier. "Have you given any more thought to the service for Dad?" I ask.

"No," she says. "I haven't." Leaves it at that.

"Uncle Andrew and I think we should do it at the beginning of October," I say, as if the date were the only issue here. "What do you think about that?"

"Sounds fine to me," she says, entirely matter-of-fact, as if she'd never had a problem with the memorial service at all.

This is too easy though.

"I'll be traveling then," she says.

"You will not."

"Oh yes, I will," she says. "I'm going to visit the Grand Canyon with Bertie—since you're obviously so interested in her all of a sudden."

She doesn't miss a trick.

"Really?" I ask. I know she's not, but I just can't help myself.

"Are you crazy?" she says.

I don't know what to say now. I've promised my uncle a memorial service at the beginning of October. I told him she agreed even. It's more than that though. I know a memorial would be the best thing for everyone—her and me included. But I don't have the vaguest idea how to start this ball rolling.

I sit quiet on the line.

"Do you really want a memorial service, honey?" she asks, but softly now, a different tone altogether.

For the record, she did this all on her own.

"Yeah, Mom," I say. "I really do."

"Then we'll have one," she says. "We can sort it all out when you come up next weekend, okay?"

"Thanks," I say.

"And you can tell your uncle Andrew for me that I think he's a pain in the ass," she says. "He should have been half as good to your father when he was living as he is now that he's dead."

She's right, of course.

But it's just as true of me, I think. Maybe even more so.

I'm sixteen years old, sitting in front of the post office at the center of Main Street. "Good luck," my father says as I open the passenger door, swing my legs out onto the street. He doesn't look terribly optimistic though.

"Thanks," I say.

Close the door behind me.

The Department of Motor Vehicles is on the top floor of the post office. Climbing and climbing, up two flights of stairs already, but not there yet. Two more flights to go. I'm here to take the test for my driver's license. I'm not a very good driver though. Can't seem to pay attention to what's happening on the road in the undivided way of good drivers.

I keep climbing the old marble stairs, worn away at the center from so many years of use, decades of sixteen-year-olds climbing to freedom—like all those little Von Trapp children, singing their way to Switzerland, only without the captain and Maria.

The test is comprised of both written and driving sections. It's given only once a month, and no one waits longer than the very next testing date after his sixteenth birthday. I'm not surprised to see five or six kids here before me when I open the old-fashioned door—milky glass in a heavy oak frame. We can't wait to become licensed drivers. DEPARTMENT OF MOTOR VEHICLES stenciled in gold, but backward now on the translucent glass when I turn around to close it.

I'm still breathing hard from the climb.

I'm not happy to see these other kids. Don't relish a public failure. It's not that driving is so hard or anything. I just get distracted.

I hand my birth certificate to a frowning old woman behind the counter—white hair set into an old woman's wavy hairdo and a forest green cardigan draped over her shoulders.

What's she got to be so dour about?

She checks my name on the certificate carefully and hands me a smallish piece of white card stock, a multiple-choice test printed on it, only twenty questions. She gives me a short little yellow pencil too, the kind without an eraser.

Everything here is smaller than I expected—the test, the lady, the pencil—more like a round of miniature golf than the regulatory power of the State.

I smile and thank her.

Maybe politeness will count for something here.

At precisely nine o'clock, she directs us to a series of small desks, all separated by beige laminate partitions. She doesn't seem at all troubled by the fact that we've been sitting together in a gaggle for almost fifteen minutes, chatting away, tests in hand. Maybe there are multiple multiple-choice tests.

Turns out not to be a difficult question in the lot anyway. Not one where my short little pencil doesn't fly to fill in a small oval of answer from among the choices, not a doubt in my heart, not a millimeter of oval left unfilled. Any concerns I had about the pencil's eraserlessness are quickly dispelled. Who needs an eraser with questions this easy? But I always knew that this would be the easy part, the written test.

I hand it back to the old woman as soon as I finish. More smiling and courtesy from me. She's smiling back at me now. I've convinced her I'm a good boy. Her teeth are crooked and yellow.

She grades my test immediately, right before my eyes. I missed only one question. Apparently it's better to use low beams in fog. Who knew?

"Congratulations," she says, initiating the smiling herself now. "You passed with flying colors."

It's hard for me to match her pleasure though. Smile back with only half a heart. It was just the written part. I place the little pencil down on her Formica countertop with a click. It's hard to imagine the written test that would outdo me. She tells me to sit down with the others to wait for the driving portion.

I try to hide my growing nervousness. I can already imagine a competent young man with straight, white teeth—the driving examiner—sharp and white, and bared to me only when strictly necessary.

I sit waiting for nearly forty-five minutes. Just staring into space—not a magazine in sight—just sitting and working up scenarios of breathtaking humiliation behind the wheel. The others are all chattering away. No one had much difficulty with the written portion, it turns out, not even LuAnn Fortin, the dumbest girl in school. Finally, the old woman calls my name.

"Yes."

"Please come up here, dear, to the desk."

Here goes: The driving portion. And you know, I might not even have a problem with it, especially if I don't have to parallel park, or do much of anything in reverse.

"I see you did very well," she says.

But she'd already told me about the written test, about using low beams in fog. She's starting to annoy me now, but I smile at her anyway.

"Wasn't so bad, was it?" she says.

What is she talking about?

"I see you parallel parked on the first try too," she says.

She should be institutionalized.

"Not everyone does that," she says. "Let me tell you."

I'm confused, but I keep smiling as I try to work this out.

"We'll mail your license in a week or so," she says.

She thinks I've already taken the driving test. I see an evaluation form in front of her, my name printed upside down at the top.

Can I get away with this?

I don't disabuse her.

Maybe I can. Caveat emptor, I decide, especially where the State is concerned. I thank her sincerely now, from the bottom of my heart. She's only too happy to bare her crooked yellow teeth again.

I race down the stairs in a flash, down and farther down, as quickly as I can. I call my mother from a pay phone on the corner. It's a very cold day, but I don't care. I'd rather wait outside. Better to remove myself from the scene of the crime. The old woman might come to her senses at any second.

My mother pulls up in front of the post office about ten minutes later. I get in quickly, shut the door behind me.

"I passed," I say.

She's stunned.

I would be too, if I were she, if I had ever taken me out on a test drive. She'd probably prepared a little consolation speech even. She drives straight home, eyes on the road, both hands on the wheel.

"How'd the parallel parking go?" my father asks that night, pleased somehow, in spite of what he must know.

We'd practiced so much together, he and I.

"Let's try it again, Matty." That's all he ever said, as sweetly as you please.

I was rarely successful.

"I did great," I tell him. "On the first try too."

In for a penny, in for a pound, right? It's not like anyone was ever going to tell him a different story. But of course, that's precisely what I'm afraid of—that the old woman will call the house, having discovered her error, angry with me for letting the mix-up stand.

But no call yet.

And the old woman can't live forever, right?

Here's what I want to know: Mustn't there have been some kid left over at the end of the day? Some kid who'd parallel parked to perfection on the very first try, just sitting there, waiting for his results. How did the old woman deal with him?

I just can't work it out.

There's another problem too. I'm still a terrible driver, my laminated certificate from the state of Vermont notwithstanding. Not a week goes by when I don't crash into something or cause something to crash into me, merging lanes like the devil himself, roaring through red lights as if that were the point.

The tickets rack up. Tragedies are narrowly averted—or they narrowly avert me, I should say. I rarely have anything to do with it. The car lives at the repair shop. I just can't pay attention to the road.

My parents are beside themselves. Silent looks of wonder pass between them—How can he be so bad at this?—every time I return with some new tale of woe.

Maybe I'll get better with practice.

"Can't we give you a lift?" they plead.

"No thanks. I'll drive myself."

They do institute one rule though: I must not drive on the highway. Never, ever.

Is that clear?

Do you promise?

Yes, yes, yes.

They must hope to eliminate highway driving until whatever shortcoming is making me so bad at this is properly diagnosed and treated. I can't blame them really. If I were paying the bills from the body shop, I'd probably have come up with a more stringent set of rules.

No, their position doesn't seem unreasonable at all.

Back in New York on Sunday night, fresh from my weekend in Darien, I pad softly around the apartment, trying to get the drift of things all over again. Telephone rings.

"Hello?"

I know it's Henry from just his hello. And I hadn't even had time to start worrying about his not having called yet. "Henry!" I say, returning the favor of his calling so soon, not making him identify himself.

"So how was the rest of your weekend?" I ask.

Who knows? Maybe I should have played dumb, pretended I didn't know who he was.

"Fine," he says, "Pretty dull. Yours?"

I'm out of my depth really from the first flash of interest on.

"Same-ish," I say. "We watched *Mrs. Miniver* on television last night."

"With your uncle?"

"Yeah," I say. "We like a tearjerker."

I realize this might not be an attractive image though—sitting with my uncle on the sofa in his study, crying in unison to a Greer Garson film. "Snatch any more kids from the jaws of death?" I ask, changing the subject.

"One or two."

He's not stupid.

"So are we getting together this week?" I ask. Apropos of nothing, just getting to the point for a change. This is *me,* asking!

"You bet," he says. "That's why I called."

Looks simple, right?

We settle on Wednesday night, after work. This was easy as pie.

I feel Olympian.

"Bye."

Until Wednesday then, Henry.

A boy I like called for a date!

This next part should be easy, right? The contact's been made, and the date's been set. Now wouldn't be a half-bad time to relax for a minute or two. I still have to think through costuming, of course, and scout for locations. Have to dream up a few conversation starters too, just for safekeeping. But that's not so bad, relatively speaking. The major hurdles have all been jumped here.

The war's over, Greer Garson Mr. Miniver's on his way home.

But I feel panicky, start pacing around the apartment in a big loop. I'm like a caged animal at the zoo—and not a resigned one either, not the defeated baboon who just sits there like a lump, entirely familiar with his captivity, letting the flies swarm all over him without so much as a lazy swat in their direction. No, I'm the new kid on the block, the tiger fresh from Kenya, just off the boat, just out of my crate—stalking the boundaries of my little cage in a continuous loop, around and around, circling relentlessly, as if my fifty-first lap might somehow uncover the exit that's eluded me the fifty times before.

I know what's going to happen here. That's the sad part. I already know. But it takes a few more laps still. I sit down in the reading chair in the corner. Put my feet up on the ottoman.

Dial.

My fingers seem to know which buttons to press intuitively, without any help from my head. The numbers are just thrumming inside me. Dial 555-PUMP to retreat from boys who like you. Boys you like back.

I'll stay on for fourteen years. I'm going to have a five-figure phone bill. I'm not hanging up until Wednesday. I'll just keep talking and talking, hunting like my life depends on it.

They'll be able to hear it too—all the next guys.

Beep.

I'll do very badly tonight. I know that too. But I can't help myself.

They'll hear how much I want a connection, the stakes I've got riding on this. I try to calm myself down.

Beep.

I just can't.

Beep.

My date with Henry doesn't make me calm like I would have expected. I'm not inclined to start reading a new novel, or to take up a new hobby—knitting, say. The idea that I might be through with hunting for a while doesn't inspire me to make a pot of tea, sit down quietly to drink it. No, it makes me want to hunt some more.

So get to work! Find someone on the Pump Line immediately! But I've already found someone on the Pump Line. Don't I remember? Someone nice too. We're getting together on Wednesday night. I'm getting together with handsome, courageous Henry.

Remember?

But I can't seem to make myself remember, or maybe because I do, there's no stopping me now. There's no getting me off this Pump Line. I'm here, and I'm staying here. Trawling with a wide net.

Not hanging up.

I keep going and going—for much longer than you'd think possible—but eventually, I come to the end of the seemingly endless supply of Pump Line dates. Scott simply runs out of connections for me. He doesn't say so, of course, nothing like that. "Hang on," he says, "while we make a new connection for you. Or press zero, and browse through the personals locker room."

I hang on, but the new connection never materializes. I just keep hanging on. Five or six minutes even, and no more next guys. The Red Sea has simply run dry, no more fishies there.

"Hang on," Scott says periodically. "We're making a new connection for you." But you can't squeeze blood from a stone, Scott. There is no next guy to connect me with. So I hang up.

Sit quietly in the corner of my living room, head hung low. Dejected now, who wouldn't be? But a little impressed with myself too, just beneath the surface of disappointment. I've outdone the entire Pump Line operation. Outdistanced Scott and his army of men. I met all his "next guys" head-on, and I was ready for more. The world champion. No one even close.

But I'm not going to rest on my laurels. No, I'm not done yet. I know what I'll do! Throw on some clothes. Brush my teeth. Grab my keys. I'm out the door.

To the Downtown Club, of course.

I don't wait for the elevator either. No, that takes too long. I take the service stairs instead, two at a time. My legs ache for three. Out on the street in a flash, hailing a cab. There's no slowing me down. I find one almost immediately.

"Twenty-third Street and Seventh Avenue, please."

I'll be there in no time. My body is vibrating in the back of the cab, thrumming with excitement and the knowledge that this is the perfect thing for me to do. Why isn't this guy moving yet? The light's green.

"Cross on Eleventh Street, please," I say, polite but sharp.

That should get him moving. So exciting back here, like fifteen presents rolled into one. He's still not moving though.

"The light's green," I say.

Don't fuck with me, driver. I've come too far to let you stand in my way.

And then we move.

It's a bright fall morning, and my first thought on waking is for a sunny yellow, cable-knit Shetland sweater that demands my immediate attention in Northampton, Massachusetts—a drive of forty-five minutes or so, most of it on the highway that's strictly prohibited to me. It looks like my parents' rule about highway driving is going to be overlooked this morning, but that's what rules are for, right?

I strap myself into the car and turn on the ignition, check the rearview mirror and the side-view mirrors and even crane my neck around as far as it will go, trying to look over my right shoulder, just the way my father always says to do.

With all these precautions taken, I feel pretty good about placing my foot on the accelerator, backing the car slowly out of the garage. The problem with all this checking though is that I have no idea what I'm checking for. The car's just sitting there, stock-still. What am I expecting to see in all these mirrors? Flashing lights? Saint Theresa, the little sparrow of Jesus, from out of the blue, nodding her head: Yes, it's safe now?

All this checking, I'm afraid, is just acting—me, starring in the role of competent driver. I never touch the steering wheel when I back the car out of the garage. I assume that whatever wheel position got the car safely in is also my best bet for getting it out.

Boom!

Feel a jarring jolt.

I pause for a second, deeply panicked: What do I do now?

I just don't know.

I've clearly hit something.

But what?

Should I stop?

Put the car in drive maybe, undo what I've done?

I'm fluttery with nervousness.

It's something big from the sound of it, whatever I've hit. From the jolt of it too.

I don't know what to do.

And in my moment of panic, I decide to keep going. That's what I decide: Just keep going. Stay the course.

I put my foot back on the accelerator and pick up right where I left off.

How can I have decided this?

I just keep going. *Through* whatever it is that I'd hit.

When I'm out in the open, on the driveway and in the clear, I get out of the car to inspect the damage. Practically none to the car. But the garage is destroyed, or at least a small corner of it anyway.

I just drove right through it, like the big bad wolf. Just blew it down. I'm amazed, standing here, surveying the rubble. I don't see how I could have done this much damage. The car was in a stationary position after all. I barely had my foot on the accelerator. But the facts are the facts: The corner where the house met the garage is gone now. Apparently it doesn't take much speed to raze the corner of a house.

Thank God they aren't home.

I'll have some time to prepare myself at least.

And where better to do that than on the highway to Northampton, where I really do need to pick up that lemony yellow sweater I've had my eye on? Maybe everything will work out fine.

So I drive to Northampton—without incident, I might add. Buy the sweater. It really is good-looking. Drive home without a hitch too, just as easy as you please. In fact, you'd never guess from my driving to Northampton and back that I'm the sort of person who could do magnificent damage to a house, backing a parked car out of the garage.

Neither of them is home yet when I pull the car into the driveway. It's only been a couple of hours since I left.

I walk inside with the sweater tucked under my arm, climb the stairs to my room. I spread the lemony sweater out on my bed. It really is lovely. I refold it, as nicely as I can, trying to reproduce the way it looked on the shelf in Northampton. Not quite. Try again.

There's another yellow sweater, it turns out. I'd forgotten all about it. Not half as nice as this new one though, so lemony and all.

Nothing left for me to do now but wait.

I walk downstairs and wander around the kitchen, then the living room, trying to pass the time. Sit down finally in the den, closest to the garage. I turn on the television and wait, and somehow I retain a calm demeanor right up to the moment my mother pulls her car into the driveway.

I feel myself growing warm, begin to sweat even beneath my arms.

But nothing still—no screaming, just complete silence. Maybe she's standing there, stock-still, clocking the damage with her mouth hanging open. Or lying in a heap perhaps on the poured concrete floor, a massive stroke brought on by the shock of her discovery.

A drop of sweat trickles down the side of my body, starting slow, just beneath my arm, barely moving at first, then picking up speed.

I keep still. I don't move from my chair in the corner of the playroom. This is an awfully long time for nothing to have happened.

Now I hear her, leather soles slapping down fast against the poured concrete, all amplified and hollow. She's practically jogging now. Here she comes. The screen door opens and the heavy back door too. Bolting into the playroom. She's not screaming though. She's too angry to yell. Look at her face—all pinched up and tight.

She's got a piece of paper in her hand. A little slip of paper, and she's waving it at me, out in front of her body. Looks like a valuable document of some kind—like the first draft of "The Declaration of Independence" or the shooting script of *The Prime of Miss Jean Brodie.*

"I'm so sorry," I say. "I was looking in the rear-view mirror, I swear I was."

"But what?" she says.

She's found her voice again.

"The side of the garage just up and moved on you?"

It's hard and sharp.

"Just overtook you by surprise?"

There's no need for sarcasm.

"I didn't mean to."

But she wants none of me, neither apology nor defense.

She's had it.

She barrels by me and heads straight for the kitchen telephone, mounted to the wall. It's got a superlong, twirly cord.

"I'm calling your father," she says.

This is strange.

We're most definitely not a wait-until-your-father-comes-home sort of family. For all the times I've watched this scene on television—helpless mothers, so June Cleaver-esque, forever threatening to call in the big guns—I don't believe we've ever acted it out before. No, we settle things on our own, she and I—the *Playgirl* in the cedar closet, the contretemps with Mr. Swenson in the ninth grade. We write my father out of scenes like these, shielding him from our terrible selves and us from his terrible inability to cope.

But not this time, I guess.

She's barking at his secretary now, "Just put him on."

Now at him.

"You'd better come home," she says into the receiver. "And you'd better listen to me the next time I tell you something."

A brief silence while he speaks.

"He's crashed through the garage."

Another silence.

"He's fine," she says.

At least somebody cared.

"I told you he wasn't ready for a car," she says. "He's a terrible driver."

That's not very nice, with me standing right here.

But I'm surprised too—surprised that my father was the agent of the car purchase, that he got it for me over her objection. It's just the opposite of what I would have expected.

It also explains why she's dragging him into this now: I told you so.

"Why don't you come home now," she says, and it doesn't sound like a question, not the way she says it.

She hangs up the receiver.

That was awfully nice of him, buying me a car. And he didn't even take any credit for it.

I look at her.

She glares back.

This could be a big problem for me.

The lovely yellow sweater begins to seem rather small in comparison.

Soon I hear my father driving into the garage.

It didn't take him very long to get here.

I join my mother in the living room, sit down in the armchair that matches hers. It doesn't matter how angry she is with me. Surely our years of close partnership—most of them at my father's expense—will count for something here, even though she seems to have forgotten them entirely for the moment.

It takes a long time before my father opens the back door. He must be surveying the damage.

I wonder if it's even possible to fix.

His face is flushed when he walks into the living room, almost as deep as the red upholstery fabric. He's enraged. This is even worse than I'd thought.

Avoiding eye contact with me too, just like her. Isn't anyone going to look at me around here? But the closer I look at him—at the slight stoop in his shoulders, at the particular squint in his eyes, like he's struggling to read some very fine print—I see he's not angry at all, he's uncomfortable. He's flushed with embarrassment, not rage.

What's he got to be embarrassed about? I'm the one who knocked the house down.

No one's said a word yet. This silence has some heft.

Then my father starts to whistle. It's a happy tune too, one of his old-time songs.

Is he crazy? Doesn't he see what this situation calls for?

He keeps whistling.

I know the words to this song:

> *I'm gonna buy a paper doll that I can call my own,*
> *A doll that other fellas cannot steal.*

He's supposed to be furious with me.

She's counting on that.

But he's blushing instead, whistling a happy tune. The Mills Brothers, no less. I'd sing along if there were any chance of defusing this situation, but I know better. I know that as well as I know the words to his song.

I glance in my mother's direction. She's pressed her lips thin, the muscles of her jaw set tight. My best prospect might be for him to keep whistling. It's annoying the hell out of her. I can see her growing angrier by the second. It's plainly legible on her face, all there for him to read.

He takes keys from his pocket, fiddles with them some—what does he need to unlock, for Christ's sake? At least his face is less red now, his complexion almost back to normal. Maybe the whistling's done him some good. It must be nice to have a little hobby like whistling, just a little something to take the edge off.

"Everything okay?" he asks, finally looking at me.

This is so wrong that there might be some irony in it. I check his face, see that there's none.

"Fine," she says, rage bubbling up over the surface of her voice. "Your son's just knocked the house down. We're fine, thanks."

"I saw that," he says calmly. Turning to me: "What happened, Matty?"

I take him through the story that she had no patience for. Grow visibly upset while I tell it too. I don't think it's for effect either. It feels real to me.

He listens with a kind face.

She looks like she might spit.

He looks upset for me. I can see it in his eyes. Maybe he identifies with trying the best you can. Trying your best but that still not being good enough.

"It sounds like you took all the right precautions," he says.

"I did, Dad. I still screwed it up though."

"Don't worry about that," he says. "We can get Milton Cheney up here to fix the garage."

He's not worried about the garage. He's still worried about something though. Looks away from me slightly, doesn't want to meet my eye for this next part. "But you and I are going to have to work on your driving some more," he says. "We've got to get you driving better."

Is that all?

He doesn't look as if he's going to say another word.

That was the difficult thing for him? Telling me I needed more driving lessons. That can't be. There's got to be more to it than this. But I can see it on his face: He's finished talking.

I'm shocked.

Not half as surprised as my mother though, her lips parted in disbelief at the stunning prospect of a carpenter from town and some driving lessons as the solution here.

She wanted a lynching.

She wanted Milton Cheney up here building a funeral pyre, log by log.

I can see it in the set of her jaw.

"Not so fast," she says, stepping forward, taking the slip of paper from her pocket and handing it to my father.

Just when everything seemed settled too.

I'd forgotten about that piece of paper.

"What's this?" he asks.

It's like a surprise plot twist at the end of a courtroom drama—when Perry Mason hands the accused a letter to read in open court. Read it, says Perry Mason. But the poor man just sits there, stone silent, all eyes on him. He can't read it! He's illiterate! He can't have read the will in advance either. Case closed.

It was such a nice solution too: A carpenter and a few driving lessons.

I watch his face as he studies the paper.

He looks puzzled.

I still can't think what a mottled little slip of paper could prove against me. It's not even three inches by four.

I walk to my father, gently take the paper from his hands. It's a sales receipt from the Northampton Shop—for the lovely lemony sweater that I bought this morning.

She must have found it in my car. Damn her.

The name of the store and the address preprinted at the top, along with a little line drawing of the storefront. Today's date and the amount of my purchase are handwritten large, in blue ink.

The salesman had a firm hand too. I can feel the impression of the numbers he wrote on the back of the slip, each one pushing itself through the paper, like an engraved invitation, or Braille.

It's curtains for me.

"Did you drive to Northampton today?" he asks.

It proves I've been on the highway.

He doesn't sound angry. Just gathering data.

If there's a centimeter of wiggle room for me here, I can't find it.

I stay calm.

"No," I say. "I didn't go to Northampton. Why?"

"Well, there's the receipt for starters," my mother says.

"I didn't," I say.

Even with all this evidence stacked against me, stacked as high as the Sears Tower, I won't admit it.

"You didn't?" my father asks, in a soft voice still.

He looks at my mother now.

They both look puzzled.

"You didn't?" she repeats, almost impressed with me.

Even she wants to believe me now.

It's the thrill of watching a high-wire artist. They both want me to make it across that thin, thin wire—so high up, thirty feet, I bet. Even though they know there's no earthly way I can.

"No," I say. "I didn't."

"Where did the receipt come from?" my father asks.

I feel small beads of perspiration forming on my brow, at the place where my hairline meets my scalp.

"I don't know," I say.

"Was anyone in your car today?" he asks.

"Not that I remember," I say, backing myself into a corner.

"Then you don't think someone dropped it in your car?"

He is rationality itself now.

This is how he plays cribbage: Establishing his victory by eliminating all the possibilities for defeat.

"I don't think so."

"Let's review the facts," my father says in a calm voice. "The receipt is from a shop in Northampton, dated today. You didn't give anyone a ride, and no one else was in your car. You can understand how it looks like you drove to Northampton."

"Yes," I say. "I can see that it looks that way, but I didn't."

It's a war of wills.

And it continues for hours, through dinner and the television news.

He insists that we play a game of cribbage later in the evening, and he keeps up the unrelenting challenge throughout.

"Are you sure you didn't go?"

But I won't give in.

"Absolutely."

He wins the first game and asks for the truth.

I stick to my story.

He wins another.

But I don't care. I won't crack.

He goes up to bed at eleven, in the thick of our stalemate.

Will this continue tomorrow? The day after? For the rest of our natural lives?

My mother comes downstairs again shortly after my father goes up to bed. She's ready to make a deal.

"Why don't you just admit it," she says. "He'll go easy on you."

I ice her out, look straight through her as defiantly as I can. "I didn't do it, that's why."

She shakes her head and walks away.

I defy them all—a lying Joan of Arc.

My father comes back downstairs at midnight, his pajamas rumpled. He won't give in either.

I've robbed him of sleep now too.

I'm watching the *Tonight Show* with Johnny Carson. Johnny's got one of those no-name stand-up comedians on. I watch the television as if I'm transfixed, for my father's benefit. Maybe he'll go away.

The camera moves back and forth—first on the comedian telling his joke, then to Johnny's gleeful reaction. Another joke, another shot of Johnny laughing.

This guy isn't even funny.

My father sits down beside me on the couch. Right next to me.

This is very strange.

He must be as uncomfortable here as I am.

On the television, it's still back and forth between Johnny and the comic. Back and forth, back and forth—so much movement for so little humor. Here on the couch, we're both stock-still, staring straight ahead. Both acting like we're transfixed now.

He puts his arm around my shoulder.

I continue acting like I'm mesmerized by the comedian, too taken up with his magnificent talent to have noticed my father's gesture. I feel the weight of his arm heavy on my shoulder. Smell the nighttime scent of him too, so close to me, the smell of sleep and fabric softener on his pajamas.

"I love you, honey," he says. Then he goes back to pretending that he's transfixed by the television again.

I wait for his next line, sure that this is just another tack in his quest to crack me, for me to admit to the drive to Northampton. We sit together for a while longer in complete silence, his arm around my shoulder not feeling half so strange as it first did. But the next line never comes. All my terrible crimes against him, and he doesn't even hold a grudge.

We sit through another complete commercial break and then some more of Johnny. My father stands up without a word and goes to bed.

Said all he wanted to say, I guess.

The next day, it was as if the whole thing never happened. I never heard another word about that trip to Northampton—not from him or from her. And you know, I could never bring myself to wear that lovely lemony sweater. Not even once. I can't imagine the trousers that would go with a sweater like that.

———

CHAPTER FIVE

A Threadbare Towel

T HE CABBY GETS ME to the Downtown Club at last. I pay him handsomely for the ride, with a hefty tip to assuage my guilt for snapping at him earlier, when he sat like a lump at the green lights, going nowhere. The overtipping doesn't make me feel much better though, and I don't hear even a hint of gratitude when he counts out my change for me.

I close the car door and run across the street to a small brick building on the other side. Jog up a flight of stairs, quick as a bunny. It's right here on the second floor, the very spot where the Ginger Mann Studio used to be—the original aerobics studio in New York City, the granddaddy of them all. Turns out I've been coming to the Downtown Club for years. Fifteen at least, long before it was the Downtown Club.

I dash into the foyer where I once paid for the privilege of high kicking to Evelyn "Champagne" King. Eight dollars, I think it cost back then, and worth every penny too. The foyer looks just the same now—windowless and dark—except for the little booth, fronted in Plexiglas—that's new.

A cashier sitting inside.

I pay almost twice as much now for high kicks of an entirely different nature here. Fifteen dollars, evenings and weekends. I don't like to think about the people who come here during the day. It's still worth every penny though, and the soundtrack's just about the same.

There's no line tonight too. That's lucky!

When there's a line here—on a Saturday night, say, when hordes of men stand waiting to be let in—there's time to think about what you're doing. Time enough—as you snake through a line weaving this way and that—for you to realize you're the sort of person who'll have sex with a stranger in a cubby no bigger than a fitting room at Bergdorf Goodman. It's not just flying up Sixth Avenue then and roaring up a flight of stairs, not just slipping inside either, all in a flash, as if you'd been propelled by steam somehow other than your own. No, on a Saturday night, after you've waited and waited, *you're* the one who got you here.

But there's no line tonight. I'll be inside in a jiffy.

When the Ginger Mann Studio closed, the wide-open aerobics room—an ocean of glossy wooden floor—was reconfigured into a warren of tiny cubbies. A series of a hundred little tombs, all with chipboard walls from floor to ceiling and doors that locked up tight, all lined up one after another in a labyrinth of dead-end paths. Every tiny cubby with its own small mattress. Every mattress covered over with a cheap, fitted sheet. A hard, foam pillow like a cherry on top. The sunny white walls of Ginger Mann were all painted dark, dark brown. The corridors black as night now, even the windows painted out. Overhead lights turned down low, as low as you can go and still call it light. The cubbies, the passageways, the darkness—*et voilà!* Aerobics studio as bathhouse. Apparently that's all it takes—just throw in a little lubricant, and you're in business.

The cashier seems not to notice me though. I'm standing with my nose not two inches from the perimeter of his Plexiglas booth, but he's acting as if he doesn't see me. It's a see-through wall!

He seems to be transfixed by a program on the little television he's got inside with him. Sounds like Bea Arthur to me. I clear my throat politely. Just want to slide my money under the Plexiglas and walk inside the club. The attendant still doesn't turn to me though. I wait politely for a moment longer, then marshal the courage to tap on his Plexiglas wall.

Knock, knock. I wait.

He looks straight into my eyes then and smiles vaguely at me, without a trace of annoyance. I don't seem to merit much of any response from him. I'm more relieved than you might think.

I pay him. Make it exact change too to cut down on the heartache. I'm not young enough to wait for change from a twenty. He passes a long, thin locker through the narrow gap between the Plexiglas partition and his countertop. He wants me to check my valuables. Feels like a miracle to me every time he slides them back out again at the end of the night—Look! My wallet, my watch! I put them in the locker one more time. He keeps the key.

Leave my father's wedding ring on.

He buzzes me through a security door at last. It doesn't fool me for a second though. Even though he makes a handy buzzing sound effect to let me in, this door doesn't provide a shred of safety. I've pushed it open once too often, by accident, just before the buzz, and it gives way every time. The buzz is a charade: The door was never locked in the first place. I can't remember now if Ginger Mann even had a security door, but I can hardly imagine it would have been necessary. We couldn't give it away. That's why we were here. But now, the faux security door makes a kind of sense, what with all the hidden sex taking shape in the dark, all along the mysterious passageways of the Downtown Club.

I missed out on sex the first time around, the seventies version— the discos and the sex clubs, the long strolls down west-side piers, multicolored handkerchiefs coded to a fare-thee-well and blooming gaily from tight rear pockets. I was too busy buying Shetland sweaters on forbidden car trips then. I was a child still. Of course I missed that iteration. And sex was definitely out by the time I got to New York in the eighties. Everyone was already convinced he was dying of sex by then. No one dared to have any more. Even the women at Ginger Mann with me, most of whom hadn't had sex since they left Smith College in 1976, even they were convinced that AIDS would be the death of them. Men were scarcely dating then, much less coupling in cubbies or lying in large porcelain bathtubs, letting strangers urinate all over them. Oh yes, the fun was well and truly over by the time I arrived.

Dark days on the sexy frontier.

But now it's back! Different, surely, from the first time around—less fun and somehow miniaturized too—like a Franklin Mint re-release or India on the "Small, Small World" ride at Disneyland. But I don't knock it. It's still sex just the same. Much more exciting than a naughty car trip to Northampton ever was.

I push open the faux security door of the Downtown Club and walk right in. So what if it's not Bette Midler anymore, singing to a room of men wrapped in plush terry towels, sipping cocktails brought to them on trays? It's all about a vending machine snack now. Heads were probably held a little higher back then too. There doesn't seem to be much joy here when you get right down to it. Like dietetic desserts: If we can't have the rich devil's food cake of fairy tales, topped off with the butter-creamiest frosting, then we'll settle for a nonfat muffin in its place—dry as dust, but it's still a kind of pleasure, right?

Another attendant, looking all of twelve years old, leads me to my tiny room now, twirling the key on a trim leather strap and singing along with Mariah Carey on the sound track, matching all her vocal gymnastics, lick for lick. He takes my dollar tip gladly—thanks me even—when he deposits me at my own little cubby along the labyrinthine path, unlocking the door for me and standing gallantly aside to let me in: My own little rabbit's hutch down the way.

Do I really wish I were at home with a boyfriend now, watching dreary situation comedies on television and eating big bowls of ice cream, rivers of microwaved hot fudge on top?

I close the door behind me.

Inside at last!

"Know what you'd like?" he asks, smiling at me over the top of his menu. I close mine. Put it down on the table.

So does he.

"Almost," I say, smiling right back at him.

I need to keep him on ice for just a little longer though. You see, Henry chose this restaurant. So I've got to find something wrong with it. Simple as that.

I pick up the menu again. Open it carefully.

Usually this isn't so hard—there's an ugly banquette maybe, circling the room like a bleeding ulcer in red velvet, or a seventy-five-dollar entrée with thirteen varieties of truffle oil mixed in—but this place isn't half bad.

"I'm a Libra," I say, turning back to the menu again. "Remember?" Explaining the delay.

"Of course I remember," he says, the edges of his mouth drooping slightly. He looks almost hurt.

I check the room for bad art, but there doesn't appear to be any. I'll find something offensive though. I always do.

"Take your time," he says. "There's no rush."

Nothing wrong with the lighting or the fixtures either.

And will you look at how fresh Henry looks in this flickering light? His face as clean as a brand-new leaf. He must have shaved just before he came here. I don't see a single whisker on that cheek. I've half a mind to reach across the table and touch it. It looks so soft. Run my fingers down the length of his jaw. I'm sure he wouldn't mind, but I think better of it. Run my eyes down the starters one more time instead.

Henry's keeping quiet now. Doesn't want to interrupt my marathon consideration of the menu.

If only this place were a tourist trap, or overlit.

I look back at the menu again.

I'm only pretending, of course, that I haven't decided what to order yet. I knew what I'd have almost the second I opened the menu: An endive salad and the striped bass, roasted whole.

Henry doesn't look the least impatient with me either, considering how long I've been dillydallying with this menu. And stalling with menus happens to be one of my patented methods for getting under people's skin too. You should see what it does to my mother. I'm still hoping he might snap. That would surely do the trick, better even than track lighting—if just a slight edge crept into his voice.

He just picks up the wine list, begins to scan it. It looks awfully long.

I'll take the first wrong thing I can find here.

He's just sitting back nice and easy, legs crossed loosely.

I take a sip from my water glass.

My stalling act nearly always works, but I've got a hunch it's not going to work with him. So composed still, relaxed even, light brown hair shining in the candlelight like a shampoo commercial.

Maybe the wine list then—too long by far, almost indiscriminate. No, I can find something more serious than that. If a too-long wine list is the best I can muster, I've failed here utterly.

Well, one thing seems sure: My stalling is a bust. I might as well own up to the fish. "What looks good to you?" I ask, before I do, my last hope flickering like the tasteful candle at the center of the table. Perhaps he'll order badly—steak with ketchup maybe. I could work with that.

"Other than Libras?" he asks, smiling at me again.

I feel the blood rush to my face—the heat of it swirling behind my cheeks, dancing behind my eyes. Blushing? God, no. I'm not embarrassed. I'm flushed from exertion, like a wrestler in the ring. I just brought him down. The newly minted champion of the bloodiest blood sport ever. I couldn't very well have a boyfriend who flirted, could I? He's just flirted himself out of the running.

But I begin to doubt myself in a stroke. This is too good to be true, right? Yes, it probably is. A little flirting is no more serious than an extra-long wine list, barely a misdemeanor.

"I took that as a given," I say, soldiering on.

It's one of our first dates too. If he can't flirt now, when could he?

It's just that I can't dispense with him until I find a reason, until I find something wrong with him first. Listen, I don't make the rules. It's simply protocol for me to find something wrong with him before I dump him, preferably something egregious.

I can't believe I look so hot to him anyway. I certainly didn't shave before I came over here. Didn't even shower. No, I stayed in my apartment, glued to the Pump Line until the very last second, dialing for my life. If I'd pushed the pound key even one more time, if I'd even thought about another connection, I'd have been late meeting him here.

"Other than Libras," he says, "I guess I'll go with the tomato salad and the striped bass."

Damn him! Taking my bass.

This would be so much easier if the restaurant were ugly. Or if he were ugly.

Maybe I don't look as bad as I think.

"I think I'm going to start with the endive salad," I say. Then pause again, but I'm not stalling this time. No, I need to choose something else, and quickly now. I can't very well order the same thing he does. On second thought, I suppose there's no harm in giving the old stall tactic one last chance. It is tried and true, after all.

Let my eyes wander around the lovely room.

You see, if this restaurant were ugly—if its walls were painted peach, if tent cards advertising novelty drinks littered every table—I could think less of him then. I could dismiss him as the kind of person who would choose a tragic restaurant. I could be done with him then and get back to my appointed rounds—to the Pump Line and the Downtown Club.

How I long to forget all about this bird in hand! Get back to my familiar shrubbery.

I've just got to find something wrong with him first.

I feel my heartbeat quicken—a momentary fluttering and a little heat: What if there's nothing wrong with him? Don't be silly. What if I'm stuck with him forever? I feel a little moisture forming at the top of my brow, right at my hairline. I hope he can't see it. Of course there's something wrong with him. The menu starts to feel clammy in my hands. I just need to find it, that's all. Take a minute and find it. And even if there's nothing wrong with him, that certainly doesn't mean there's anything particularly right with him.

"Then what?" he asks.

I don't know what he's talking about.

"After the endive salad," he says, reminding me where I left off.

He says it just as sweetly as you please though, not rushing me at all. He only wants to know what I've chosen for a main course; if I've decided, that is. He looks prepared to wait forever. The very edge of an immaculate white T-shirt peeking out from the neck of his navy sweater.

Never mind. I'll just have to find another way to skin this cat.

"I was thinking of the veal chop," I say, never having thought of it before this instant. I hate veal. The only thing going for veal is that it sounds like the antithesis of striped bass.

I keep looking all around me. I know I'll find something.

But he's not making it easy for me, sitting there so handsome in the flickering light of this perfectly nice restaurant.

"Is everything okay?" he asks. Sounds a little concerned.

"Fine," I say, looking straight back at him. "Why?"

"You seem distracted," he says. "And you're looking all around like something's the matter."

He wasn't supposed to notice that.

"No, no," I say quickly. "Everything's fine."

For the record though, the napkins are a little coarse.

"Because we can go someplace else, you know."

"I know," I say, brushing it off. "I like it here."

"Or you can call this date quits if you want to," he says, just a little slower now, making sure I understand all my options.

"I know that too," I say, looking right back at him.

I hate him, seeing through me like Saran Wrap.

Then he smiles at me. His blue sweater suits him awfully well, nice with his eyes. I can't help smiling back. Like when he kissed me when I walked in the door to meet him—on the lips, but not too much. I couldn't help kissing him back.

Here's what I want to know: How could this perfectly nice man be big enough, substantial enough? That's the real problem here. How could he possibly turn everything around for me? Because that's what I need. I need someone to turn everything around.

And where's the thrill, by the way? I have practically no desire to sleep with him.

Relax. He's going to trip up sooner or later. And when he does, I'll pounce. I'll be out of here before he hits the ground even.

Well, I might sleep with him first, just to see.

I sit back in the meantime, smiling right back at him.

He looks awfully good though. And this is the second time in a row he's brought me up short.

You'll never guess what he does for a living either, the bastard. He's a child psychiatrist—my fantasy-boyfriend job. You know, the one you project onto handsome strangers at the gym and the Downtown Club, when you keep circling them and circling them through all the looping passageways. When you endow them with the very best that you could hope for.

He launches into a self-deprecating little story about a dinner he cooked a real disaster—when the veal turned out like shoe leather. It's funny enough, I suppose. Designed to make me feel like a genius for choosing veal off a menu.

Careful what you wish for, I guess.

My mother watches the swimming lessons sometimes. Sits on the old bleachers by the water's edge, legs crossed ladylike. Green paint chipping and splintery wood all around her. Other times she just drops me off, leaves the motor running even. "Don't slam it," she says. I try to close the door just right.

Bertie and I walk down to the water. She slips her blouse off over her head. There's the top of her navy swimsuit, underneath. Clean white racing stripes running down both sides, elegant shoulders too. Her skin like a silken sheath over lean muscle and bone, tanned to gold from all those hours at the lake.

Dashing in a slim pair of Bermuda shorts now. So much tanned leg still, even after the long shorts leave off. She unfastens the shorts, and lets them fall. There's the bottom half of the navy suit.

I have a hundred little swimsuits—sweet little numbers with interlocking circles, broad red stripes. Little white liners sewn in like undies, drawstrings and elastic waists to make doubly sure.

Bertie and I wade into the lake together.

She's tall as a mountain, with shining black hair that hangs straight to her shoulders. Shining so bright you can see your face reflected in it—a Prell commercial come to life. Prettier than the local girls by far.

She stands behind me in the water now—hovering and crouched down low, pressing her shoulders on top of mine. She drapes her long, long arms on top of my shorter ones. Presses to demonstrate the way she wants me to move them, the way she wants the strokes to look. I fit comfortably beneath her wings.

"Like this," she says, canting one wrist slightly, as she cants mine too, with the slight pressure of her hand on top of mine. "Now pull the water toward you," she says, pulling her arm toward me and pulling mine with it, like a puppeteer. "Just like this."

She's nearly as tall as my father and every bit as solid, except I'm comfortable as she hovers. "No, no," she says, "not like a rake."

She brushes against me easy as you please. This is nothing like those tennis drills with my father—him on his side of the net, me on mine. There's nothing loaded here at all.

"Keep your fingers glued together like this," she says, pressing my fingers together with the pressure of her own. "So they're like a cup when you pull them toward you."

So happy to be standing here like this, with Bertie crouched over me like a lean-to, protecting me from the elements.

"You'll move much faster through the water that way."

Big like my father and easy too. Who knew it could ever be so easy?

Standing beside her on the dock as she rattles off her commands.

"Feet together," she says.

I place them side by side, watching her too, standing next to me. She demonstrates as we go, places her long, slender feet side by side.

"Now curl your toes over the edge."

We wrap them around the edge of the dock. Willing them to nearly ninety degrees, clamping on.

"Knees bent," she says.

I bend them.

"Arms back."

And back they go.

I'm ready, I think. But she squeezes the butterfly of my shoulder blades together. Not quite yet. She wants me wrapped up tighter still. So I clench a little harder.

"Go, tiger."

Now! I push my legs as hard as I can, release them like springs coiled tight from the edge of the dock, throw my arms out in front of me.

All to please her.

Oh yes, I unfurl myself. Chin tucked under, just like she said. I fly though the air and slice into the water. I think it was good. I really do.

"You've got to keep your legs together," she says when I surface, swimming back to her on the dock now.

There's always something more.

"And your arms farther out front," she says. "Right out in front of you, like this."

I try again.

"No, no," she says, when I do. "Not so deep."

Am I having fun?

"Just skim the top of the water like a bird coming in to land."

And then one more thing. So we do it again. And then again. But she always sticks with me, I've got to give her that. Bertie's attention never wanders. She's as demanding as my mother, but focused on me. Bertie only wants me to swim better. Only asks for things I can give.

I can keep my arms out front. Oh yes, I can. I can keep my legs together and my chin tucked too. I can unfurl my legs like little steel springs.

I can't do much about my father hiding in his study, or my mother ranting in the kitchen, but I can hold my arms out in front of me.

So I do.

I'm sitting with Goldstein on the Upper East Side. It's nearly three months now since he called me on the carpet for my spotty attendance record—ten sessions at least. I haven't missed a single one since. Funny how the prospect of an angry, male voice on the other end of the line is enough to get me out onto the sidewalk—in the face of real-life client meetings and full-blown sinus infections, rain even. I'm hailing cabs now with time to spare.

Just want to be good, I guess.

"It's funny, I know, but it doesn't seem to bother me," I say.

Goldstein's just asked me—for the three hundredth time since I first told him, months ago now—how I feel about my mother's affair with Sheila.

He nods at me from across the room. Runs his hands back and forth over the thighs of his beige corduroy trousers. I'm hot just looking at those pants—it's sweltering in here, the middle of July, and he's dressed in corduroy still.

"And I would have expected to feel jealous about it," I say.

Perfect attendance notwithstanding, I can't report any magnificent progress here. It's been nine months now since my father died, and I still can't get within fifty feet of him. "It was all years before I was born, I suppose." Filling up the sessions with the Pump Line still, and lately with entries from my mother's little black book too. "I was just a little ovum then," I say. "Tucked away nice and neat. I suppose even a blind man can see that Sheila Gray had nothing to do with me."

And just think of all the things people do in nine months: They have babies, for Christ's sake! Knit elaborate sweaters with huge cowl necks, but all I have to show for my nine months is an improved attendance record with an old man on the far, far reaches of the Upper East Side.

"So it doesn't upset you at all?" he asks. Looks a bit skeptical.

I guess I'm supposed to be upset.

"I don't think so," I say.

"Even though she made you go to a psychiatrist when she found out that you were gay?" he asks. He's trying to stir the pot a little, heat things up. I can hardly blame him, but he's a bit of a novice though. I could give him lessons in that department, if he'd like.

"Not really," I say. Her making me go to Dr. Norton Esty doesn't upset me at all. "She just wanted to make sure I had someone to talk to," I say. My mother never thought any less of me for being gay. I'm sure of that.

"So it doesn't bother you," he says, in the affirmative now—nodding his head and pretending he agrees with me, clearly at the pinnacle of his disagreement.

"I do wish I hadn't had to be told though," I say.

Maybe that'll count for something.

He looks interested, so I continue.

"Wish I'd been able to figure it out on my own," I say.

"Hmmm."

"Or seen it coming, at least."

He runs his hands back and forth over the worn corduroy trousers again. Looks like I might be onto something here. Don't ask me what though.

"You wish you'd been cleverer," he says, nodding a bit.

I spin into overdrive at the suggestion: "I wasn't around for a minute of it," I say. Startled by how angry I sound. "I can hardly begrudge myself not working that story out." And why so defensive? "A middle-aged woman on a weekend trip when I was ten, and a reappearance twenty years later. Nobody could work that out. Nothing to be clever about there."

I sit quiet, spent almost, when I've finished ranting.

He opens his eyes wider when I look at him. He's clearly intrigued, but he stays quiet too.

I have no idea what that was all about.

"You like to see things coming," he says. "Don't you? Just hate to be surprised."

I nod slowly.

"Why do you need to be so clever?" he asks, almost whispering now.

"I don't know," I say.

It's true. I don't.

"I didn't have a clue about Bertie either," I say. "And I was there for every minute of that one."

All those evenings—hour after hour—sitting on the landing at the top of the stairs, just sitting there in shorty pajamas—crisp in seersucker, cool in a smart gingham check—eavesdropping on the two of them in the kitchen, barely a room and a staircase away. Legs stretched down a step or two in the dark, just dangling down as comfortably as you please, all settled in for an evening of espionage, and delighted at the prospect.

"I listened to every last word they said." The hem of the pajama bottoms just above my knee. "Listened to the Scrabble tiles scrunch around in the velvet bag." All three buttons of my pajama top done up nice and neat. "Heard them clatter onto the Formica counter when they spilled out."

I listened to the hum of the refrigerator even, to every peep and creak and sigh. I listened so carefully you would have thought my life depended on it, and still not the slightest intimation about the two of them.

"I'm not clever at all," I say.

I feel as if I might cry.

.   .   .

It's a short walk from my apartment, only six or seven blocks or so—straight out the front door of my building and up the street, to another glassed-in booth where another minimum-waged attendant will sell me another overpriced admission—this time for two.

Push the heavy front door open and walk out onto the sidewalk. It's a lovely night at least—the end of May. And I've dressed just right for it too: A trim navy shirt and a pair of old-time corduroys.

Halfway down the block, I run into a familiar-looking woman out walking a dog—a little fox terrier. I'm pretty sure she lives in the building across the street from mine. I recognize her tweedy hat, like the kind James Joyce wears on the covers of all those Penguin paperbacks.

I half smile at her. She smiles back with all her face. Now I recognize her for sure. She gives me a small wave too. Her little dog stands stock-still on its leash, head cocked in my direction, twiggy legs trembling ferociously.

"Spring at last," she says.

I can't imagine how the little dog walks on those quivering legs.

"Yes," I say. "It's a beautiful night."

Just its legs shaking though, everything else as steady as a rock.

Happily, I don't feel the least pressure to say another thing.

"Heaven," she says.

It sure is. It's my idea of heaven: A little commentary on the weather, just that—no pressure to amuse her, or schedule a dinner date or any kind of coffee outing. Thrilling to think I'll never find out where she works, who made her lovely hat.

"Night," she calls out.

I check my watch. It's only half-past six.

There's plenty of time to walk there and buy the tickets still. Plenty of time for an easy stroll.

I turn the corner and walk north.

Past the doormen on lower Fifth Avenue—a little bored-looking in their spiffy blue uniforms. Some splayed out on wooden stools just inside their front doors. It is a bit quiet now, I suppose, a little boring for a doorman. All the pedestrians who were rushing home from work just half an hour ago, clogging up the sidewalks and jockeying for space—they're all inside now. Swinging their briefcases like machetes, clearing paths. They've taken that aggression indoors, to their wives and children.

I'm just strolling up the avenue, swinging my arms a bit—trying for unencumbered, but falling flat. I'm perfectly encumbered, in fact.

I'm meeting Henry in twenty minutes.

Even the tension from the corners has dissipated—practically no one bucking to cross against the lights or playing chicken with the oncoming traffic. Only one or two optimistic souls trying to hail cabs.

I keep walking north. Stop for an apple at the deli on Thirteenth Street. We won't eat until after the movie.

Henry's probably just stepping out of the shower now—all lathered and rinsed, shampooed and conditioned, waiting until now to shave, beard softened by the steam and hot water.

Turn right onto Broadway.

He'll want to be especially alluring tonight. This is date number three, after all. Time to put up or shut up.

I take a bite.

It's hard to believe we've reached this crossroad so fast. Feels like only yesterday he beeped into my life on the suburban Pump Line, when I was nursing my battered face at my uncle's house in Darien.

This apple tastes like it's been on sale since October. Its shiny red skin fooled me. Lovely to look at, but loose around the fruit inside. I throw it in the trash can on the corner.

Oh yes, I can see it all already. I've been on this date a thousand times. We'll be slightly nervous when we meet. Halting small talk as we walk inside. And hyperconscious of each other, sitting together in the dark. Definitely not touching—oh no—but somehow more conscious of each other than if we were. I'll be more tuned in to the gentle rise and fall of his breathing chest than if I laid my hand right on top of it.

There's the theater up ahead. So much bigger than everything else on the block. Seven theaters and just two films. We're seeing the arty one, of course, probably showing in a tiny theater in the basement. They'll need all six upstairs for George Clooney.

Henry's not pushy either. He'll wait a good long time before he makes a move, before he lets his leg drift across the line of demarcation between us—just the very edge of his left thigh kissing mine. So lightly at first, I probably wouldn't even feel it if I hadn't been waiting for it. He'll need the muscle control of an Olympian to keep that thigh in place, only barely touching and no more. He'll wait to see whether I answer in kind, whether I leave my leg there, resting lightly against his—maybe even pressing back slightly—or move it away.

Salty popcorn in the clever plastic holder, hands free, but not required at this juncture. I'll keep them folded in my lap.

Just a small fusion of corduroy, outer thighs pressing lightly against each other in the dark, so much urgency and so much lightness, more dramatic by far than the subtitled movie on the screen up front. All unfolding in two center seats, about ten or fifteen rows back.

Oh, what the hell.

I'll lean my thigh back into his.

Why not?

There's no line at all when I approach the glassed-in ticket booth.

Dinnertime, I suppose.

"Thank you for coming to Loews," the girl says from inside the booth, speaking into a small microphone.

There's no microphone on my side of the glass wall. Just a metal grate at about mouth level—or mouth level for a shorter person, about Adam's apple level for me. It's built into the Plexiglas between us.

"Can I help you?" she asks.

She speaks directly into the microphone, and when she's finished speaking, she lowers her gaze slightly and looks into it too, into the little black mouthpiece at the end of it. Keeps her gaze trained there, as if that were the way to see me—through the long black stalk that grows up from her ticket console, curving gently to her lips. Like looking at me through a microscope.

I smile to warm her up.

Nothing. She's still not looking at me though.

People are probably very rude to her here. She must be steeling herself against mistreatment, speaking in a monotone, refusing to establish eye contact with me. I just keep smiling.

At least she's looking at me now. Her face a mask.

The Loews people probably never even thought to tell her to smile while she was saying her lines, much less speak with some inflection in her voice. They can't think of everything. And I can't help feeling as if I've done something wrong, that she's right to punish me this way.

She's wearing a horrible uniform—brown polyester smock, matching brown hat. Maybe this isn't about me. I'd probably be furious too, wearing that smock—a Loews insignia sewn onto my left breast—sitting in a glass cage all day.

"Your hair looks great," I say, committed now to winning her over.

Her hair is great too, I'm not just flattering her to be nice. That's only part of it. Long black cornrows with blood orange beads woven in, and all the ropy rows scraped upward and tied together at the top, like a lovely spray of tulips tied loosely with a pretty yellow ribbon. The little brown hat sits at the top, an utter irrelevance, like the care instructions florists attach to out-of-the-way stems. You wouldn't even see it, looking at her casually through the Plexiglas.

She's risen above that uniform.

I smile again to convey the depth of my feeling for her—a wide-open smile. But nothing comes back still, not a thing. No smile to answer mine.

I'm smiling still, but awkwardly now. If she's heard me—and I think she has—she's a very rude person. It must take her three hours to do that hair every morning. I'd think she'd like a compliment.

I feel my affection for her leaching out of me now.

Goddamn her and that microphone. I'm glad all these movie chains are bankrupt. "Two for *Destiny of Fools,*" I say, clipped, almost British. Madonna on David Letterman. That'll show her.

These movie places deserve to go out of business.

"Seventeen dollars, please."

With employees so coldhearted and mean.

I do my best to toss a twenty into the little well beneath her Plexiglas window—no mean feat, considering that a twenty-dollar bill is only a piece of paper. Considering how hard it is to throw paper with anything like precision. It's impossible. Still I try to convey with the flick of my wrist that a twenty is nothing to me. See, Miss Minimum Wage.

"From a twenty," she says, flat as a pancake.

The bullets of class warfare ricochet off her Plexiglas booth.

I should have let Henry get the tickets.

She slides three crisp dollar bills into the well, along with the tickets that whir out of a metal slot on her console.

He offered to get them too.

"Enjoy the show," she says.

Oh yes, she's got that script down cold.

I decide not to thank her.

Will myself not to.

It's going to be a silent exit for me, a stinging rebuke for her. But I can't quite reach the tickets inside the little well beneath her window. It's awfully small, and the angle's all wrong. Plexiglas comes down too far.

She slides the bills and tickets forward slightly, helps me out.

"Thanks," I say, in spite of myself.

I'm sitting on a wooden stool at the kitchen counter, swinging my legs loosely, careful not to let the toes of my sneakers bump up against the lower cabinets. That just makes her angry.

I'm watching my mother make a cursory dinner—hurling pork chops under the broiler, tossing a salad with breathtaking indifference. Closing all the cabinets and drawers a little loudly.

She gathers up the cutlery into one fist—tines and blades and handles all sticking out in every direction like a gruesome weapon in a kung fu movie—a wad of napkins in the other hand to stanch the bleeding. She takes a few steps toward the dining room, then pauses, changing her mind. I can hear her sigh: The kitchen's so much easier.

I can make out her thoughts as easily as if she were speaking them out loud, as if they were coursing through my own head. I've got her tuned in like an FM radio station.

She drops all the cutlery onto the kitchen table, must nearly have thrown it down by the clattering it makes on the Formica. I rush to help her pick out the right pieces from the chaos on the tabletop. I don't say a word.

She talks constantly as she does these things, talking to herself really, but addressing me, cataloguing my father's shortcomings as she goes. "We never talk," she says. "Not a word. He just walks in and sits down to dinner. Acts like this is a restaurant, and I'm just a waitress here."

I never interrupt.

"Shows absolutely no consideration for my feelings," she says. "For everything I do around here. No, he takes it all for granted. Treats me like a scullery maid."

I stare at her with all my might, blurring the edges of everything in my field of vision that isn't her. Keep the outline of her navy blouse clear as a bell, let the yellow refrigerator melt behind her like butter in a hot pan. It's a magic spell: If I keep her alone in focus, I can cause her to go on like this forever, preferring me to my father for as long as it lasts.

"And after dinner," she says, "he just disappears into that study of his. Goes in and closes the door behind him, stays there all night. Not a second of adult conversation around here."

There must have been a time before these wonderful, horrible complaining jags of hers, before my little-boy jealousies found their perfect outlet in this conspiracy, before I liked to watch my father brought low.

I'm eight.

"But you," she says, letting something soft into her voice now, "you'd never treat me like that, would you?" She stabs three potatoes with a fork and tosses them into the microwave.

I shake my head with all my heart. I never would.

"Never a dinner out either," she says. "Not even on the weekends, when every other wife in town goes to the country club for dinner and dancing."

I'm thrilled to be taken into her confidence like this, to be so much higher than my father in her esteem.

"And never a party or a trip either," she says. "No, it's just not right.

Every weekend, with him off alone in the woods, walking and walking. Looking for what, I'm sure I don't know."

I've already learned to chime in with a sharp-edged detail—never too much though, never more than a word or two. "The Cunninghams are playing in the mixed doubles tournament this weekend," I say. Throwing another log on the fire, stoking her up.

"I don't know why he ever got married," she says. "We don't do a thing together. He just sits locked away in that study of his as if I didn't even exist. I don't know how much longer I can take this."

I've got her all to myself now.

Congratulations, I guess.

We're sitting side by side, Henry and I, sunk down deep into plush velvet seats that rock forward and back with the least pressure against the padded backrests, like old-fashioned porch swings set on hair triggers.

It's freezing in here, like a meat locker. I have goose bumps on my arms. It's just the end of May, but they have the air-conditioning turned to August. A lady down front pulls a ski sweater on over her head. My eyes have adjusted to the blackness now. I can see as well in here as if it were high noon. And when the scene changes—a quick jump cut to morning—the light from the screen makes me squint, makes it high noon in here for real.

Stadium seating—that's what it's called. We're set so high above the row of seats in front of us that Wilt Chamberlain could be sitting in front of me right now, rocking away, and I'd still see the screen just fine. Not that I'm paying much attention to the movie at the moment. No, I don't have that luxury yet.

A dark-haired woman on screen moves in breathtakingly close to the handsome leading man.

I still have to work out how to sit here comfortably with Henry.

It looks like she's going to kiss him. That's how close she's standing. But just when you'd expect her to lift her face upward, to close her eyes languorously and present herself for kissing, she opens her mouth instead.

It surprises me.

She starts to speak.

White-lettered words appear at the bottom of the screen a couple seconds after she finishes. Nothing she said required her to stand so close though, not if you believe the translation anyway.

You'd think it would be easy to get comfortable in these seats too—like big, business-class rocking chairs, all padded and upholstered in burgundy velvet—but it's not. There's this armrest to work out, for instance. Only one to share between us, and it isn't immediately clear to me how we're going to do that.

The actors on screen are still standing too close for comfort, speaking straight into each other's faces.

Maybe if I put my arm like this?

Henry brushes his forearm against the inside of my wrist. Doesn't move it right away either, like an accidental brushing. No, he lets it linger there. His arm feels warm and dry against the sensitive skin inside my wrist. Nice at first, but I don't want to leave it like this. I don't want to risk his skin growing sweaty against mine.

I try to pay attention to the screen.

Move my arm just a little.

That woman is still standing so close.

And my seat rocks every time I shift position. I move my arm on the armrest just a little more, a little farther away from him still. Yes, this is much better. I can sense him nearby now, but we're not actually touching.

I should be paying closer attention to the movie. Who is this woman? She could be the one from the beginning, I guess, the woman on the bicycle.

Henry leans into me now. I feel the solid pressure of his shoulder resting against mine. We're fused together, just below the neck.

But the woman on the bicycle was prettier than this, I think.

He shifts in his seat again, and his shoulder vanishes.

Usually I pay extremely close attention at the movies. Usually I'd know precisely who this dark-haired woman is. I look at Henry in profile, in the reflected light of another daytime scene. He's looking straight ahead, lips parted slightly. The light from the screen flickers off his face—brightish first, then darkening. I watch his eyes dart around the screen. He's really paying attention. I'm sure he knows exactly who this woman is.

He looks back at me now, smiles.

This is hard work.

I smile back at him.

What I'd really like is to stop this seat from rocking. I concentrate on keeping my body still, but the more I concentrate, the harder I rock. I just can't keep the pressure of my back constant against the padded backrest.

The Pump Line is so much easier than this.

I feel a small breeze on my cheek.

Turn my head, to its source.

It's Henry. Leaning in like he wants to kiss my cheek or—no, whisper something in my ear. It's going to be hard for him to zero in on my ear though, the way I'm rocking back and forth.

What if he asks me who the woman on the bicycle is? What will I say then? I feel myself swing out in front of him, then back behind. I can even see the clean hairline behind his right ear. I'll just have to make something up, I guess. Try my best to lean into his mouth. He whispers in my ear. I feel the breeze of his words against my neck. I can't make out what he's said though.

"What?" I whisper back, almost silently, more mouthing than whispering.

Neither of us wants to disturb the other four audience patrons, sitting half a mile away.

He whispers again.

I still don't understand him, but I'm too embarrassed to admit it a second time. So I pretend I've heard him. Nod my head in agreement, trying to look as knowledgeable as possible.

What if he's asked me to stop rocking in my seat?

I turn my head back to the screen.

All this rocking must be very annoying.

At least I recognize this woman.

There it is! You just shift your weight into your legs. That stops the rocking entirely. Look down at my legs, planted firmly on the ground. What a simple solution! My seat's not rocking one bit now.

Looking down at my legs just in time to see one of Henry's drifting toward mine—drifting, drifting, almost in slow motion. I keep my feet planted firmly in place. Looks like I'll be an eyewitness. Watch as Henry's thigh collides lightly with mine, more like a kiss than a collision though. He leaves it there too, resting against mine, connected thigh to thigh now.

I look back at the screen. I'd better start paying attention. He could ask another question any time, you know.

It feels pretty nice too, letting my shoulder rest casually against his. Feeling his thigh press lightly into mine.

I have to pay better attention to the movie though.

He reaches for my hand now, wraps his fingers loosely around the top of it. Who could pay attention to the film? He squeezes, then releases it. Lets his palm linger though, just resting on top of my hand. It feels warm, awfully nice.

He's focused on me.

Not sweaty at all.

Not like the halfway attention of the next guys on the Pump Line, just waiting to push the pound key for another connection.

No, it doesn't feel like he's going anywhere.

Or the ones at the Downtown Club either, moving in fast and retreating even faster.

It feels like Henry's here for the long haul.

Not a comfortable feeling at all.

Inside my room at the Downtown Club—not five feet by seven, even—the lights so dim I can scarcely make out the bed in front of me, I stand quietly for a minute after the attendant drops me off, calm and quiet for just this moment.

Makes for a nice change of pace.

This is how I would have expected to feel after my date with Henry, just like this. But the calm burns away in a flash, and panicky flutterings overtake me.

I'm wild again. Jittery legs, bouncing up and down. I need to be naked already. Need to rip these clothes off. And so I do, piece by piece.

But I need to fold them too—also fast, folding each article as soon as I remove it. Neatness counts here. I know from experience. Like a downhill skier, I need speed with control. That's the idea. I want to get out into those corridors as fast as I can. Want to screw like a bunny, hopping this way and that down the mazelike bunny paths. But I also want my clothes folded nice and neat, little bundles all tied up with twine, just like Farmer McGregor would do, keeping his barn spic and span—all my clothes folded and stowed away on the wall-mounted shelf beside the door.

Kick off my shoes.

There's the rub, you see: I want to be Peter Rabbit and Farmer McGregor too.

Shimmy out of my trousers. Hold them out in front of me at arm's length, like a discerning shopper in a department store. I give them a crack with a sharp flick of the wrist, smoothing out the wrinkles in a flash. Fold them neatly in half, then in half again, into a tidy little package now. Place them nicely on the metal shelf, cool to the touch.

You see, I know the red-faced shame of finishing up here, concluding my debaucheries at the Downtown Club, and ready to leave, only to come back to my clothes all tangled up in a heap. All the evidence of my earlier desperation glaring back at me—seams and sleeves and trouser legs every which way, an orgiastic jumble—the cheap cotton of underpants peeking out from wool.

Sweater next, up and off. Fold it fast, department-store style. Ralph Lauren's got nothing on me. Place it carefully on top of the trousers.

Do you want to be the person so hungry when you arrived here, in such a mad rush, that you couldn't spare the thirty seconds it would take to fold your sweater?

Trust me, you don't.

T-shirt, up over my head. Lay it flat against my chest. Quick, fold it fast. Put it right on top. Underpants next, slip them off and fold them too—a little origami in cheap cotton. Even my socks, one on top of the other, identical twins, folded in half and placed at the pinnacle, at the tippity-top of the chilly metal shelf on the wall beside the door.

Don't get me wrong. It's not as if I'm going to feel great when I leave here today simply because I've folded my clothes. I'll feel pretty lousy, in fact, if history is any guide, slightly sapped and a little sad. They'll just be a small boost to my self-esteem, these nicely folded clothes.

I may be wasting my time coupling with strangers in the near dark, avoiding more emotionally fulfilling relationships with any number of available men, statistically reducing my chances of ever making a true and loving connection with every mindless fuck, but whatever else happens here along the labyrinthine paths tonight, at least I'll have folded my clothes when I came in, stacked them up neat as a pin.

Naked now, just another body here—and that's exactly what you want to be, just another body—with a standard-issue, threadbare towel wrapped loosely around my waist, just like everyone else.

Anything to avoid being me.

I slip my shoes under the bed, side by side.

Some of them go for costumes here: A cherry red Speedo in a sea of white towels—so sad, like Bette Davis in *Jezebel*—or jockstraps.

They miss the point.

It's like the Pump Line here, only better—no voice!—a place to let your natural body loose, set it free. Not a mirror to be found. Take on the simple identity of no particular identity.

Call him Joe, just your average Joe. Let him go too, let him wander through the corridors as silent as a stone, sniffing out all the simple pleasures a body can find.

Go, Joe, go.

Leave all the complications behind for a change, the guilt and the fear that all your crimes will be uncovered—that they should be too if there were an ounce of justice in this world. Just fold them up and stow them away too for a spell.

Walk out into the hallway now. Check the door behind me. Make sure it's locked.

Free as a bird to begin my laps now, my twirling paces.

Here I go.

CHAPTER SIX

—

Chinchilla Jackets

I'M BACK IN DARIEN AGAIN, on a sunny Sunday. It's the middle of
September now. "Are you ready?" my uncle calls to me from across
the court. He's desperate to start playing games, start keeping score.
It's the second time he's asked.

"Sure," I say.

We've only been warming up for about fifteen minutes though.
Haven't gotten anything like a rally going yet, but then my uncle
doesn't really want to hit the ball back to me. He'd rather try for a win-
ner than warm up. Started charging the net like a wild rhino after
about three practice forehands. It doesn't look like he has a backhand
to speak of.

"Do you want to take any practice serves?" I ask, walking toward the
net. I don't want to shout. There are people playing on both sides of us.

It's nice here. Red clay courts with wrought-iron lounge chairs in
between, green-and-white canvas umbrellas overhead. Water foun-
tains even, right out here on the courts.

This place is nothing like the little club where my father taught me
to play, up in Vermont. We swept our own courts there, wrote our
names in pencil—first come, first served—on a sign-up sheet fluttering in the open air outside the tiny clubhouse.

"First ball in," he says. "Okay?"

I nod my head, bigger than normal though, so he can see me from across the court. My uncle spent the better part of the morning negotiating a court time for us. He had to lend me a shirt too. Mine didn't have a white collar.

"Here goes," he says, tossing a ball up into the air.

I can see from the way he tosses it though that he's going to serve it into the net. That toss is too low. He tries a second one—sending it up, again not nearly high enough—and he sails that one into the net too.

My father could have solved his problem in short order, I bet. Some days he carried the green bucket straight out to the baseline. Watched me practice my toss—no serving, just the toss—over and over, until he was satisfied that I had it right.

"More out in front of you," he'd say.

I kept tossing, let the balls fall to the ground after I did, so we could see where they would land.

"Try for one o'clock," he'd say, drawing the face of a clock around me in the clay, making a small *x* with the tip of his racquet—out in front of me, and to the right—right where he wanted the balls to land.

I watch my uncle grow frustrated on his side of the net—red-faced and sputtering. Four bad tosses now, four serves into the net.

I help him gather up the balls.

I don't say a word though. He'd just be annoyed with me if I offered any advice. I walk back to the baseline instead. Lift my face to meet the warm September sun, and stand vaguely ready for a serve that isn't likely to clear the net anytime soon—not until he changes that toss anyway.

It's just three weeks now until the memorial for my father. A small cocktail party in his honor, it turns out—the culmination of exhaustive, three-way negotiations that took the better part of the summer.

"You can tell your mother to fuck herself," my uncle told me, when I reported her snap veto of his suggested church service, inviting anyone with a word to say to step up to the microphone on the altar.

"Cheesy as a Jerry Lewis telethon," she said.

And I reported every word back. Once she'd relented on the service itself, there seemed no harm in going back to my old tricks in the pot-stirring department. So familiar and all.

"Millions of innocent viewers held hostage by a windbag in a cheap tuxedo," she said. And in my father's case, it may have turned out to be an awfully quiet afternoon, even more uncomfortable for everyone involved.

She was right, of course, but I didn't tell my uncle I agreed. Oh no. I acted appalled as I repeated back her every word.

"Just as controlling as ever," he said to me.

And I to her.

She vetoed his second suggestion too: A kind of cabaret evening, with musical selections drawn from my father's library of ancient vinyl records. "The thing to remember about your uncle," she said in her most measured voice, as if she were teaching me something—how to roast a chicken maybe, or perform a tonsillectomy, "is that he's a moron."

I shuttled back and forth between them all summer long, no one as happy as I—essential at every turn, the Rome to which all roads led.

We settled on a cocktail party in the end, almost by default, having eliminated nearly every other form of human gathering. It's to be held on the first Saturday in October, in the late afternoon. There'll be hors d'oeuvres passed and quiet background music. It'll be fine, I think—terrible but fine.

My uncle finally manages to hit a serve over the net, into the service court too. I return it easily, to his backhand side. He smashes it into the net. I was right. He doesn't have a backhand.

My father made me practice every shot.

My uncle's taking a new tack on his serve too. Not even attempting that hard first serve anymore, now that we're keeping score, now that he gets only two tries to serve it in. He's settled on a kind of dink shot instead—soft as a cloud and arching high, high up in the air—the sort of serve an old woman would be ashamed of.

It's not very effective, that serve, but I give him credit for it anyway. He's taking a page from my father's playbook: If something's not going right out there, he used to say, you'd better figure it out and change it fast.

No sense repeating the same old mistakes.

. . .

It feels a lot like Christmas morning. I'm tingling as I lie here. It could be Christmas, I suppose, or her birthday, more likely—an occasion of some sort on the very near horizon.

I'm lying in bed with a baby blue blanket tucked all around me. I grab onto it with both hands, up near the top, right around my shoulders. Grab onto the satin border in matching baby blue that runs all across the top edge. I pull it taut, so it looks like an icy road in winter, all shiny and slick.

Here we go.

I run the satin border back and forth across my lips—back and forth—silky friction—back and forth—in icy blue.

I must be very young.

I've already tried to wake them once this morning, sauntered down the hall, having dreamt up something to ask for even—a glass of milk maybe, where my Spirograph might be.

He picked his head up off the downy pillow, hair all messy from sleep. It's never messy in the daytime—no, all crisp part then, combed into place. He lifted his sleepy head and looked my way with eyes that didn't quite focus, unaccustomed still to the morning light, but she snapped at me before he could say a word: Get back into bed, she said, in a very angry tone.

I froze in place.

Now, she snapped.

Still it's going to be a lovely day. There'll be presents later and cake, company too. I thrill to it all as I lie here, running the satiny border back and forth across my lips. Decorations in the living room. We'll be all dressed up. And it's not even my birthday. No, it's all for her.

Such an angry voice: Get back into bed.

My father opens the door. Walks into my room smack in the middle of a back and forth, baby blue ribbon midway across my lips. I freeze in midswipe. I know it's wrong.

He's wearing a pair of white pajamas with navy piping all around the edges. Hair combed neat. Very handsome, like Cary Grant in *Indiscreet*. He looks perplexed when he sees me.

It's not plausible that he's just woken up, not the way he looks. It's not just the hair either, parted too neat, every strand in place. No, it's the pajamas too—snowy white and freshly ironed, as if he'd just taken them from a costume closet. As if he were waking up in a movie or a play.

I must be making this up.

He's clean shaven too.

I drop the blanket. Stare hard at his pajamas, hunting for an edge that isn't piped. Concentrating takes some of the edge off my mortification.

"Good morning, lazybones."

The shame of discovery all mixed together with the pleasure of the silky swiping. His look of concern has vanished now. He seems to have pushed the image of the baby blue blanket right out of his head, swept the silky ribbon far away from my mouth.

"Good morning," I say.

Doesn't he remember that I was awake already?

"Time to get up."

Finally.

He walks over to the bed and picks me up.

What?

Yes, just like a groom carries his bride across the threshold—one arm supporting my back, the other under my knees.

Hang on a second.

I hold on tight around his neck.

This is crazy.

Spy patches of skin through the gaps in his pajama top, slivers of chest and stomach in the stretches between the big pearly buttons. He carries me down to the kitchen.

I don't believe this for a second.

Some of the patches have manly hair, others don't.

I'm already six or seven. He wouldn't carry a seven-year-old to breakfast. This is just another detail casting a long shadow of doubt over the entire episode: His carrying me down the stairs like a bride.

"Here's the plan," he says, when we're sitting together at the break-fast nook. I nod. I like to be in on a plan. I hope it involves lots of his carrying me around.

Where's my mother during all this?

The next thing I know, the four of us are sitting side by side on the sofa in the living room.

But there are only three of us. Who's the extra person?

That's odd. It's Sheila. There we are though—my mother and fa-ther and Sheila and me—sitting on the sofa, like blackbirds in a row.

It wouldn't be natural to sit like this—all in a row. And haven't I already said that Sheila came to visit only the one time, when I was ten? No, there's just no way to square the chronology here. It falls apart so quickly, disintegrates like moths' wings between my fingers, just a chalky residue left behind.

I don't see a cake or any decorations either. Just two extremely large boxes on the coffee table in front of us, all wrapped in shiny gold paper. The kind where you remove the wrapped top from the sepa-rately wrapped bottom, then reach down deep for the present inside. Boxes like these exist mostly on television, where there's not time for a proper unwrapping, or for the mess. Lucy Ricardo, reaching in. But there they are: Two golden boxes with elaborate red ribbon work at the top, sitting right in front of us on the coffee table.

My father catches my eye to let me know it's time. Raises his eye-brows, just like we agreed.

"Come on, Mom," I say, egging her on.

"Time to open the presents," he says.

She looks at me, then at my father. Opens her eyes wide: You mean these lovely golden boxes are for me?

"Yes, yes!" I scream.

Sheila hasn't said a peep. Just sits there, pretty as a picture, like in the old-time photograph, "Morocco, 1955."

My mother leans forward toward the box directly in front of her. Raises her shoulders slightly and takes a deep breath, luxuriating in the gift. I smell its lovely fragrance too: Some white flower whose name I've never known. She slips the top off the golden box and places it neatly on the floor beside her.

I can't wait to see what's inside!

She can't reach inside from where she's sitting though. It's too high off the coffee table—so she stands, wearing a nice blue dress.

She looks lovely.

She reaches her hands into the open box and pulls out something stupendous and furry, all silvery and gray.

"Ooohh," she purrs. "Chinchilla."

It's a fur coat!

She twirls around in a circle, holding the fur by the collar so it flares out as she twirls, like a chiffon skirt on a ballroom dancer.

She'd never do anything like this

She slips the coat on. It looks beautiful on her. She flips the collar up around her neck, sinking into the softness of fur against skin the way you sink your body into a warm, warm bath. She raises her shoulders so the fur collar reaches even higher—obscures her cheeks, reaches just beneath her eyes.

It's hard to imagine my mother doing any of these things. She does have a beautiful chinchilla coat though. No two ways around that.

"It's pretty," I say, reaching out to touch it. Softer even than skin.

My mother leans toward my father and kisses him on the cheek.

"It's beautiful," she says.

My father blushes.

There's a momentary calm, a short pause in the action, like someone's changing reels. "Open the other one," I say, turning to her.

She's sitting on the sofa again, wearing the chinchilla still.

I can't wait to see what the matching box has inside.

"No, that one's not for me," she says.

How would she know?

"That's right," my father says.

It must be mine!

"That one's for Sheila," my father says.

Feel a stabbing in my chest.

Shouldn't it be for me? But the action is unfolding so fast there's nothing I can do to alter it. Sheila leans forward now, just like my mother did.

Stop!

But nobody hears me.

Sheila removes the top from the second golden box. Places it on the floor beside her. Maybe there's a third box, somewhere, for me? There really should be, don't you think?

Now she stands, just like my mother did, reaches deep inside the golden box. Her hands and forearms disappear. She pulls out a second fur coat. This one's brown.

She twirls around just like my mother did, just like neither of them would ever do in life, slips it on.

"Sable!" my mother exclaims.

"Fantastic!" Sheila says.

Just the two of them, lush fur collars flipped up around their necks. What about me?

I'm walking all around the gallery with Constance Bronstein, one of my most dependable collectors. She's about fifty, newly divorced—wearing a strappy floral dress as a concession to the heat, and enough jewelry to choke a horse. Her cash settlement looks like it's burning a hole through her bright red Kelly bag.

Just the two of us here, walking very slowly.

I'm careful to walk just as slowly as she likes. A tad concerned that my assistant, Janie, might turn up, interrupt our leisurely stroll. I did notice a huge stack of invoices on her desk this morning. But I don't worry too much about Janie. She's smart enough to hightail it back into the office if she sees I've got a client with me out here. She knows it's much easier for me to seal the deal when I've got the place all to myself.

We've been standing still for almost a minute now, Constance and I, silent as stones. These are good signs.

"I just love this one," Constance says, staring at a picture on the wall, a huge color photograph of a fat lady from the circus. Dirty folds of fabric and heartbreaking folds of skin.

I smile at her and nod—try to look as knowing as humanly possible. "I knew you'd understand these," I say. Adjust the collar of my trusty summer uniform: Trim khaki suit with an open-necked shirt, nice brown loafers without socks.

"So cinematic!" she says.

Whatever the hell that means.

"You've always had a beautiful eye, Constance." I keep repeating her name. People like to hear their names.

She smiles at the compliment, looks back at me. I lock in on her eyes, never let go. This is how I make it happen.

The show that's hanging in the gallery now is just about the worst one we've mounted all year. Derivative Diane Arbus— big, sloppy photographs, all bright colors and camp. It's the dog days of summer though. I don't begrudge myself. We'll get back to work in the fall, when it's a little cooler out.

Plus, I've sold the hell out of these pictures. Made a fortune on this fat lady alone. Sold six prints already from an edition of ten, and I've got three weeks to go still.

"Yes," she says, "I really love it," turning back to the photograph when she's had her fill of me. She knows I'll be right here if she wants me. "But you know," she says, "I like that one over there too," pointing to the far wall now.

"Exactly," I coo back at her.

We head in the direction of the far wall. Stop about five feet in front of another large-format photograph, this one of a dark-skinned black man—dirt caked onto his purple-black face, wild eyes blazing.

"I'm not sure which one I like better," she says, looking back up at me.

This is going even better than I'd hoped.

"Well, they'd be heaven together," I say, all innocence.

Just then, I hear the front door opening behind us. Must be Janie. I've got to keep her from ruining this perfect spell I've cast. Got to get her into the back room as quickly as possible.

Constance and I turn toward the door.

"Henry," I say, a little loud—up on the first syllable, down on the second—the way surprised people do.

What the hell is he doing here?

We've been going out for a couple months now, just plodding along. It hasn't been easy though, what with my escapades on the side and his unfortunate tendency to speak his mind—his inching forward, my leaning back.

Let me tell you: If he jinxes this sale, it's going to get a lot harder.

Constance looks at Henry in the doorway—all sweaty in a pair of shorts and T-shirt—then back at me. She looks as if she doesn't like this development any better than I do.

Henry walks straight up to us—a little like a refugee from 4-H camp. Thin legs and knobbly knees. I think those are the same shorts he was wearing last night.

"What are you doing here?" I ask. Try to keep the annoyance from leaching out, for Constance's benefit.

"I was in the neighborhood," he says.

Nothing to do but introduce them, I guess. Henry extends his hand. Constance shakes it grudgingly.

I locate his musky smell in the air between us. A faint spiciness mixed with his own warm skin. I like it too—in spite of myself.

"Could I have a quick word?" he asks me.

"Not right now," I say. Doesn't he see I'm working here? "Constance and I are in the middle of something."

He looks a little uncomfortable at this, but I couldn't care less. Barging in here, unannounced.

I smile at Constance, back to wooing her again.

"No problem," he says. "I'll take a look around."

I was hoping he'd leave.

This isn't going to be easy, getting Constance back in the mood. I start turning her around, but she's harder to maneuver now. Like steering a big boat. Finally I manage to get her pointing in the right direction again—big black man dead ahead, wild eyes raging.

"You're so right to like this one, Constance," whispering now, for her ears only. "Look at that skin," I say.

She looks at the picture, a little absently at first.

I stay quiet. Face the wall, feigning rapture, but I only have eyes for her. I'm watching her like a hawk out of the corner of my eye, praying that she catches fire again.

But she doesn't. She's like a bird at the end of a long branch now, head jerking this way and that.

Damn you, Henry.

"Let me put the two of them side by side for you," I say, careful not to phrase it as a question. Questions can be answered in the negative. "I think you'll see they're wonderful together."

She turns toward me, fingering one of her large earrings, then looks vaguely in Henry's direction. "No," she says, a little listless now. "I don't think so."

"Let's take another look at the other one then," I say, redirecting her to the fat lady.

She pinches up her face. "I think I'll wait on that one too," she says.

Nothing to be done for this. Nothing that doesn't smell of desperation anyway. I smile at her.

"I'll come back another time," she says.

Maybe she will. But I doubt it.

"I'll be here," I say, trying for cheerful.

She offers me both her cheeks for kissing, first the left, then the right. Her skin is just as cool as can be. Then she walks straight out the front door.

She was close too.

"Henry," I say, when she's safely gone, not at all surprised by the hardness in my voice. "You just cost me ten thousand dollars."

"How?" he asks.

From a distance, he looks like a little boy in his summer getup, but he's aging fast as he walks quickly in my direction, growing larger by the second.

"That woman was on the verge of buying two pictures," I say, hearing my voice grow louder. "Before you barged in here."

"I'm sorry," he says, but he doesn't sound sorry at all. He sounds annoyed.

"This is my workplace," I say.

What does he have to be annoyed about?

"You can't just march in here whenever you feel like it."

"I called you," he says. "Left a message."

Yes, I definitely hear it now: He's angry too.

"That's no excuse," I say. "Coming in here, dressed like that."

"Fuck you," he says, as fierce as I've ever heard him.

I'm frightened. Henry's not a shouter. The skin on the side of his neck is fiery red, just where I imagine his jugular vein must be.

"I've been locked out of my apartment all day," he says, pure fury now. "Thanks to you."

Me?

His eyes are as wild as those of the huge black man in the photo in front of me. "You took my keys when we left your apartment this morning," he says.

I feel a sinking in my chest.

Nothing ever turns out clean, does it?

I check the pocket of my suit jacket. Confirm that he's right: Two rings of keys. Oh well. I hand him his.

He exhales deeply.

That explains the shorts, I guess.

It's brighter out here in the hallway of the Downtown Club, brighter than it was inside my little room. No matter though. Let it be as bright as it will. I've already left the distinct edges of my personality behind—all my recognizable features and my clothes. I'm just a boy with a clean white towel wrapped around his waist.

It's a big, complicated racetrack here—loop the loops galore. You really have to learn your way around. I start to walk with the other men, all of us silent as mutes. The only sounds the occasional gasp of pleasure, a slap coupled with a moan of delight. And the Whitney Houston CD, of course, pumping out her greatest hits.

Just a lovely boy in a threadbare towel, that's all.

But why am I walking so fast?

I'm twisting and turning through the corridors and passageways, twirling big-time now. And nothing so simple as a golden ring on a measly ring finger. Oh no, not this time.

But so much faster than all the other men.

Now it's my whole body twirling, my legs carrying me in giant loops, in huge twirling circles all around the Downtown Club.

Maybe it's the excitement—my first lap so fast I can scarcely take in the sights.

I'm free.

I can feel my pulse racing beneath my skin, blood pumping just beneath the surface. No trace of me here, only a body moving through these corridors. You'd never know it was me. No voice, no little Persian rug.

My eyes haven't adjusted to the semidarkness of this place yet, and I still can't seem to slow myself down. I don't know why I'm moving so fast, like a greyhound through these elaborate passageways. I can scarcely see the men on display in their little rooms—what with the darkness and my speed—doors opened invitingly, men offering themselves for my delectation, all nearly invisible to me.

Slow down already!

Not an only child or a semi-orphan here. No son of an unfaithful wife.

My legs must need to move as fast as they're moving right now. So I let them. Why fight it? Negotiating the corridors as politely as possible, racing by all the leisurely Sunday drivers ambling slowly in my path, taking in all the sights. I can't seem to join into the spirit of the thing. If anything, I wish I could race around these corridors even faster.

I make another complete loop, still too fast, but I feel a sea change coming. Feel myself begin to calm slightly in the middle of the next large loop. My body starts to slow itself down. My legs must be tired of racing.

I readjust my towel, just a little looser, a little lower slung.

Quick exhalations give way to a more leisurely breathing, even my whirring thoughts start to unravel. I'm simply here now, my twirling a leisurely amble. Just seeing what there is to see.

At last!

My twirling takes on precisely the meditative quality that you're looking for in a stroll around the Downtown Club. My eyes begin to adjust to the darkness too. Like a baby who's cried and cried for no apparent reason, really worked himself up to ever more desperate sobs, until he simply stops, until the nameless circumstance that caused all those tears in the first place is simply burned away in significance, if not in fact. Baby just doesn't have the energy to cry anymore, the exertion of his sobbing has calmed him down.

I should be used to this. It happens every time.

Not to worry though. I'm walking comfortably now—nice and slow, this way and that, through all the complicated passageways of the Downtown Club. Send my gaze easily into the open rooms on both sides of the corridors: Men standing in their doorways, men reclining on their beds—all visible to me from the corridor as I stroll.

Readjust the towel lower on my hips.

Dip into room 314. Close the door behind me. Sweet kisses from a tall blond. He pushes his back up against the side wall to make more room for me in this tiny room.

The skin on his arms feels as soft as his kisses. He runs cool hands down the length of my back, softly too, from the nape of my neck all the way down to the small of my back. And then he lets them travel all the way up again, hands moving softly up and then softly down.

It's heaven for a while.

Until I grow slightly bored with his kisses.

"Have fun," I say, smiling, walking out then as easily as I walked in.

How easy it all turns out to be here!

Dipping into another room just down the hall, a solid-looking Mediterranean, built like a fireplug. He's much shorter than me actually, now that I'm inside, standing beside him. Shorter and more than a few years older too, but thick and solid. He's clutching me tight and rubbing his body roughly against mine. This feels nice too. He pulls me down onto his bed.

Dipping in, dipping out—like a hummingbird as I go. Room to room, hovering and dipping. So free and easy here. I can do whatever I please.

Easy with the men in the corridors too. I smile at them nicely when I pass. They're not obstacles in my way anymore. We're like a confederacy of brothers now. I can spare a smile for any of them, for all of them. It won't be taken the wrong way either—no come-on, just an easy meeting in a dimly lit passage.

Walk right by an elderly man, down on his knees in the doorway of his cubby, the picture of him framed by the metal doorway. Arms hanging at his side, his eyes large for me and every other man here, importuning: Come inside, please. He doesn't look as if he's having much luck.

I feel for him, but he's not my problem.

Walking and walking, in glorious loops. You can never have the lay of the land completely here. That's the wonder of the place. Always new arrivals, and men who were here long before you too—men whom you'd desire mightily, if only you'd seen them.

But you haven't, not yet anyway.

They were otherwise engaged, behind closed doors when you

walked by before. Or you were behind closed doors when they walked by. Like a Marx brothers movie, a closed-door comedy of errors. So you keep walking and walking—really, you must—in large circles that make even larger loops, eventually making up all the many passageways of the Downtown Club.

I stop by the open door of a beautiful black man in a deserted corner. Stand waiting, hopeful. No response though—no nod, but no quick aversion of the eyes either. I hold my ground, right outside his door. The prospect of rejection not enough to scare me away. I'll just stand here and see what happens. I might be surprised.

He shakes his head finally, in quick little strokes: No thank you. But he smiles back kindly as he does. No offense?

I rewrap my towel. My feelings are hurt, but I walk right on. Try to pretend it never happened.

Of course, you could skip all this walking if you wanted. Just plant yourself in your room like a geranium in a window box, keep your door wide open. Let all the men pass you by—let yourself be observed— you can be the doggy in the window here.

I prefer the walking though. The freedom of the large loops and the small byways. Walking the paths again and again, making triply sure— no stone left unturned. You never know what you might turn up.

And then I see him. This is the one I will commit to. He's a doctor. Everything in me knows it. Strong and trustworthy, just the one to take care of you in a pinch. Tall and dark-haired too. I can just picture him on his rounds at the hospital, clipboard in hand. He looks stable and handsome, well educated too in his clean white towel, like a medical smock on him.

He's all these things as I pass by his open door.

I loop around again—choose a small byway this time. Get back to his room fast. Pass his open door again, more slowly now.

He smiles me inside.

Lovely kisses and lovely suckling and lovely rubbing and all these things with my soon-to-be new lover, the doctor. And when we're done with all that, we lie together so comfortably on his little bed. Intimations of a lovely future for the two of us, my brand-new boyfriend and me.

Who turns out to be a retail specialist from Armonk.

. . .

We're all three sitting at the kitchen table—my mother and father and me. It's the dead of winter now, just past that point when the snow and ice and dull gray skies begin to feel as permanent as tattoos. Late February, early March. It's one of those three-day weekends—Presidents' Day maybe, or the one that comes after that.

I'm visiting my parents in Vermont.

It won't be long now before my father kills himself. Just six or seven months, I think. But I'm oblivious to all that.

I've made a pot of extremely strong coffee—espresso maybe, or something with chicory mixed in. Whatever the latest affectation may be. We each have a sunny yellow mug in front of us. I've noticed though that I'm the only one who's drunk from his. Makes me feel superior.

"Are you warm?" my mother asks.

I assume she's speaking to me. I'm wearing one of my old-time sweaters—one of the brightly colored numbers, stowed away still in my bedroom upstairs. I feel the tightness of the boy's sweater on the man's frame. "Not at all," I say, looking up at her. "Why?"

But I see she's looking at my father. She was speaking to him.

He doesn't say anything, but he does look warm, a little flushed. Dressed in light blue shirtsleeves, not even an undershirt beneath. His face is growing ruddier before our eyes, as if someone were flipping through a color wheel, fast—from pink to scarlet, projecting every deepening gradation on my father's cheeks. He must have the flu.

"Are you feverish?" she asks, reaching over to him, laying the back of her hand against his forehead.

I feel fine.

I'm planning my escape. Calculating the earliest train I can propose to take me away from here, back to my life in New York. There's a snowstorm coming. A "weather alert" has been flashing across the bottom of the television screen all day, interrupting songs on the radio too. I don't want to get stuck here.

"Just a hot flash," he says. "Probably the coffee."

My mother looks skeptical.

"I'll be fine in a minute," he says.

His skin looks filmy with perspiration.

"I thought only women got hot flashes," I say.

They look at me in unison. It's funny. They've been in step all weekend, like synchronized swimmers, toes pointed high. I've been the odd man out up here. Not that they'd ever exclude me. No, it's a product of my own choosing. I'm the one who moved away, after all, started a new life. I'm the one who threw them back together again.

"Not at all," my mother says, sounding knowledgeable. "Men get hot flashes too. It's very common."

She's an expert on all things medical.

"We're at that age now," she says, smiling, looking at my father again.

Actually, they're about ten years past that age, but who's counting?

I'm thinking the four o'clock train.

And I can see my mother's right. My father's face is less red already. He's looking more comfortable by the minute.

I take another sip of the coffee, bitter and wonderful.

"Your coffee's terrible," my mother says.

I like it even more.

"I'm worried about the storm," my father says.

This will be a nice segue, I think—breathing in the aromatic coffee, tracing the easy conversational line from "storm" to "train" in no time flat.

I look up at my father.

He's bright red again. Looks fired from within now.

Something's not right here.

"We need to lay in supplies," he says, talking faster now, sounding rattled too. "We could get snowed in, you know." His face is sweating. "Run out of food," he says, undone. "What if we can't make it down to the road?"

The driveway's only a hundred yards long.

I look at my mother, ready to take her back. Ready to roll my eyes in league with her again, but she's got her eyes trained on my father still. She looks upset.

"Honey," she says, murmuring, "try to relax." She reaches out and places her hand on top of his. "We have plenty of supplies here."

I don't know that I've ever heard her voice so soft.

"And we can always get to the road," she says. "Don't worry about that."

But I've had enough of this. "I think you've both gone crazy," I say. This is ridiculous.

My mother shoots me an angry look. I know not to disregard it.

"Are you sure?" my father asks, ignoring me, looking at my mother still. He sounds like a child, nearly consoled.

"Yes," she says, softly still. "I'm sure." Nodding her head now too.

She stands up and walks over to the sink. Takes a pill from a container on the windowsill, one of many. Runs a glass of water. She brings them to my father.

"Here," she says.

He takes them from her without a word, swallows them down.

"Everything's fine," she says, though it's hard for me to tell whom she's talking to. Then she sits down heavily behind her bright yellow mug and lifts it slowly to her lips.

"Here's the next guy."

"Here's the next guy."

"What are you looking for?"

"Here's the next guy."

I don't even hear what they're saying anymore. Can't force myself to listen.

"Here's the next guy."

The beeps don't even bother me. I scarcely hear them now.

"Here's the next guy."

"What are you looking for?"

"Here's the next guy."

I don't hang up the receiver though.

"Here's the next guy."

Somehow I just won't lay it back down into its cradle. It fits so nicely there too, hand in glove. Just won't do it.

"Here's the next guy."

No, I hang on instead. Receiver at the ready, pressed up against my ear. I'll wait for that next guy until the twelfth of never. And for the one after him too, if it comes to that.

"Here's the next guy."

It's not like I think these next guys are getting me anywhere. This is just a bad habit now, like smoking cigarettes or biting my fingernails. I just keep doing it now, one more nasty little habit—I just keep waiting for the next guy.

"What are you looking for?"

The thrills aren't half as thrilling as they used to be.

"Here's the next guy."

But I keep dialing in all the same.

"What are you looking for?"

Paying fifteen cents a minute.

All this calling should have turned out so differently. I should have found the perfect boyfriend already. I should be holding him tight. No memory left of the hours and hours I've wasted here.

"Here's the next guy."

That's one thing in Henry's favor: I've found him already. And he's a good man too. That's another thing.

"Here's the next guy."

You know, I don't think Henry's ever mentioned his cock to me, not even once—how big it is, or if it happened to be throbbing. The guys on this line could really take a lesson from him in that department.

"What are you looking for?"

Yes, he's a real gentleman, that Henry. Puts up with me too. Let's not forget about that.

"Here's the next guy."

But here I am.

And here I stay.

"What are you looking for?"

You know, this is a real first.

I think I may be done for.

I'm going up to Vermont today. My uncle's coming up tomorrow morning. We're going to help my mother get ready. It's too much, I think, to ask her to do it all alone. The memorial service–turned–cocktail hour is the day after tomorrow.

But somehow I can't take the train today.

Can't see me waiting for the uptown local to the station, the way I usually do. Or waiting in a long line there for a ticket behind all the people in front of me—invariably wanting monthly passes and requiring no small amount of check writing and picture ID showing and finding the one supervisor in the entire commuter rail system who can initial a personal check.

I'm too jittery today—frightened of all that dead time, standing around the station, waiting for scratchy track announcements over the old-style P.A. system. Too much time to wonder how I'll get through the party, what on earth I'll say to all the people who shake my hand, kiss my cheek.

I feel my hands clammy and my forehead too. It's a beautiful fall day though. It's not the weather. Nerves, I guess. I take a tiny pink pill—Xanax—from the small container Henry gave me. I wasn't far off on that shrink fantasy, was I?

In the long run, of course, taking the train would be much easier, faster too, but right now, that train would probably kill me. Sometimes it's better to take a little longer in motion than to melt down in wait. Sometimes you just need to keep moving.

So I run to the car rental place instead, the one on Fourth Avenue—Sunshine Rentals—and pick out a small blue car from the teeming lot. Virtually indistinguishable from all the other blue ones, and not so different really from the white ones or the red ones either, but I choose it.

I ask the man in the office if it has a CD player.

He tilts his head to one side, silky blond hair falling in the same direction. Looks back at me, squinting, as if I might be pulling his leg.

Apparently they all have CD players now. Who knew?

His hair moves every time he does, in fact, lurches forward with every step, then swings back, comes to rest again just below his ears.

He hands me a long form with several carbon copies attached.

Hair sways toward me with the forward movement of his arm.

His form puts me in mind of Penn Station all over again, looks as if it could stop me moving for a good long while. Like Amtrak, only on a preprinted form this time. I don't panic though. I simply begin to fill in the blanks, and eventually he hands me the keys to the little blue car.

Thank you.

I rush back out to the lot, my own hair like a dreary brown helmet, I'm sure, not moving an inch. It takes me a while to find the little blue car again too. I thought I remembered exactly where it was, but it turns out I don't.

There it is—next to the one with the Tennessee license plates.

I hang my suit bag on the plastic hook in the back, and lay my overnight bag in the floor well of the passenger's seat. Shotgun, we used to call it, back when it mattered if you knew to use low beams in fog.

Slip into the driver's seat now and close the door behind me, all vacuum packed and sealed up tight. I hate the smell of new leather. I'd like to go back into the office and ask the man for an older car, but I can only imagine the paperwork that would entail. So I start the ignition instead, and push down on the buttons that open the two front windows.

I dig a few CDs from the overnight bag on the floor and lay them out—just so—on the passenger's seat beside me. Feel a wave of sadness when I spot the Blockbuster case inside. I load the *Best of Dusty Springfield* into the little slit of CD player, like slipping a shiny dime into a parking meter, only horizontal, and right on the dashboard of the car.

Push the lighter for good luck.

It's a long drive.

I wish I could say that my driving skills have improved dramatically since the day of the yellow Shetland sweater, but I can't, not honestly at least. I suppose they may have improved a little bit, matured with age maybe. I may well be at the low end of competent by now.

I saw the video yesterday when I was roaming through the classics section at Blockbuster. *September Affair,* I read on its spine. I pulled it from its place in the perfect row of videos. Not much interest in the classics, I guess. "Starring Joseph Cotten and Joan Fontaine," all in loopy red script on the front of the cardboard box. A photograph of Joan Fontaine in a trim traveling suit. The synopsis on the back just as I remembered it: The story of Sheila and her married doctor, except Sheila's a violinist in this version.

I rented it on the spot.

It seemed only fitting to say good-bye to my father and that lovely married doctor on the same weekend.

I drive all the way to First Avenue, then turn left, heading north. There's not much traffic today.

"Just drive all the way up First Avenue," that's what the silken-haired man behind the counter told me. "Until you can't go any farther."

I didn't write any of it down. It didn't seem very complicated to me.

"Make sure you get into the left lane," he said.

I remember that distinctly. It seemed very important.

"In ten blocks or so, you'll drive over the Willis Avenue Bridge."

I wrote that down—Willis Avenue Bridge—on the back of the Sunshine Rental envelope, with all the carbon copies stuffed inside. I check it now, just to be sure. There it is: Willis Avenue Bridge.

"When you cross the bridge, you'll see a sign for New England," he said. "Just follow the signs."

It sounded simple enough. But First Avenue just doesn't end. He never mentioned that First Avenue is infinite. I don't see any bridge either, not even on the far horizon, just more road. And it's getting uglier too. Starting to feel very *Bonfire of the Vanities* to me, driving along First Avenue in what can't possibly be Manhattan anymore, looking for a bridge I've never heard of.

Now I'm frightened.

I pull the car over to the side of the road and turn off the ignition.

Doesn't something awful happen to that man in *Bonfire of the Vanities*? Doesn't he run someone over, or get shot? What if the man at Sunshine Rentals made up the Willis Avenue Bridge? I press the button on the dash that locks all the doors. Click. Reach for my overnight bag in the well of the passenger's seat. It doesn't feel like much of a joke to me: Making up directions.

I dig out my cell phone. Dial the numbers and press send.

"Henry?"

He'll know what to do.

"Matthew," he says. He sounds surprised. "I thought you'd be on the road by now."

It's nice to have someone to call.

"Am I interrupting you?" I ask.

Some little girl could be drawing her heart out at this very minute, a chunky blue crayon gripped tight in little fingers, trauma gushing forth onto a thick sheet of construction paper. But I suppose he wouldn't have answered the phone then, would he?

"Not at all," he says.

"Do you know where the Willis Avenue Bridge is, by any chance?"

"Sure," he says. "It's all the way at the end of Third Avenue."

"No, it's not," I say, bouncing back at him, as sharp and fast as a hard rubber ball. I sound like my mother.

But I'm sure the guy behind the counter said First Avenue. I pick up the rental envelope again, but it just says "Willis Avenue Bridge" on the back, just like the last time.

"Yesss," he says, dragging it out, clearly annoyed with me, but trying to keep it in check. "It's at the end of Third Avenue."

I've really got to work on this. I know how awful it is to be on the receiving end of her speeding bullets, and still I shoot them out, right and left, without the least provocation.

"I'm sorry," I say. "I got bad directions, and I'm a little lost."

"Not to worry," he says. "Can you get yourself over to Third Avenue?"

"I think so," I say. "I'll call back if I can't."

"I'll be here," he says.

I start the car again and turn left. Drive south on Second Avenue for a good long time, then back up Third Avenue, to the very end.

Yes, there it is.

The Willis Avenue Bridge. Just where Henry said it would be.

—

CHAPTER SEVEN

Monochrome Outfits

"**D**ARLING," SHE SIGHS, a little exhalation mixed in with each syllable, as if she were fortifying herself with a breath of air before explaining something I really should have understood on my own. Sounds like she's talking to a remedial math student. And I was always good at math.

I've just walked in from my drive.

I see the evidence of preparations under way: Cases of wine and sparkling water stacked up tall against the far wall. Empty chafing dishes in shiny stainless steel, waiting to be filled with finger food and heated up with Sterno, the small blue flames flickering underneath. My father's cocktail party is the day after tomorrow, almost a year to the day since he died.

"What are they doing in here?" I ask, pointing to a pair of navy wing chairs, fitted one on top of the other, like interlocking pieces of a jig-saw puzzle. They belong in the far corner of the living room. Everyone knows that.

"They're on their way to the cellar," she says, shrugging her shoulders. "The caterer wants better *flow*." She doesn't look impressed.

My mother wets a thick yellow sponge and begins wiping down the countertops. They already look spotless to me. I walk over to another group of cases, a lower stack by the window: Every kind of booze under the sun. I try to imagine what I'll order. Try to imagine who'd order Wild Turkey.

It was a good decision to drive here. Kept me otherwise engaged.

"I have three words for you," she says, really enunciating now—for the lecture hall, for a whole class of remedial math students.

I turn to her.

"Yes," she says. "Three little words." Volume turned up loud.

What's she talking about?

She moves away from the sink, toward the center island, standing behind it as if it were a podium. She tugs at the hem of her navy turtle-neck and straightens up a little taller—just the way you would if you were standing in front of a room full of people.

I should feel a little less stupid now. This isn't about me.

"Statute," she says, vowels as broad as Katharine Hepburn's. She's from the Main Line now, just the poshest math teacher ever. She raises her index finger in the air—first word—so even the stoners in the very last row can see.

But it's just me here in the kitchen with her.

She waits a beat: "Of," still a little loud, raising a second finger, making a "v for victory" sign. Another beat. "Limitations," she says, and there's the ring finger. Three words, three fingers—a veritable Boy Scout's pledge waving in the air. She's gone from zero to sixty in under three seconds, like those sporty cars on television commercials. I have no idea what she's talking about.

"Yes," she says, again with a little sigh mixed in, "there's always a statute of limitations."

It's as if I'd asked her a question—name the capital of North Da-kota maybe, or some other question far too stupid for asking—and then developed a specific case of amnesia. I remember everything in the world except the question I just asked. Don't know what to make of it when she says, "Bismarck," with a little sigh.

"What are you talking about?" I ask.

"Statutes of limitations," she says, as if nothing could be clearer. Happy enough to demonstrate her mastery of the plural case too. "It's a legal term."

"I know that," I say.

"Do you?" she says, giving me a knowing look—a canted face and a raised brow. If this were a soap opera, they'd cut to a commercial now.

"Of course I do."

Her knowing glance doesn't make her look nearly as superior as she'd hoped, I'm afraid. Tilting her face like that only draws attention to the sagging skin at her jawline.

I'm feeling an unfortunate desire to please rearing up though, threatening to overtake me in a stroke. Maybe it's tenderness for how old she looks. I try to hold myself back from defining the term out loud. Will myself not to. I know her little patter has nothing to do with any actual statute of limitations.

But I can't help myself. I really want to be the teacher's pet. "It's the length of time you have after an accident," I say, in spite of myself, "to make a claim against the person who caused it." I feel smaller now for having spoken. And even more certain that the span of time between an injury and its resulting lawsuit has nothing to do with what's going on here.

"Exactly." She nods, smiling. Pleased with the dark-haired boy in the third row.

"I still have no idea what you're talking about," I say.

She looks at me as if I must be playing dumb. She's blinking hard, as if no one could be this stupid in actual fact.

"This isn't a courtroom," I say.

"Darling, do you think I don't know this isn't a courtroom?"

I may not know what she's up to at the moment, but I've got a general sense for her game: A big offense is usually her best defense. I just don't know what she's defending against yet.

"I'm just telling you that there are always statutes of limitations in place."

"Yes," I say, "I think I've got that part down. You've said it four times now."

I feel tired. It's a long drive here.

She makes a small moue with her lips.

I lean against a tall stack of wine and soda, let them bear me up.

"Don't do that," she says.

I move away from the cases.

"Maybe you could move onto the next part," I say. "When you tell me which particular claim of mine you're not going to allow."

She looks at me for a beat, as if she might speak, then squeezes out the sponge over the sink instead, forcing out the excess water. "What makes you think this is about you?" she says eventually. She doesn't stop squeezing until she's gotten every last droplet.

It's a fair point, I think.

Very little in this household ever has been.

"Let's get back to Henry," I say.

Goldstein smiles at me like a proud papa from across the room. Getting down to work at last.

I smile back at him. He's a nice old man.

It's rare for me to be so direct: Why, oh why, Goldstein, I asked— within the very first minute of this session too—with lovely Henry banging down my door, a child psychiatrist of my very own, why am I trudging around the Downtown Club like a fat man on a crash diet, just walking and walking, hoping all that exercise will somehow justify the chocolate cupcake of my dreams? Why do I sit on the Pump Line for hours on end, the hungriest telemarketer who ever lived?

"Where's your father in this?" he asks.

But I don't have a clue.

Don't know a thing about that.

I can see he does though.

Goldstein looks like he's hit pay dirt over on his side of the room. A lock of white hair fallen down onto the middle of his forehead, not yet pushed back into place. That only happens when he thinks he's onto something big.

Oh yes, I know all the signs.

Just don't know what to make of them.

"Can you see your father in this relationship with Henry?" he asks. His voice is soft and kind enough to break my heart. He really wants me to get the answer right. But I don't know where my father is. I haven't got a clue.

"I don't know," I say finally, after a respectable pause. Vaguely ashamed of myself.

I wish I could start this session all over again. Come out of the gate a little slower this time.

I wish I knew the answer to his question too.

I'm sure he does. Oh yes, I'm sure he's got this dance choreographed to a fare-thee-well. Nearly everything refers to my mother or my father here—nearly every event in my contemporary life. I can take my pick: Him or her. Sometimes I choose right, sometimes I don't. I don't know how to answer his question today though, asking about my father directly.

And he's not spilling any beans yet. No, he'll make me rehearse all the steps first, just practice and practice. Move through the steps, and then once more from the top.

"Really?" he asks.

He'll keep leading me through the dance until I see the pattern for myself.

"Really," I say.

It's awful when I see it, lovely too—like a magnificent natural disaster. Will you look at how beautiful that twister is? We both sit silent then, letting it sink in. Oh yes, we've been through this plenty of times before. What a hollow feeling in my stomach there'll be—such an emptiness there when I see it at last, what this resemblance is all about, how far I'll go to sabotage myself.

He always makes sense in the end. Goldstein's an excellent choreographer. Only I have no fucking idea where my father is in this, old man—that's what I'd like to say. But I don't, of course. There's no need to be vulgar.

He wants me to stick with Henry. That much is clear. Yes, it's obvious in his voice and his posture and the soft-looking wale of his corduroy trousers even. Everything in this room wants me to stay with Henry, but I don't want to. So what do you make of that, pants?

"Why do you think you keep rejecting these perfectly nice men?" he asks.

I don't know.

"What are you so afraid of?"

He keeps talking, but I can't even hear him anymore.

"Getting out before they turn their backs on you."

Stick, stick, stick—that's all I hear.

"Because they'll turn their backs on you eventually, right?" he says. "They're bound to disappear."

Stick.

"Without a trace."

Oh!

Really?

But he left plenty of traces, Goldstein—all over the backyard, they were.

"Why do you opt, always, for the ones on this crazy telephone service of yours instead?"

It's called the Pump Line, Goldstein!

"Always on the verge of hanging up on you."

Stick with Henry, stick with Henry.

"So seductive and entertaining."

But I don't want to stick with Henry.

"Fun while they last," he says. "But focused entirely on themselves."

No! I don't believe it. Not those sexy boys on the Pump Line!

"Turning to the very one who's guaranteed to turn away."

They're not exactly the spitting image of her—with her salt-and-pepper hair and funny turtleneck outfits.

He can't be right. Can he?

I just don't know.

I suppose I could stick with Henry for a little longer.

Goldstein's looking straight at me now.

I don't really want to though.

Stick, stick, stick.

He'll never say it out loud though. Not a word of it.

He doesn't need to.

I don't have to be vigilant anymore, not after she's puffed herself up, going on about statutes of limitations. Don't have to keep my eyes trained on her either—ready to jump right in—in case she needs me.

No, I'm free to let my eyes wander all around the kitchen now. I look at the piles of snowy white cocktail napkins on the counter. Four tall piles, tied up with blue ribbon.

Look at her ring on the counter too, near the soap dish. A simple gold band with a milky opal set in. So familiar sitting there—the matte gold against the shiny white countertop. Sometimes she takes her rings off to rinse the dishes. Puts them next to the soap dish when she does.

She has rings she wears all the time—her wedding band, the big diamond—and a couple of others that she puts into rotation only every once in a while. Like this one, the milky opal. The other rings aren't there though—the wedding band and the diamond. Funny for her to have taken off just the one.

Wait. She has the others on still?

That's not her ring, that opal.

It's familiar, but not hers.

Then I hear the Billie Holiday again. She never turns the stereo on, especially not the CD player. I don't even think she knows how. Now I know.

It's Sheila's ring.

Sheila must be here.

Why didn't she just tell me Sheila came back? How long did she think she was going to keep it a secret? No wonder she looked distracted. All that rubbish about statutes of limitations.

I start to move in the direction of the living room.

"Where are you going?" she asks.

But I already know what I'm going to find there.

"Just going to turn the music up a little," I say.

I'm not giving anything away though—not yet, not until I have the actual goods in hand. She follows me through the hall, moving a little faster than she normally would. She's got more ground to cover if she's going to keep up with me.

I walk into the living room.

"Sheila, dear," she says, arriving a second after I do, just after I've said hello. "Give us a minute," so matter-of-fact. "Will you?"

"That was nice," Henry says, in a soft voice.

Can he be serious?

"Mmmmhh," he purrs, like a cat luxuriating in a small triangle of sunlight.

I guess he is.

Henry and I are lying close together, silent and still. We're lying face-to-face. His arm drapes easily over my shoulder.

It was okay, I guess.

At the very beginning with Henry—several months ago now—it *was* very nice. There was definitely a touch of the rocket's red glare about it. Of course there was. Just enough excitement in bed to keep it all on track, to keep it moving forward.

One of Henry's legs rests lightly against mine now. We're thigh to thigh.

I remember lying in bed with my father once, a light film of urine drying on my tummy and legs. I'd wet my bed and sneaked into theirs. Lying in the middle, between them. Lying on my right side, facing him.

I think there has to be some sexual heat, at least at the beginning. Even Goldstein needs a little of the rocket's red glare to work with.

I thought my father was asleep. Saw the even breathing, the regular rise and fall of his stomach and chest. He was on his side too, his left side, facing me. I thought it was safe.

By now though, the sun has set on the initial thrill with Henry. Maybe not quite set, but it's definitely lower in the sky. I close my eyes to help him now—augment his generous handiwork with sexy images from my daily travels.

My father was asleep. I was sure of it. Saw the even breathing with my own two eyes. The regular rise and fall of the blanket and sheet. So I reached out and touched his chest. Ran my fingers down the length of his stomach. I thought it was safe. Only his eyes sprang open when I did, like in a cartoon. Cartoon sound effects even—booiinngg!—eyes opened wide.

It's still Henry, of course, lovely as ever—with just a little dose of tall guy from the hardware store thrown in, or older man from the flea market, his Dalmatian on a bright red leash.

Henry and I stay very still now, lying here in place.

So what if there's a little dose of man from the hardware store thrown in? I don't think it matters.

My father's eyes were wide, wide open, looking straight into mine.
Oh no!

What have I done?

Who knows now if it ever even happened?

He looked confused, then startled, then deeply distressed. All in a matter of seconds, and all through wide-open eyes.

Henry and I lie facing each other. We're awfully close. I try not to worry about the blemish on my chin or the very real possibility of stale breath. I worry still, of course, but I try not to. And I don't worry enough to shift my face away.

My father exhaled deeply through his nose, mouth closed. His eyes, wide open still, looked directly into mine. I heard his breath at the back of his throat, like the sound of the sea, like the sound of waves breaking far out on the water. It sounded like deep distress, or disgust.

He didn't say a word.

I thought my father was sleeping. I thought it was safe. And it wasn't even his chest really. I only touched the cotton T-shirt under which his chest lay.

Sex with Henry turns out to be altogether different from the men at the Downtown Club. More comfort, less drama. Henry doesn't want to leave me. That's the difference. I'm not fighting against the inevitable with him.

Henry's not like the guys at the Downtown Club at all, up in a flash, trying to work out which threadbare towel is his. No, he's not going anywhere. He's staying put. I feel sure of that.

My father exhaled deeply.

I knew I was very bad.

He exhaled deeply and turned over, onto his other side.

Didn't say a word.

I looked at his back then, rising up like Mount Rushmore from the sheets. His T-shirted back rising up high.

What if Henry leaves me?

I close my eyes for a second.

Give them a little rest.

My father feigned sleep, on his right side then. It was the kindest thing under the circumstances, don't you think? He was still awake though. I knew that. Awake and extremely disconcerted.

When I open my eyes again, Henry is lying exactly as he was—very close still, facing me.

Sheila stands up from the sofa, from where she was nestled in a downy corner, legs tucked up underneath her. Still holding the book she was reading when I walked into the room. She looks down at it in her hands now, as if she were surprised to see it there. She puts it down—open still, facedown—on the arm of the sofa, like a big chintz bookmark to keep her place.

It's an old collection of stories by Alice Adams. She must have gotten it from my bedroom, from the bookshelves on the far wall.

I stand in the entryway, just inside the living room door.

She'll ruin the spine, putting it down like that.

She's had the run of the house, I guess.

Dressed like my mother, except all in green—green knit top, same-ish green trousers. The look suits my mother better though. Looks a bit like a prison uniform on Sheila.

I look for the golden ring, just to be sure, the one with the milky opal set in. Search out the long, slim finger of her right hand, where she wears it. It's not there, of course. It's in the kitchen, next to the soap dish. Sheila's a little coltish now, smiling warmly but awkward, not quite sure what to do or where to look—first at me, then over my shoulder, then down at the book on the arm of the sofa.

She reaches for the remote control on the coffee table.

"No," my mother says. "Leave it on."

Sheila knows how to work a CD player.

My mother's standing right behind me.

All in green my love went riding—that's what I think. It's the title of a cummings poem, but that's all I can remember, just the title and not a word more. I can feel my mother just over my left shoulder. Even before I heard her voice—ordering Sheila to leave the stereo on—I could have told you precisely where she was standing. Sheila looks frozen in place now—told not to turn the stereo off, but not what to do instead. I've turned them into fourteen-year-old girls again: Caught them smoking cigarettes in the lavatory. Oh yes, I've caught them red-handed.

"I'll leave you two alone," Sheila says, walking toward the study.

Neither of us responds. My mother walks over to the club chair by the window, perches lightly on one of its arms.

I hear Sheila climbing the stairs.

I sit down on the sofa, at the opposite end from where Sheila sat, nearer to my mother. As soon as I'm settled though, I stand up again. Walk over to the stereo and turn it off. I don't care if she wants it on. I can't bear to listen to Billie Holiday right now. "My Old Flame" in that warbly voice of hers: *I can't even think of his name.*

I pick up the book from the sofa's arm while I'm at it. Close it and inspect its spine for damage—almost hoping for some. Place it down carefully on the coffee table. Book as Fabergé egg.

"So is this what all that statute of limitations nonsense was about?" I ask, sitting down on the sofa again.

She doesn't say anything.

"I'm not entitled to lodge a complaint about you and Sheila anymore," I say. "Is that it?"

"No," she says. "Not really."

She surprises me though: She doesn't look uncomfortable in the least, doesn't sound it either. I would have thought I'd have her on the ropes now, but she's as cool as a cucumber.

"Maybe," she says, shrugging her shoulders, as if it hardly mattered.

"I know all about—" I start to say.

"Sheila told me about your walk," she interrupts.

"She did?"

Of course she did.

My mother nods.

How could I imagine that she wouldn't? My desire to bring her low has deserted me now.

"Why didn't you just tell me?" I ask.

"Honey, that was forty years ago," she says.

I'm confused.

"For about three minutes," she continues.

"You mean . . . ?"

But Sheila's still here.

"Of course not," she says.

She looks back at me now as if I were simpleminded, eyes squinting slightly. It's the honest, life-sized version of the math class routine she did when I first walked in the kitchen door. Maybe she's telling the truth.

"I haven't been sleeping," she says.

I am simpleminded. What does that have to do with anything?

"I haven't slept for months really."

She's never mentioned this before.

"Have you seen a doctor?" I ask.

"Even with the sleeping pills I'm not sleeping."

She stands up from the arm of the chair, where she was balancing, and sits down properly now, settling into the lap of the chair itself.

"Maybe you could . . . ?"

But I have no idea what, maybe, she could do. I'm willing to take the problem on—I already have, in fact. I took it on the split second I heard it—the way I do with all her troubles. It's my problem now.

"It helps having someone in the house," she says.

I'm glad to hear it. I really am. Glad she can find some relief. Of course I'm jealous too. She didn't ask me to stay. It's the last thing I would have wanted, but now it's the only thing, now that she's asked someone else.

"Has Sheila been here the whole time?" I ask.

Where did they put her when I came to visit?

"No," she says, shaking her head. "Just off and on, over the last couple months."

Since things started heating up with Henry. I feel guilty now, having left her in her hour of need.

"Why didn't you just tell me?"

"I didn't want to worry you," she says. "It'll get better."

I wonder if Henry knows about sleeping disorders.

"You'd just have thought there was a problem here if I told you Sheila came back."

That's not what I would have thought.

"I know about Bertie too," I say.

That's what I would have thought.

"What do you know about Bertie?" she asks.

I thought I didn't want to bring her low.

She looks confused again, and again, the expression on her face looks honest. Maybe I'm being too enigmatic; maybe I should just come out with it.

"I know you had an affair with her."

"No, I didn't," she says, calmer than I would have expected.

So why can't I bring her low?

I give my father's wedding ring a good old twirl. It's the first time I've worn it in front of her. I meant to take it off before I got here. Even reminded myself to while I sat in gridlock outside of Hartford, but then I forgot. I can't tell yet whether she's noticed it.

"I know about the time you pretended your car was broken but it wasn't."

"I don't know what you're talking about, she says.

No raised voices, no dramatic effects either, but I hear a trace of annoyance now.

"I *know*," I say, underlining it for her.

"Bertie and I were never lovers."

She says it simply—no sighs, no long vowels, none of the affectations of a United Nations translator.

Maybe it's true.

"You weren't?"

"Of course not."

"Not even for a minute?"

"Not even for a second."

"So why did you stay for an extra night at Uncle Andrew's house?"

She just looks back at me, puzzled. She doesn't know what I'm talking about.

"You pretended your car was broken when it wasn't, so you could stay an extra night."

"I don't remember that," she says.

"You had Bertie with you," I say. "You stayed an extra night."

"I don't remember that at all."

"Well, you did."

"Probably to get a break from your father and you."

I believe her.

I see Sheila wandering around in the backyard now, heading out toward the brook. I never heard her come back down the stairs though, or walk out the back door either. She'd make a good spy, Sheila. Moving all around this creaky old house as quiet as a cat.

"So you're not a lesbian?" I ask.

"I'm afraid not."

I'm standing on the corner of Fifth Avenue and Ninety-first Street—right outside the Cooper-Hewitt—waiting for Henry. He read in the paper that the exhibit of twentieth-century chairs is closing next week, on the first of October. It's months now since he first invited me to see it with him, since that little boy toppled over in his own twentieth-century chair, at that café in Westport. The exhibit's already served its purpose in my view: I only needed Henry to invite me, and he did that four months ago. But Henry can be sentimental. He wanted to come. Sometimes it's easier just to go along with him.

I check my watch. Three o'clock. He should be here any minute.

I light on a man in a striped jersey in the meantime—broad stripes of navy and red, a clean white collar. The kind of shirt lacrosse players wore in high school. He's about ten feet away, looks like he's waiting for someone too. Nice enough looking—tall with dark brown hair.

I really fix my gaze on him now. Keep it trained there too. It's an unbroken chain of looking.

He hasn't noticed me yet.

I will him to look back at me now, to return my gaze. I send out the strongest telepathic waves I can muster, straight to the heart of him—just beneath a broad red stripe in that jersey: Look back at me now.

And then he does. He turns his head slightly, just enough to take me in. There! He sees me now.

I smile slightly, nod.

He swivels his head back, looks away fast.

I feel a pang inside my chest.

A grown man in a little boy's shirt. Never mind him. Just move on. Henry's going to be here any minute.

I play the same strange staring game with all the men in a fifteen-foot radius of where I'm standing—the man in the tan windbreaker; the skinny guy farther on, little girl by the hand; even the heavyset man turned in the opposite direction, only his lumpy ass pointing my way. None of them very promising.

I see the traffic light turn yellow.

I see Henry too, across the street.

It's the I'd-walk-off-with-you-right-now game—staring and staring with all your might, hoping the object of your gaze will take you off with him right then, saving you from the one you're supposed to meet in front of the Cooper-Hewitt. I just made it up.

It's too late now. Here comes Henry, halfway across the street. He sees me now too.

"Am I late?" he asks, walking up to me, smiling.

"Not at all," I say.

Henry looks right at me, gives me precisely what I wanted from these other guys. Kisses me on the lips too.

"You're right on time," I say, smiling back.

"Shall we go in?" he asks.

We climb the marble stairs and pay our admission. The exhibit we're looking for—Chairs of the Twentieth Century—is located in two small rooms at the far end of the ground floor. It looks a bit pathetic when we walk inside it. Dusty old chairs lined up, one after the other, and pushed up against all four walls of the room, a double strand of chairs down the center—like the Virginia Reel.

Chairs in the shape of everything but chairs here: There's a paper clip chair and a Brillo pad chair with a small clearing in the steel wool for your ass to rest in. Each chair less functional than the one before it, and every single one of them annoys the hell out of me.

There's a series of small plaques hanging on the walls too—one for every chair: "Mushroom Chair (1976). Marie Laurel and Joseph Henschel, Swiss. Painted acrylic, foam, and steel. Continuous production by Vitra." Henry reads the plaques, leaning close to the wall. He checked his glasses with his briefcase, by mistake. He doesn't seem to recognize the stupidity of this enterprise.

We come to a leather chair in the form of an oversized baseball glove. I see the heavy white overstitching, just like the real thing. Feel my stomach turn at the insistent cuteness. Henry reads the plaque.

"Does it say it's for people with personality disorders?" I ask.

"Shhh."

We move on, past chairs in the form of birch-bark canoes and roller-coaster cars, a green felt chair like a head of broccoli and a woolly black one like a little French poodle.

When we're finished looking at the chairs in the first room, we walk through an arched doorway into the second. On the other side of the arch, just inside the second room, there's a plain, wooden chair—like the kind you'd see in school, back when you were young. It's for the guard to sit in during quiet moments. We stop and look at it. It's more elegant by far than any chair in the exhibit. Simple and functional, everything a chair should be.

"Oh sure," I say, looking from the chair to Henry, beside me, "but where's the vomit-inducing novelty?"

Henry's face turns to stone, his eyes to slits. "Will you relax," he hisses, grabbing my arm. My hand brushes against the sleeve of his soft sweater as he yanks me off to the side of the room. Feels like I've been naughty in the supermarket, like I'm about to be threatened with an extended wait in the car.

"You don't need to be half as clever as you're trying to be," he says, whispering angrily.

"I'm not trying to be clever," I say, angry right back.

He'd know it if I were trying to be clever.

"Knock it off," he says, his voice hard still. "I'm not going anywhere, okay? You don't have to entertain me every minute, or freak out every time I turn to read a fucking wall plaque."

Then he hugs me.

My mouth falls open, but there's nothing left for me to say. Across the room I see a vibrant red sofa, shaped like a pair of curvy, bee-stung lips.

"Are you sure?" I ask.

She smiles.

I didn't realize it would sound so foolish.

She laughs softly and leans her head back against the club chair.

Foolish sounding, but I really want to know.

"Pretty sure," she says, looking back at me. "I think I'd know if I were a lesbian."

I smile now too. Find a little of the same easiness, just a few seconds later. It's a relief to be in synch with her again. I rest my head against the plump downy cushion of the sofa.

"Especially at this late date," she says.

So I was wrong.

"You're not so old," I say.

My case had seemed so ironclad to me too: The walk with Sheila, the dinner with my uncle.

"It's nice to think of though," she says, leaning her head back again, sending her gaze up toward the ceiling.

It's nice to think of being a lesbian?

She's smiling still, but looking a little wistful now.

I've lost her.

"Nice to think it could be so simple."

I don't know what she's talking about though: If *what* could be so simple?

I smell the lavender candle she's lit in the kitchen.

"Just trade in one model for another," she says.

Oh, I see. Picture the wide-open lot at Sunshine Rentals. All those blue cars looked the same to me. "Like a big car lot," I say.

I see a small pleasure wash across her face.

Funny how the scent from that little purple candle travels all around the house.

"As if that were the problem all along," she says.

At least I gave her a laugh, asking if she was a lesbian. But then she dismisses the pleasure. I see that too. Watch it drain right off her face. Turn serious right before my eyes.

"You know, honey," she says, looking straight at me, "practically nothing comes down to sex in the long run."

It sounds like an overstatement. I look out at Sheila, wandering around by the brook now, just a green dot on the landscape, colored leaves at her feet. You'd never even know who it was from this distance.

"Do you know that already?" she asks.

I feel my chest seize up with defensiveness. I think of Henry, back in New York. Goldstein too. They've both figured it out.

"In the end," she says, "a lot more comes down to eating dinner together. Sleeping in the same bed."

Maybe they're all light-years ahead of me—Henry, Sheila, all those next guys even, working their keypads in search of the enlightened. Surely it can't come down to nothing though?

"A lot more comes down to watching movies," she says.

Yes, I get the point. She doesn't have to list every one of her daily activities. I think of *September Affair* in my bag upstairs, think of Sheila's handsome, married doctor too.

"Was there ever really a married doctor?" I ask.

She looks back at me, confused. I look down at my hand on the chintz sofa cushion. I'm being foolish. I know that.

"Now what are you talking about?" she asks. Sounds like she's getting a little tired of this though. I can't say that I blame her.

I look up at her again. I'm embarrassed to have brought him up now, but I've lived with him for such a long time, that married doctor—like a dream you keep hoping for, letting too many daylight hours slip right through your fingers.

"The doctor from London," I say. "You told me Sheila had an affair with a married doctor from London."

I pause to see if it registers on her face. It's almost there.

"They flew to London together," I say. "Then Sheila turned around and flew right back."

She lifts her head slightly.

"Remember?"

Now she remembers.

"That was me," she says.

It turns out I really don't know anything.

"*You* and the married doctor?"

She nods.

"You cheated on Dad?" I say.

"No," she says, dragging it out. "It was two million years ago. Before I ever met your father."

This scenario never occurred to me.

"It really happened," I say, more for myself though than for her.

She nods again.

"I miss your father," she says.

I don't.

We sit quietly for a minute.

I guess I miss him a little.

I know what's coming next.

"I should have seen it coming," she said. "I could have stopped it from happening if I'd been on the ball."

There it is.

She waits for me now, quiet as a mouse.

"No," I say. "I don't think so."

She waits some more. Wants me to continue. Her face looks uncertain though. Even though we've been rehearsing this scene for nearly a year now, she looks as if she can't quite count on me to speak my lines on cue.

"No?" she asks.

"I really don't," I say.

She keeps waiting, silent and expectant. She needs me to say my next lines—that she's not to blame, that there's nothing she could have done. Her look still says she doesn't trust me though. But I'm not the one who left her, am I? Not the one who put a bullet through his head.

"No," I say. "I think it was me."

She looks startled now.

That's not our script.

"What?" she says, in a louder voice.

We've never done it this way before.

It just popped out.

"I wished him gone for as long as I can remember."

"That's not true," she says, louder still, with certainty.

She just wants me to read from the script.

"But it is," I say. "I always wished him gone. I'm sure I must have wished him dead."

"You did not," she says, ferocious as a tiger now.

How would she know?

"Then I could have you all to myself."

She looks back at me, stunned now. Is it possible she doesn't always put two and two together? She looks more upset than when we started even. That wasn't my intention though. I didn't mean to upset her.

"I remember once," I say. "Maybe it was Christmas, or your birthday."

She's studying me closely now, eyes squinting. She's searching my face for a clue about where I might be heading, what I might say next.

"I made you a change holder," I say.

She's peering at me now. Can't trust me anymore.

"From an egg carton."

Hanging on my every word.

"I cut the top off," I say. "You know, the part that latches down over the eggs." She nods. But I see a flash of annoyance behind her eyes. I suppose she knows what an egg carton is.

"I painted all the little wells different colors."

So this is what it feels like to have her full attention.

She nods, waiting still—waiting to see how it all turns out, how this homely crafts project will tie me to my father's death.

"You were sweet when you opened it," I say.

It looks like she's hungry. That's how avid she is. Maybe this was always the way to get her attention—just by telling the truth.

"You unwrapped it slowly," I say. "Made a big production about how much you liked it."

She smiles, keeps nodding.

It only stands to reason, I suppose. Hearing the truth must be much more interesting than hearing someone parrot back what you want them to say.

"Then he brought out this massive box for you."

She cocks her head slightly, as if she can't quite locate this particular box in her memory of boxes.

"A big golden box."

She's still searching for it.

"You opened it in a flash," I say. "Brought out this tremendous fur coat—all silvery and unbelievably soft."

She looks perplexed.

"I was livid," I say.

She takes it all in.

"Sitting there with a shitty egg carton in my lap."

Nodding again.

She understands the story now.

"Just one problem," she says.

Now it's my turn—I nod right back.

"Your father never gave me a fur coat."

"The one in the closet," I say.

"No," she says, shaking her head. "I bought that myself."

And I was pretty sure of this one.

"He gave it to you," I say.

"I think I would remember that." She's calm again. All the volume has left her voice.

Yes, she probably would remember a chinchilla gift. And I thought I was like a video camera, just taking it all in, recording every scene.

"Well, that's hardly the point," I say.

Anyone could see my backpedaling though. It was very much the point. I'm still thinking of that fur coat, even as I try not to. I can see her opening that golden box as clear as day.

"That kind of thing happened all the time," I say.

It turns out I'm an unreliable witness.

"Nearly every day," I say.

"So you had a rivalry with your father?" she says, harder than I would have expected. "Big deal."

Well, it is to me.

"All kids do," she says. "But you're not a kid anymore, honey. You'll never be a kid again."

There's a strange relief in her calling me old, like the weight of a thousand golden boxes lifted from my shoulders.

"You had nothing to do with his death," she says, much softer now.

I'm still not sure.

"Trust me, you didn't."

How about all my expert manipulations? The way I put him in hot water every chance I got.

"Honey," she says, standing up from the club chair now, walking over to me on the sofa. "Just think how much pain he was in," she says, standing in front of me, blocking my path in case I opt for running. "Think how helpless he felt—to have ended it the way he did. Just think of it."

It's true. It must have been awful for him.

She sits on the arm of the sofa now, rests her hand softly on my shoulder.

"He was in agony," she says.

I stay quiet.

"You've got to take it easy on yourself," she says. "We both do. That much hurt, that much pain—you couldn't have done anything about that."

I feel the truth of her statement down deep in my stomach. Down twenty thousand leagues, even deeper. Like a heavy stone lying quiet on the ocean floor, hidden beneath all the swirling activity closer to the surface, the kicked-up silt and sand of Bertie and Sheila and every last man tromping around the looping passageways of the Downtown Club.

"Please don't torture yourself with this," she says, looking right at me, holding my gaze firmly as she speaks. "You're a good boy. You deserve to be happy."

And I actually feel like a good boy for a change.

"Will you try?" she asks.

Feel my eyes welling up.

I nod.

We sit quietly for a minute. It's rare for us.

I lean into her, sitting on the arm of the sofa still. She wraps her arm around my shoulder. Squeezes it hard.

"So you thought I was a lesbian, eh?" she asks, a small smile lighting her face when I look up at her.

I smile back.

"You know," she says, "when Sheila first met your father, she told me she thought he was gay."

"She did?!" I say, nearly squealing.

My mother nods, smiling still.

"Well, did you?" I ask.

The thought has never even occurred to me.

"No," she says, shaking her head. "Your father wasn't gay. Trust me, that wasn't the problem." I watch the smile drain from her face. She looks older now, less fixed without it too—as if she might drift away. She's gazing out the window, to the suicide spot. "Your father was like a little boy on a very long sleepover," she says. "A little scared. He just wanted to go home."

We fall back into another silence then. The second in as many minutes. It's probably a record for us.

I lean back into the sofa.

"You know," she says, after a spell, her voice easy as you please again. "I think I still have that change holder somewhere."

I know she does.

"Somewhere in my bureau," she says.

Top drawer, right-hand side.

When I wake up on Saturday morning, the sun is streaming in my bedroom window. Looks sticky on the sunny surfaces, like butterscotch. I check the clock on the bedside table. Feel glad to have slept late for a change.

Nice sleepy feeling still.

It's a sunny day for my father's send-off. I'm glad for that too.

When I grab hold of the linens to pull them back, I see my father's wedding ring, soft gold against the white cotton sheets. It surprises me. I've never slept with it on before. I hadn't meant to last night. The skin down by the ring has swollen up around the band. It looks like it should hurt—angry red skin puffing up—but it doesn't. Not at all. I give it a small tug, but it doesn't budge. Feels like it's moored in place.

I wash my hands under warm water, run a bar of soap back and forth across the ring. I've seen my mother do this. Soon it slides right off, easy as you please. I place it carefully on the rim of the sink. Clink. Hear the metal of the ring kiss the porcelain. The ring's left a mark on my finger, a thin white band where the gold pressed down, several shades lighter than the rest of my hand. I can see it in the mirror when I brush my teeth.

I walk down the hall to my parents' bedroom and put the ring back in the top drawer of my father's bureau, where I found it. The strip of white on my finger has almost disappeared already. Feels like a relief to me.

Back in my room, the sun's shining in my window still, but it's shifted slightly now—just a few minutes later—lights up the glass-fronted cabinet in the corner, where my abandoned sweaters lie folded up neat. They're all lit up a shade or two brighter in the morning sun— a riot of woolly color, safe behind glass.

I head downstairs for a coffee.

"Morning, darling," my mother sings out, happy to be at the center of so much activity. The caterers are here now, and she and my uncle are already busily at work, bickering over the placement of the drinks table in the living room.

"I was thinking in front of the picture window," he says.

"I'm sure you were," she says, sounding solicitous. "But that would be a disaster." My mother couldn't care less where the table goes.

"In front of the window sounds great to me," I say.

My uncle beams like a little boy. My mother smirks. And Sheila sits quietly at the kitchen table, reading the newspaper.

I find the keys to the little blue car on the counter and head out the back door. Can't help stealing a glance at the phone, sitting on the counter, when I pass. Push buttons and pound key, both. Weekend mornings are always rich on the Pump Line, a promising brew of sleepyheads fresh from bed and guys who haven't been to bed at all, wired still from their evenings out.

I get into the car and fasten the seat belt. Start the engine and back the car out of the garage with a tidy little three-point turn. Sadly, there are no witnesses though. I head slowly down the long driveway. Feel the tires rumbling over the gravel and hear the ping of small stones, kicked up and echoing around the underside of the little blue car. I look both ways before I pull out onto the sleepy street.

Henry's train will be here soon. I want to be there when it pulls into the station. I may not be the best boyfriend in town, but at least I can be a punctual one. It's awfully nice of him to come all this way for me. Put up with my crazy family too. I wish I knew I'd do the same for him.

Who knows? Maybe someday I will. And in the meantime, showing up early seems like the least I can do. I want to be the first thing he sees when he steps off that train—like the nice old cabbie with his snappy red tie. I'll give Henry a ride anywhere he wants this morning. Show him all the sights. Take the long way home.

ACKNOWLEDGMENTS

A thousand golden boxes, filled with gratitude, to:

Dick and Laura Snyder, the truest friends a person could have;

Jordan Pavlin, my editor at Knopf, whose intelligence goes hand-in-hand with her charm;

Judy Clain, my generous first reader, who helped me dare for a second;

George Hodgman, a most incisive reader and friend;

Chip Kidd, who gave me a book it's my pleasure to hold;

Betsy Lerner, my agent and friend, who brought more wit and warmth and intelligence to this enterprise than I could have imagined; and

Michael Haverland, who makes everything turn out fine.

A NOTE ABOUT THE AUTHOR

Philip Galanes is a graduate of Yale College and Yale Law School. He lives in East Hampton and New York City. This is his first novel.

A NOTE ON THE TYPE

This book was set in Fairfield, a typeface designed by the distinguished American artist and engraver Rudolph Ruzicka (1883–1978).

Composed by Stratford Publishing Services, Brattleboro, Vermont
Printed and bound by Berryville Graphics, Berryville, Virginia
Designed by Robert C. Olsson